The Hockey Hero Comes Home

The Hockey Hero Comes Home

by

R. A. Petrarch

Chapter 1

Jasper Jarvis

Nothing compares to scoring a goal. Absolutely nothing. It's better than waking up on the first day of summer holidays, knowing you have a full two months, school-free, ahead of you. It's better than bagging a huge score of candy after a night of trick-or-treating on Hallowe'en and better than opening presents on Christmas day. It's better than tricking your mom into believing that yes, you really *have* brushed your teeth when she asks at bedtime, when all you did was chew a piece of minty gum. Better than going a record four days without showering, and better than finding that faded five-dollar bill, which you were sure you must have spent, in the front pocket of the jeans that have just been washed. It's even better than secretly staying up well past your bedtime and watching a scary movie on TV. At least, this was true in the world according to twelve-year-old Jasper Jarvis.

To say Jasper was an ice hockey fan is an understatement. He lived it and breathed it and was absolutely obsessed by it. Every person, place, or thing in Jasper's life mattered only in how it related to hockey. Take school, for instance. School was important, not because of the things he learned during class, but because he got to play mini-stick hockey during recess. Or take his parents. They were important, too. A little bit because they had jobs and took care of him and his brother, but mostly they were important because they were old enough to drive and could take him to the rink for practice on Saturday mornings. Even his annoying brother, Jake, had his uses. He could play goal, well, really more just stand in net and whine that he was bored, while Jasper practised his shot in the driveway. Yes, everything and everyone had a role to play when it came to Jasper and hockey.

If you asked Jasper, and you can bet he'd be hoping you'd do just that, he would without a doubt tell you that the best part of playing ice hockey was scoring a goal. There was nothing in the world that compared with it. The feeling of streaking down the rink, sharp skates skimming along the top of the ice and gaining speed with every stride, made his heart race. Jasper was quick on his skates for someone his age, and he could zip past the other team's defencemen, dodging left or right before they had time to think, always one stride ahead and out of reach. Sometimes he wished he could play without a helmet on, just so he could feel the cold arena air whooshing through his shaggy blond hair. As an added bonus, he was convinced he would look fantastically cool in doing so.

Jasper's obsession with hockey noted, it is not surprising that on a cold Saturday afternoon in mid-January in the small town of Paris, Jasper was to be found at the Grand River Sport and Community Complex in his team's locker room, dancing from foot to foot in anticipation, waiting for the game to start. Oh, and that's Paris, Ontario....Canada. Not Paris, France. Just in case there was any confusion. One's small and sort of empty, having more trees than people, with its biggest claim to fame being the "cobblestone capital of Canada". The other is a world-famous metropolis home to some of the most precious works of art and architecture the world has ever known, and is also the city of Light or Love, depending on who you ask. Again, just so there's no confusion.

Jasper loved game days. He couldn't help it. It was as if pure adrenaline started to pump through his veins as soon as the family car rolled within sight of the rink and the countdown to the first face-off began. He couldn't wait to be suited up in his gear, gliding down the ice, with the puck on his stick and the goal in sight. He loved the feeling of the cold arena air against his warm face. He loved the sound his skates made as they scraped across the ice. He especially loved that moment right before the first puck dropped. The moment when the tension was highest, anticipation all around, when no goals had been scored and the possibilities for the game were endless.

Jasper didn't like to brag, and consequently never did, but he was good at playing ice hockey. Very good. So good in fact, he played in a league with boys that were two and three years older than he was. Last season, he had scored an incredible 377 goals. Jasper was big for his age and he was incredibly fast. No one could keep up with him, not even the captains of the other teams. For most kids, it was just their families and friends who came to watch them play. Not so, for Jasper. Complete strangers came to watch him play hockey, and sometimes they would even yell advice and shout encouragement from the stands. This was more distracting than anything else and made Jasper nervous. Still, he was flattered they had bothered in the first place. If you asked Jasper, and again, you can bet he would be hoping you would do just that, he would say that it was all about the team, not just him. Winning or losing, succeeding or failing, what mattered most was the team.

Nevertheless, he was so good that sometimes very important people would come to watch him play. Jasper had the impression that these people were from The Show, the Big League. There would

be whispers of "There's scouts here, can you believe it? He's so

young," or "Men from the big league. Always knew that kid would go

far". The arena would be much fuller than was usual and people

would point and stare as Jasper made his way to his team's locker

room. His mom would make sure his jersey was extra clean and his

hair was combed nicely, which embarrassed Jasper and made him

wish everyone would stop looking. All he wanted to do was play

hockey, but when the scouts were set to attend a game, he'd have to

sit through his mother's lectures during their drive to the arena. Mrs.

Jarvis would harp on about the need for Jasper to outshine his

teammates, to make an *impression,* to *succeed.* As far as Jasper

could tell, his mother had been obsessed with him succeeding in life

since before Jasper was born. To Jasper, this seemed like an awful

waste of time, but he kept that to himself. When his mother was on

one of her rants, she was unpredictable, screechy, and generally

terrifying. A bit like a cat whose tail has just been stepped on,

except louder and behind the wheel of a car.

Jasper knew these scouts were important people. As he

understood it, it was up to them to decide if hockey would be his job

when he was older. The idea was pretty awesome, even if being a grown-up seemed a long way off. Jasper loved to spend hours just skating and practising his shot, loved every minute of every game he ever played, and the idea of getting paid to do it was so fantastic, it was almost too good to be true. Of course, Jasper knew that it was possible. Sidney Crosby's job was hockey. The same with Jonathan Toews and Steven Stamkos. Hockey had been Mario Lemieux's job and Wayne Gretzky's too, and now they got to coach younger players. Jasper couldn't imagine anything greater.

As much as Jasper hoped the scouts would decide that hockey would be his job when he was a grown-up, what he was even more interested in was whether or not one of these scouts, these all-powerful, all-knowing, suit wearing hockey gods, could get Sidney Crosby's autograph for him. *That* would be the coolest thing ever because Sidney Crosby was the best and no one played the game like he could.

Jasper never enjoyed the attention, from the scouts or from strangers. Sometimes, it got embarrassing. As I'm sure you know, it doesn't feel very nice to have people talk about you like you're not there, or to talk about what you can do well and what you need to improve on as if you can't hear them. Jasper especially didn't like when people would whisper to each other and then turn to stare at him. His face would feel warm and sometimes his throat would feel tight and tingly. Whenever people stared at him, Jasper would do his best to hide or slink away. Once, in his rush to get away from three hockey moms eyeing him up and down, Jasper turned too quickly, nearly ran into a little girl holding an ice cream cone, lost his balance and ended up, head over skates, in a garbage can. His mother pulled him out by his ankles, absolutely mortified. Jasper came up covered in popcorn and licorice and laughing loudly, suddenly relieved and happy. Even if the extra attention could get annoying and embarrassing, Jasper's only real complaint when the scouts came to see him play was that sometimes all the extra kerfuffle would delay the start of the game. In the end, the only thing that mattered was hockey and scouts or not, victory or defeat, secret whispers or loud cheers, all Jasper wanted to do was play.

On this particular Saturday afternoon, Jasper's team, the Brantford Badgers were playing the Paris Parasites. The Badgers and Parasites had played against each other before. The Parasites were good, but Jasper knew the Badgers were better. They could win this game if they worked hard, and that's exactly what Jasper's team did.

The Badgers got off to an early lead, scoring twice in the first ten minutes. Jasper played centre, and so he got a lot of scoring

chances. The first goal was his, and he assisted on the second. The

first period was about to end when the Parasites scored a nice goal

to make it two to one.

After a few words of encouragement from their coach at the

intermission, the Badgers came back with full force, scoring another

three goals, with two of them being Jasper's. The second period

ended with the score of five to one.

Just before the third period was set to begin, Jasper looked

to where his family sat in the stands and groaned. His mother was at

it again. Her face was red and her hands were balled up into fists in

front of her mouth. She was literally shaking with excitement....or

anger. With Mrs. Jarvis it was difficult to tell the difference. She was

watching the ice so closely it looked like she thought the whole

arena might disappear if she blinked. She took Jasper's hockey

games very seriously.

The referee dropped the puck and the third period was

underway. Mrs. Jarvis was convinced Jasper needed more ice time,

and so she brought a stopwatch to each game and tracked every

second. It was not unheard of for Mrs. Jarvis to take her stopwatch to Jasper's coach after the game and wave it in his face, loudly

demanding that Jasper be given more ice time. Jasper was convinced

that even if he played the entire game, which would be unfair and

exhausting, his mother *still* wouldn't be satisfied.

Mrs. Jarvis also had the distasteful habit of hollering

commands at Jasper during his games, and today was no exception.

"*Take the shot!*"

"*Stop passing and SHOOT!*"

"*Hustle......HUSTLE......HUUUSTLEEEEEE!*"

Surely, Mrs. Jarvis thought she was doing her son a great

favour. However, Jasper was quite happy to have his cage-cover

helmet firmly in place because with each bellowed order, his face

flushed a deeper shade of red. To be fair, Mrs. Jarvis wasn't the only

one screaming advice from the stands. The arena was filled with the

shouts of parents trying to play the game for their kids, but just like

everything else in life, Mrs. Jarvis was obsessed with being the best,

even when it came to embarrassing her son while he played hockey.

In fact, she had gotten so loud and unruly, the league had banned

her from attending anymore of Jasper's hockey games. Today, she

had snuck in wearing a wig and big, dark sunglasses. She was doing her best to keep her screams to a minimum, so as to avoid detection.

As for Mr. Jarvis, he sat quietly and sheepishly next to Mrs. Jarvis,

mortified by his wife's behaviour but too scared to ask her to keep it

down. Jake, that whiny know-it-all and younger brother to Jasper, sat

primly reading a book, trying to look intelligent and important.

Jasper wished they would watch him play, *really* watch,

instead of trying to play for him, like his mother did, or sadly stare at

one spot on the ice, like his father did, or occasionally glance at the

scoreboard like Jake did. Watching his family made Jasper feel sad

and strange, like there was something that just didn't fit. It was like

they were playing for two different teams, he and his family. How

could they not care for something that Jasper loved so much?

There was no time to think about that now. They were

moving through the third period and as Jasper's coach always

reminded his team, you had to keep your mind on the game at all

times. As the third period went on, it was clear the game was won.

The Paris Parasites were losing steam and Jasper was starting to

feel that familiar sense of triumph and happiness that only came

with winning a hockey game. This didn't stop Jasper from scoring a

fourth goal, however. When it came to hockey, Jasper always worked

hard, no matter what the score. He treated every minute of every game like it was still zero all.

The buzzer sounded and the game was over. The players lined up to shake hands. Jasper was the captain of the Badgers and he led the way. He made sure to shake everyone's hand because that's what a good hockey player did.

"Good job!" Mrs. Jarvis yelled from the stands. "I'm so proud of you! You showed those Parasites!"

Jasper flushed and shrugged as a Parasite skated by. Jasper left the ice and made a beeline for the locker room. Mrs. Jarvis was shouting to him.

"Jasper! Jasper, honey, wait!"

Jasper pretended he couldn't hear and waddled along the rubber mats with his skates as fast as he could.

"JASPER!" Mrs. Jarvis screamed and Jasper stopped. That one was too loud to be ignored. His mother stomped over to him, her blonde wig slipping backwards and her huge sunglasses sliding down her nose. She bent down to face him. "Honey, there's someone I want you to meet."

Jasper suddenly felt tired. *Here it comes*, he thought. Grown-ups and their talking. It wasn't out of the ordinary for Mrs. Jarvis to bring people to talk with Jasper after a game was over. Usually, they were important looking people with important sounding things to say. Jasper would do his best to pay attention, but after a game, all he could really think about was the juice and snacks waiting in the locker room. He was sweaty, and his ankles were getting stiff, but his mother had that I'll-start-shouting-if-you-give-me-a-hard-time look on her face, so Jasper just smiled and said, "Okay."

Mrs. Jarvis took Jasper by the hand and trotted him over to where a tall, skinny man with a perfectly trimmed moustache stood. As Jasper approached, the man smiled, revealing perfectly square, large white teeth. There was something unfriendly about him and the way he smiled, like it was all for show. As it turned out, the man was a hockey scout and had come to speak with Jasper and his family. For the most part, the man talked, Mrs. Jarvis listened, and Jasper waited, hoping the fruit punch wouldn't be gone by the time he got to the locker room. As much as he loved hockey and the idea of playing hockey for the rest of his life, adults talking was boring and Jasper's mind tended to wander.

Jasper was so caught up in thinking about which super power he would choose, if he had to choose just one, that at first, he didn't notice the woman glaring at him from the stands. The second Jasper's eyes met hers, the woman jumped to her feet.

"You aren't that good," said the adult, her face twisted in sneer.

"I'm sorry?" Jasper said, not knowing what else to say.

"Are you an idiot, too? I said you aren't that good," the woman said. "Look at you, talking to a scout while my kid gets nothing. You hog all the ice time so no one else gets a chance to shine. My boy is so much better than you are. You don't deserve this!"

Jasper glanced up to his mother. She was hanging off every word the scout had to say and hadn't even noticed the woman in the stands.

Jasper's throat felt tight and there was an unpleasant clenching in his stomach. He didn't even know this woman. Had he really taken ice time away from her son? Jasper felt guilty and the happiness from his team's win disappeared in an instant.

"I don't-" Jasper began, but the woman didn't let him finish. She stomped off down the aisle, massive backside swinging heavily from side to side and permed hair flopping angrily.

Jasper watched her go.... but he wasn't the only one. It was then that Jasper first noticed the top hat, and the woman who sat with it upon her head. The woman who wore a shiny, black top hat turned her head to watch the angry woman leave, and once she had, the woman in the top hat turned back and laid her staring eyes on Jasper. There was no emotion on her face. No surprise, no interest, no confusion. Just blank. She stared and stared and stared. Jasper was suddenly sure that she had been staring at him all afternoon. The large, dark eyes in her pretty face blinked slowly. Jasper looked away, embarrassed.

Jasper felt all too aware of how heavy his hockey equipment was and how much his ankles were aching. He could still feel the dark eyes of the woman in the top hat on him, and he wanted desperately to get away. Luckily, it looked like his mother was just finishing up with the scout.

"No, thank *you,*" Mrs. Jarvis said as the scout handed her his business card.

The scout turned to Jasper and flashed his tired smile again, before turning towards the arena's exit.

"Isn't that lovely, honey?" Mrs. Jarvis said, smiling down at the crisp white business card in her hand. She hadn't noticed

Jasper's drooped chin or his red-rimmed eyes.

"Yes," Jasper said, his throat burning. "It's awesome."

Chapter 2

The Woman in the Top Hat

By the time Jasper had changed out of his gear and the Jarvis family was in the car on their way home, the angry hockey mom and the woman in the top hat had been pushed out of Jasper's mind. Now, he had more pressing, and more stressing, things to deal with.

If there was one thing that could be said about Mrs. Jarvis for certain, it was that she was never satisfied. Ever. She always wanted *more.* Bigger, better, faster, stronger, tougher, smarter, and more expensive. Whenever, wherever, and for whatever reason, she turned everything into a competition. Mrs. Jarvis was obsessed with being the best.

In the Jarvis household, every minute of every day was spoken for.

The family ran on precise daily schedules and every room had its own clock. There was no free time. Every toy, shoe, sock, plate, fork, paperclip, figurine, sweater, and napkin had its place. A place for absolutely everything, and everything always in its place was the daily standard.

Mrs. Jarvis, who would've been known as Victoria to her friends if she had any, was a bossy and brash woman who always seemed to be shouting. She had no indoor voice, just a really, really LOUD-BELONGS-ON-A-FOOTBALL-FIELD-IN-A-THUNDERSTORM kind of voice. She was built like a Viking and had a face to match. She was big, brown-haired, and broad shouldered, standing nearly six feet tall. In the right light, she even had the shadow of a beard. She ran her family like an army commander runs a regiment and she had no time for silly things like emotions or fun. In a word, Mrs. Jarvis was wholly unlikeable and at times could be quite terrifying.

Mr. Jarvis, who also had a first name, Albert, which nobody used, was a squat, disproportionate man with dark hair and dark eyes whom you might've thought, upon meeting him, had no voice at all, as Mrs. Jarvis tended to do much of his talking for him. He was a man of few words and even fewer opinions. His face was round and overpowered by a large nose that he never fully grew into. His arms were like two fat sausages on either side of his body that swayed from side to side as he waddled about, often following behind Mrs. Jarvis. Over the years, Mr. Jarvis's face had had reason to display a sad, lost look so many times that now, his face was just stuck that way.

Mr. Jarvis sat in the passenger seat while Mrs. Jarvis drove. Jasper and Jake sat in the back seat with some of Jasper's hockey gear piled between them.

"That was a great game today, wasn't it?" Mrs. Jarvis asked Mr. Jarvis. "I think Jasper played really well, don't you?"

Mr. Jarvis opened his mouth to answer but before he could get a word in, Mrs. Jarvis chattered on.

"We'll have to make sure he works hard during practice. We want to impress those scouts next time they're in town, don't we honey?"

This last bit was directed at Jasper, who nodded.

As far as Mrs. Jarvis was concerned, every available moment of every day had to be used to *achieve* something, or to *improve* on something else. Jasper and Jake were each enrolled in an endless list of after-school activities and clubs, and Mr. and Mrs. Jarvis spent all the time they weren't at work shuttling the kids from practice to practice and from lesson to lesson. Each week, Jasper had to endure piano lessons, violin lessons, Spanish lessons, German lessons, swim class, extra tutoring lessons in math and science, vocal coaching, modern dance class, guitar lessons, soccer games and practices in the summer, and hockey games and practices in the winter. The hockey, of course, Jasper didn't mind. As for everything else, he had never shown any interest in, or desire to continue, any of it. Despite Jasper's pleas, Mrs. Jarvis insisted that he keep up with all of it and she wouldn't be satisfied until he was fluent in Spanish, could sing like Pavarotti, paint like Picasso, and swim like Michael Phelps. Mrs. Jarvis wanted the best for her children, and she was going to get it, no matter how unhappy she made them in the process.

"Wasn't that fantastic?" Mrs. Jarvis asked, not needing an answer to go on. "Another scout came to meet with our Jasper. I'm so proud of you dear!"

"Thanks, mom," Jasper said.

"Now, if only you would put as much effort in your swimming and your art. I *know* you could be just as great at those," Mrs. Jarvis said. She sounded cheerful, but there was an edge to her voice. Jasper heard it. Mrs. Jarvis had never been happy with Jasper's "lack of ambition", as she called it.

"I just don't like those other things as much as hockey," Jasper said.

This was a familiar familial argument.

Mrs. Jarvis straightened in her seat and Mr. Jarvis sunk farther into his. In the rear-view mirror, Jasper could see his mother's cheeks flush pink.

"Why is that, sweetie?" Her voice was sweet, but its edge sharpened.

"They just.....don't make me happy. Not like hockey does," Jasper said.

"Maybe if you tried a little harder," Mrs. Jarvis said. She was breathing fast. "All I want is the best for you. Why don't you want the best for yourself? Why don't you want to be the best?" Her voice was getting louder. Loud and scary. This was the mother Jasper knew so well.

"I just," Jasper began quietly and glanced over at Jake, saw the sneer on his face, then continued on, much louder. "I just don't think being the best is all that important. No one can be the best at everything."

Mrs. Jarvis swallowed hard. She tightened her grip on the steering wheel. Her knuckles went white. She was shaking.

"Not that important," she said. She turned sharply to look at her husband, and the car swerved jerkily with her. "Did you hear that?"

Mr. Jarvis jumped in his seat. He opened his mouth and took a breath and was just about to speak, but Mrs. Jarvis pressed on. Mr. Jarvis never had a chance.

"What could possibly be more important than winning?" Mrs. Jarvis said, her voice louder still.

Jasper didn't answer. If he stayed quiet, the storm might pass.

"Nothing," Jake said. This brought a smile to Mrs. Jarvis's face and she calmed immediately. She adored Jake, and Jake knew it.

Unlike Jasper, who dragged his feet at anything that wasn't hockey, Jake loved the attention his mother heaped on him. Jake loved to win, and Mrs. Jarvis loved him for it. Jake was a sore loser and an even worse winner. Anytime he won anything, whether it was a swim meet or an art show, he would shout and jeer in the faces of the other participants and Mrs. Jarvis would be right there with him. Jake was like his mother in every way, right down to the curly brown hair, dark eyes, broad shoulders and "winning" attitude.

Jake worked hard during every German lesson and dance class, every soccer game and guitar practice, not because he actually enjoyed any it, but because he loved to brag to other kids about all the things he could do that they couldn't. What Jake truly loved was being better than someone else at something, and it didn't matter who or what. Oddly enough, hockey was the one thing Jake had given up on a long time ago. Once it was clear he would never, ever be better than Jasper, Jake lost interest. If he couldn't be the best, Jake wasn't even willing to try.

"Oh Jakey-wakey, you tell your brother that!" Mrs. Jarvis said, drumming her fingers happily against the steering wheel.

Jake grinned at Jasper.

"Winning's all that matters, Jasper!" he said. "Mom says so!"

Jasper fought the urge to body check Jake clear out of the car. Instead, he stared straight ahead and said nothing.

Jake grabbed Jasper's hockey stick and poked Jasper's side. Hard.

"Didn't you hear me?" Jake asked. "Or have you gone stupid

all of the sudden? *Did widdle Jasper swip on the ice and hit his iddle head?"*

"You tell him, Jakey!" Mrs. Jarvis said, giggling.

Believe it or not, this was normal. Mrs. Jarvis and Jake would tease Jasper about not wanting to win at everything, and Mr. Jarvis wouldn't say a word. As always, Jasper did his best to ignore them.

"I heard you," Jasper said.

Jake poked Jasper's side again, even harder than before.

"Doesn't mean you're not stupid!" Jake said, poking Jasper again and again while Mrs. Jarvis laughed.

Jasper pushed Jake away. Mrs. Jarvis always let Jake act like a brat and it made Jasper angry. Besides, his team had won today. He thought that would have been enough for them.

But it was never enough for Mrs. Jarvis. Not ever.

"Oh, Jasper, your brother is just having a little fun. He just wants to see you succeed. Isn't that right, Jakey?" Mrs. Jarvis said.

"Yes, mom!" Jake said, and fluttered his eyelashes.

Jasper wanted to shove Jake's head into the smelly hockey bag sitting between them.

"That's my awesome little guy!" Mrs. Jarvis said, sounding ever so proud. "You should try and be more like Jake, Jasper," Mrs. Jarvis finished, and all the sweetness had gone and her voice was hard again.

At first, Jasper said nothing. He didn't want his voice to crack or waver when he spoke. He bet if he looked in the mirror, his eyes would be red and shiny again.

"I thought hockey was supposed to be fun," he said.

Mr. Jarvis, as usual, said nothing.

Jake and Mrs. Jarvis though, they laughed. Howled, really. They laughed so loud and so long, that Jasper wondered if they might never stop.

"Fun!" Mrs. Jarvis said, choking back more laughs. "Fun?! Who ever said anything about fun?" She barked out some more laughter.

Jasper didn't answer. His throat felt tight again and he didn't feel like talking.

"Oh, Jasper," Mrs. Jarvis said, between a few more bursts of laughter. "You really should try and be more like your brother."

Jasper's stomach sank and they drove on. Mrs. Jarvis was always telling Jasper to be more like Jake. Mrs. Jarvis loved to loudly, and publicly, compare her sons. She heaped compliments onto Jake and criticisms onto Jasper and Jasper felt like he would never be good enough for her.

As soon as the family arrived home to 44 Peter Drive, Jasper and Jake were sent off to their bedrooms to work on their homework while Mrs. Jarvis got dinner started. Mr. Jarvis, whom Mrs. Jarvis had little faith in, was not allowed to help with anything so important as dinner, and so slunk off to watch TV.

Once in his bedroom, filled to the ceiling with books and educational toys, Jake dutifully pulled out his German workbook, while Jasper prepared for a mini-stick shootout with the wall. Jake had the bigger bedroom, so Jasper naturally played mini-stick hockey in there instead of his own room. As an added bonus, it annoyed Jake.

"Stop it with that stupid stick. It's such a waste of time!" Jake said, rolling his eyes.

"You just don't like hockey because you aren't very good at it," Jasper said. "If you played more, you might actually like it."

"*EHRNT*. Wrong. Hockey is for losers," Jake said, not looking up from his workbook.

"Really? You think learning to speak German is more fun than playing hockey?" Jasper asked, not taking his eyes off the tennis ball as he shot it at the wall.

"Fun, fun, fun. Learning German isn't fun. It's *useful*. Why do something if it's not *useful?*". Jake often repeated things Mrs. Jarvis had said, just like a parrot.

Jasper sighed and said, "You sound like mom."

Sometimes, Jasper just couldn't understand his family. They all seemed to think the same way and act the same way and be happy doing it. He didn't fit in, and he knew it. Jasper and his family had been playing by different rules since day one.

"Good!" Jake said, haughtily writing in his workbook. "And mom *looooooooves* me for it!"

Jake giggled and smiled and then began to hum to himself.

Jasper just kept shooting the tennis ball at the wall and said nothing. He always tried to make himself believe that his mother loved him and Jake just the same, the way all parents are supposed to. Moms and Dads weren't supposed to have favourites. The thing was, Mrs. Jarvis didn't smile at Jasper the way she did at Jake. Whenever Jake brought home an artwork that had won 1st place, or a perfect spelling test, Mrs. Jarvis's face would break into the warmest, happiest smile. Her eyes would twinkle and for a moment, she would stop and relax and enjoy being a proud parent. She might even stay happy for the rest of the day.

Jasper could never seem to make her do that, and he really did try. His 3rd place finish at a swim meet and almost perfect piano recitals only ever earned him a tired smile and a quick hug or pat on the head. Even winning a hockey game or scoring the most goals would only make Mrs. Jarvis happy for a few minutes. Then, as always, the attention shifted back to Jake.

"BOYS!" Mrs. Jarvis said, her voice booming from downstairs. "Dinner is ready!"

Jake closed his book neatly and carried it with him down to dinner, obviously feeling very important. No doubt, Mrs. Jarvis would spend all evening helping Jake with his homework while she ignored Jasper.

Jasper followed his brother downstairs, passing about ten

photos of Jake on the way. Each picture showed a beaming Mrs. Jarvis, and an even sort-of-smiling Mr. Jarvis, holding an apple-cheeked and grinning baby Jake. In the background of one picture was the Eiffel Tower, Niagara Falls in another, and the Great Pyramid of Giza in another. When Jake was a baby, Mrs. Jarvis had wanted to "get him off to a good start" and so she had taken him travelling all around the world. Jasper hadn't been allowed to go because he had started school by then and Mrs. Jarvis would never let him miss that. He had stayed with his uncle, Fredrick, while the rest of the happy family went all over the world having their picture taken.

In amongst the large and glossy pictures of Jake covering nearly every inch of the walls, there was one, very small, picture of Jasper as a baby. Everyone in the photo, including Jasper, looked miserable. The family stood in front of a grey wall in an empty room that Jasper didn't recognize. Baby Jasper was crying and Mr. and Mrs. Jarvis looked exhausted. Mrs. Jarvis especially. She looked very thin in the photo, with sunken cheeks and her bony arms struggling to keep hold of baby Jasper. Jasper walked by these photos everyday, but he never liked to look at them.

"Jasper!" Mrs. Jarvis said. "What is taking so long?"

Jasper scampered down the hallway and slid to a stop next to the dinner table, which earned him an annoyed huff from his mother.

"Sit," Mrs. Jarvis said.

Jasper sat. On the table lay a selection of equally unappealing dishes. Mrs. Jarvis was obsessed with the wondrous health benefits of bizarre foods from all over the world. She was always reading health magazines, or researching on the internet, and insisting to Mr. Jarvis that they absolutely had to have a rare citrus fruit from Thailand or a root vegetable only grown in Ecuador. To Jasper, it usually looked, and tasted, just like tree bark or grass. He could say that with some certainty, since he had once plucked up the courage to try the real thing, just to be sure.

Jasper forced himself to eat a few mouthfuls of something dark green and crunchy that tasted bitter and sour. Beside him, Jake happily chewed away at his food in-between big smiles at Mrs. Jarvis. Jake never missed an opportunity to suck-up to their mother.

"How's your German lesson, sweetie?" Mrs. Jarvis asked, ruffling Jake's hair.

"*Gut!*" Jake said, putting on his best German accent.

Mrs. Jarvis frowned.

"Jake, sweetie, what have I told you about speaking nonsense at the dinner table?"

Jasper nearly laughed out loud, but covered up quickly by pretending he was chewing furiously on his sour green mush.

Mrs. Jarvis smiled a smile that did not reach her eyes.

"I was just saying that -" Jake began, and Jasper stifled another laugh. Jake was getting in trouble *for speaking German*.

Jake pinched Jasper under the table.

"Nothing. I meant good. My German lesson is very *good*," Jake said, flashing another big smile. As usual, Mrs. Jarvis had no idea how silly she had made herself look. To no one's surprise, Mr. Jarvis said nothing. He just sat quietly and ate away at his pile of green and brown mush. Whether he liked Mrs. Jarvis's cooking or not, no one knew. He never said a word about it.

Mrs. Jarvis smiled at Jake.

"That's good, sweetie. You make your mommy so proud when you work so hard. Jasper," Mrs. Jarvis said, jabbing at her green mush with a fork. "You need to practice your violin tonight."

"But, mom -" Jasper began, but Mrs. Jarvis was an expert at cutting people off.

"But nothing. You need to practice the violin. You've been spending too much of your time playing hockey and you've been letting everything else slide." Mrs. Jarvis said all this without even looking at Jasper. She kept her eyes on her food, occasionally glancing up at the clock on the wall, ever mindful of the valuable minutes ticking by.

"I don't even like the violin. It hurts my fingers," Jasper said.

"You just need more practice," Mrs. Jarvis said.

"And I'm awful at it. The neighbour's cat howls whenever I play."

"You need to practice more," Mrs. Jarvis said again, the steely edge coming back into her voice. Jasper knew it was time to give up. His mother wasn't going to budge.

"Can I at least play some hockey after dinner?" Jasper said, wanting to avoid his violin and the awful sounds it made for as long as possible.

Mrs. Jarvis opened her mouth, looking like she was about to

shout at him, but Jasper rushed on.

"It'll be easier for Jake to do his homework if I'm not playing the violin. It's so noisy. I can practice violin later, once Jake is done, and if I play some hockey in-between, I won't be wasting any time!" Jasper said, forcing a wide smile.

"Stop smiling. You know how I feel about your smile," Mrs. Jarvis said, and Jasper's smile disappeared.

Mrs. Jarvis didn't like it when Jasper smiled because Jasper only had one dimple, on his right cheek. According to Mrs. Jarvis, having only one dimple, rather than a pair, was a "genetic imperfection" and she didn't want Jasper putting his flaws on display. It looked uneven and odd and such a thing just wouldn't do for Mrs. Jarvis. Jasper did his best to hide his smiles from his mother, but occasionally she would catch a glimpse. The wider his smile, the deeper the dimple, and the more irritable Mrs. Jarvis would become.

Mrs. Jarvis thought for a moment, torn. Jasper's plan made sense, and anything that helped Jake made Mrs. Jarvis happy, but Mrs. Jarvis also hated to give Jasper his way.

Finally, she smiled a dimple-free smile and reached out to pat Jake's head.

"All right, that's fine," she said. "I'll help Jake with his homework after dinner. Now, everyone, eat up."

They ate in silence. Jasper pushed the greenish-brown muck around his plate and pretended to eat some whenever he thought his mother might be looking, which wasn't often.

As dinner drew to a close, Jasper asked to be excused.

Mrs. Jarvis didn't even turn her head. She just waved her hand and continued leaning over Jake's shoulder, watching closely as he worked through his German lesson.

I could get abducted by aliens, Jasper thought sadly, *and she would probably wait until after she finished reading Jake's bedtime story to start looking for me.* Then, even more sadly, Jasper thought that his mom would probably just be relieved that the aliens hadn't taken Jake.

The garage was littered with tennis balls and broken hockey sticks and dull skates and pile after pile of rubber hockey pucks. After a minute of searching, Jasper pulled out a pair of hockey gloves, his favourite driveway stick, and a stack of pucks. He piled everything on top of the hockey net stored in the garage and then shifted the lot outside.

In an instant, the scene was set. To an outsider, it would've just looked like a battered hockey net at the top of a driveway, but to Jasper, it was overtime in game seven of a Stanley Cup final between the Chicago Blackhawks and the Toronto Maple Leafs. Time didn't matter to Jasper's imagination as he played along side Doug Gilmour and Mats Sundin and they faced-off against the likes of Jonathan Toews and Bobby Hull.

"It all comes down to this," Jasper said, imagining a cheering crowd. "This is it. The winner of this game takes home the Stanley Cup."

Jasper stick-handled the puck from side to side and then went top-left.

"AND HE SCORES!" Jasper ran around in circles, high-fiving his imaginary teammates. "Jarvis has done it! He's won the Leafs the Cup! It's been years since the Leafs have brought Lord Stanley home but *JARVIS HAS DONE IT*!"

All the while, Jasper kept taking shots on the empty net. Top-right, bottom-left, five-hole. Sometimes, when Jake wasn't being a complete brat or Mrs. Jarvis was working late, Jasper would ask Jake to wear the goalie pads they had in the garage and stand in net. Any goalie was better than no goalie. Pretending you were the star player for the Toronto Maple Leafs could only be fun for so long. Sometimes it was nice to have someone to play against.

Jasper kept taking shots on the empty net, practising his wrist shot and slap shot, shooting again and again, wanting each shot to be perfect. Eventually, his arms began to ache and his nose began to run. It was cold outside and he hadn't thought to wear a hat. It was the middle of January and early evening meant a darkened sky.

Jasper took one last slapshot and hit the puck with everything he had. It streaked towards the net, bounced off the cross bar and then rolled back down the driveway.

Mrs. Jarvis hated it when he left pucks out in the road because she couldn't stand the sight of her house looking less than perfect. Plus, she was on thin ice with their neighbours as it was, and she was loathe to give them a reason to complain. Jasper ran down the driveway after the rolling puck.

Then, he saw her again. The puck continued its wobbling trek across the street, but Jasper had stopped cold, his eyes wide.

At first, Jasper was more surprised to see someone else on

the quiet street. Most people were in their homes by this time of night, eating dinner or watching TV. It was too cold to be outside.

When he recognized her as the woman in top hat, Jasper's stomach clenched and adrenaline pulsed through him.

The woman in the top hat stood in the middle of the road. She wore a tight-fitting, smart-looking, dark grey dress. It was old-fashioned and rather plain. The folds of her heavy skirt ruffled soundlessly in the breeze. Her waist, as narrow as her dress was wide, was cinched in with a corset laced tightly overtop her bodice. Her boots were as black and shiny as her top hat. She wore bright yellow gloves on her hands.

She said nothing. She had that same blank look on her face that she had had at the arena. She stood and stared and watched Jasper. She did not move. She might not even be breathing, for all Jasper could tell.

The runaway puck now forgotten, Jasper glanced quickly at his front door, guessing at the distance. Could he outrun her? Would she chase him? It struck him as a bad idea to turn his back on this woman.

His heart pounding, Jasper took a step backward. He kept his eyes on the woman. She slowly glanced down to the foot that had moved, then her eyes came back to stare at his face. The rest of her body did not move. She looked pretty and angry, bored and interested all at once.

Then, it began to snow.

With a shock like seeing a statue suddenly start moving, Jasper watched as the woman very delicately and slowly unclasped the large, yellow briefcase she carried with a *snap!* A muffled clanking came from inside it as she rooted her gloved hand around. There was something heavy in there.

The woman carefully pulled out a long, bright yellow object which Jasper knew at once to be an umbrella. The colour of her gloves, briefcase, and umbrella matched exactly. The umbrella was much too long to fit in the briefcase, no matter what angle it was shoved in there. Jasper's breathing quickened and his heart beat faster. It was like watching a cartoon come to life and it didn't seem at all real.

The woman primly snapped her briefcase shut and then noiselessly opened her umbrella. Snow piled softly atop it. Her eyes never left Jasper's face.

Jasper stared back, fighting the panic he felt rising in his throat.

Around them, the snow continued to fall. It was really coming down now. It was Jasper's cold feet that got him moving. He took one step back, and then another, and another. His heart was pounding. He tripped over his hockey stick lying in the driveway but before his backside could hit the ground, he caught himself with his hands. In a mad dash, he ran back into the house, slamming the door behind him and locking it.

He was breathing hard but his was mouth was clamped shut. He thought he might scream.

He stood there, back pressed against the wall, waiting and listening. When his breathing had slowed, he pulled the curtain back from the front door and peered out the small window there. He expected the glass pane to be filled by the woman's face, staring back at him. But of course, the woman was gone. She hadn't even left any footprints.

Chapter 3

Uncle Fredrick Featherstone

Saturday was Jasper's second favourite day of the week for several reasons. Beyond being part of the weekend, which meant no school and usually a hockey game to play, it was also the day before Sunday, which was Jasper's favourite day of the week, because Sunday could mean Uncle Fredrick Featherstone.

One Sunday a month, Jasper went to visit Featherstone Farm in Paris, Ontario. Those Sundays took a lot of waiting to get to, but they were always worth it. It was on just such a Sunday Jasper found himself in a world of trouble, though it started normally enough.

As per usual, the family awoke to Mrs. Jarvis shouting.

"WAKE UP!" Mrs. Jarvis hollered down the upstairs hallway, her voice shattering the silence in all the bedrooms. "It's time for family yoga!"

Jasper sat up and rubbed his eyes, blinking in the morning light. He thought maybe his mother was actually a robot who didn't need sleep. Mrs. Jarvis's heavy footsteps stomped down the hall and

Jasper hurried to get out of bed. Mrs. Jarvis hated to be kept waiting, especially when there was yoga to be done.

As Jasper changed into some shorts and a t-shirt, shivering in the cold and wishing he could do yoga wrapped in a blanket, Mrs. Jarvis walked into Jake's bedroom across the hall. Jasper's door was open a crack and he silently watched as a smiling Mrs. Jarvis gently shook Jake awake, patting his head and stroking his hair, softly telling him it was time to get up. Jake smiled and blew a kiss at his mom, which she playfully caught and tucked in her pocket, saving it for later.

Mrs. Jarvis sharply turned her head to glare across the hallway and Jasper scampered away from the door. He jammed a sweatband over his head, lunged deeply and stuck his arms out to either side. If she asked, he would say he was stretching.

Mrs. Jarvis barged across the hallway and swung Jasper's door open. It banged against the wall, leaving a mark.

"Jasper," she said. A moment before she had looked relaxed and happy, but now the dark circles under her eyes and deep lines in her forehead were obvious. She looked harsh and hard and her smile had gone.

"I'm stretching!" Jasper said, lunging deeper and waving his arms. "See. Stretching." His big smile was not returned.

"Downstairs. Two minutes," Mrs. Jarvis said, and left the room without another word.

Sunday morning family yoga was the worst.

The night before, Jasper had had the idea that maybe, just *maybe*, he would tell his parents about the woman in the top hat. How he had seen her at the arena and then again on Peter Drive. How she had been creepy and strange and had just stared and stared at him. However, as the family clumsily made their way through their Sunday morning yoga routine, with Mr. Jarvis huffing and puffing and sweating through his shirt, and Jake falling over again and again as he tried to do the hardest moves, and Mrs. Jarvis's face grower redder and redder as she barked commands, Jasper thought that, perhaps, now was not the time.

Instead, he looked forward to seeing Uncle Fredrick and visiting the farm in Paris.

If Jasper had to think about it, he would probably say Uncle Fredrick was his most favourite person in the whole world because Uncle Fredrick was just as fun as any kid and was the biggest hockey fan Jasper had ever met. Jasper loved his family very much, even his mother, who was sometimes scarier than a roller coaster and far less predictable, but things were just *different* with Uncle Fredrick. Jasper never had to explain himself to Uncle Fredrick because Uncle Fredrick already knew. At home, Jasper felt like he had to be perfect, like there was always something he should be doing to make his parents happy, but with Uncle Fredrick, he could relax. There was no shouting, no homework, no "it builds character", just plain old fun.

Featherstone Farm was far from the city, with a small farmhouse perched atop a gently sloping hill in the centre of a huge cornfield. There was a pond at the foot of the hill, right at the edge of the cornfield, and every year when it got cold enough, the pond would freeze over. For as long as Jasper could remember, he had gone to visit his uncle one Sunday of every month and in the winter, they would play pond hockey for hours and hours. Jasper loved it there. Uncle Fredrick was a fantastic hockey coach, helping Jasper practice his stopping, turning, shooting, and passing. When Jasper finally tired of playing hockey for the day, they'd head inside and Uncle Fredrick would let Jasper watch as much TV as he wanted, usually sports highlights, and he always had plenty of sweets on hand, which Jasper was never allowed to eat at home.

The yoga DVD came to an end. Mr. Jarvis was bent over, sweat dripping from his forehead and puddling on the floor, and he looked like he might be sick. Jake limped towards the kitchen, claiming he was about to die of thirst, and Mrs. Jarvis hurried behind him, fretting and fussing over his ankle and patting his head.

Jasper cautiously followed. It was traditional for the Uncle Fredrick Argument to follow the Sunday Morning Family Yoga.

In the kitchen, Jake had his ankle propped up on a chair and was sipping a glass of water. Mrs. Jarvis knelt by Jake's foot, tenderly holding an ice pack there.

"How's my little guy doing, hey?" Mrs. Jarvis said. "You did such a good job with your yoga today. I bet your core is just so strong now and all your chakras are perfectly aligned."

Jake smiled and wiped his forehead on his wristband. "Thanks, mom. I tried the harder moves today. Did you see?"

"Yes, of course sweetie. You were the best!" Mrs. Jarvis said. "And you know how much mommy loves it when you're the best!"

Jake purred with happiness.

Jasper cleared his throat. Best to just get it over with.

"Mom?" he said.

No answer.

"Mom?" A little louder this time.

Mrs. Jarvis shifted. Jasper knew she had heard him, but was pretending she hadn't.

"Mom!" Jasper said, louder still. This one was too much to ignore because now even Jake was looking at Jasper expectantly.

Mrs. Jarvis turned her head to glare at Jasper. She knew what he was about to ask, and he knew what her answer would be.

"Yes?" Mrs. Jarvis asked with a prickly sweetness that made her sound like a witch.

"Can I go and get ready for Uncle Fredrick's?" Jasper asked, trying to keep his voice calm. Mrs. Jarvis could sense fear, just like a dog.

Mrs. Jarvis sighed loudly. For some reason, she hated it whenever this one Sunday, the best day in the whole month, rolled around. Jasper could tell that she didn't much like Uncle Fredrick and what she liked even worse was letting Jasper go visit him out on his farm.

"Wouldn't you rather spend the day here, Jasper?" Mrs. Jarvis asked. "You could practice your violin some more, or work on some of your paintings or even," she swallowed and closed her eyes for a moment, "Play some hockey with your brother in the driveway."

This was often Mrs. Jarvis's tactic for getting Jasper to do something he really didn't want to. Mrs. Jarvis seemed to think that being allowed to play some road hockey with Jake was something special indeed.

Jasper wasn't tempted. Not even a little. It was Uncle Fredrick's or bust.

"But, Uncle Fredrick's got the huge pond at his place and it's so much more f-," Jasper caught himself just in time. "It's so much better for practising. I can practice my skating and my stickhandling and my shooting with all that space." If his mother had a heart, this was the way to it. His mother could be convinced of almost anything if the end result meant winning a prize or a trophy or a contest.

Mrs. Jarvis thought for a moment, torn. On the one hand, she didn't like Uncle Fredrick and Jasper suspected she also didn't like it when anyone had fun. On the other hand, it would mean lots of good hockey practice and skill building. The battle was always the same, but Jasper had yet to miss a trip to Uncle Fredrick's farm.

"All right," Mrs. Jarvis said, finally. "Go pack your equipment."

Jasper took off before she could change her mind.

"Even your neck guard!" Mrs. Jarvis called after him.

Jasper had changed out of his yoga shorts and into his Leafs jersey and jogging pants in thirty seconds flat. His mother had been known to change her mind when it came to Uncle Fredrick and Jasper didn't want to push his luck. He rushed to the garage and gathered up his skates, gear, helmet, and stick and was soon out on the front porch, waiting for Uncle Fredrick in the cold Sunday morning air.

The street was quiet. More snow had fallen in the night and none of the neighbourhood kids had been out to play yet. Everywhere, the snow was flat and fluffy and perfect. The trees lining the Jarvis's front yard swayed delicately in the breeze. There was hardly a sound, just a soft calm.

That calm was shattered by the arrival of Uncle Fredrick.

One moment, the soft sounds of branches creaking and birds

delicately chirping filled Peter Drive and the next, Uncle Fredrick's beat-up, wood- panelled station wagon was chugging down the centre of the street, cutting deep tire tracks into the fresh snow.

Jasper cheered and waved as the car pulled into the driveway. The motor coughed and clunked and sputtered before falling silent. Uncle Fredrick sprang out of the car.

Uncle Fredrick was a tall, stocky man. Whereas Mr. Jarvis seemed to be carrying too much bulk for a man his height, Uncle Fredrick was well proportioned. He was big and jolly, just like Santa Claus, and was at least six and a half feet tall. His face was round and friendly and more often than not, fixed with a smile. He had blond, fly-away hair that was grey in places and almost always covered in a toque he had knitted himself. He had the largest, rounded, bluest eyes Jasper had ever seen and they gave his face a lovely, twinkling cheeriness. Uncle Fredrick wore denim head to toe, all day, every day, and a pair of heavy work boots that were most likely older than Jasper.

"Jasper, m'boy!" Uncle Fredrick boomed, spreading his arms.

Jasper jumped into his uncle's arms and gave him a bear hug.

"Uncle Fredrick! I'm so happy you came!"

"Of course! It's Sunday, isn't it? We have some serious practising to do!"

"Tell my mom that," Jasper said. "She doesn't want me to go. Again." Jasper and Uncle Fredrick shared a chuckle at Mrs. Jarvis's expense. With Uncle Fredrick around, Mrs. Jarvis didn't seem so scary.

"Where is this mother of yours?" Uncle Fredrick asked, looking up at the porch.

Right on cue, Mrs. Jarvis strode out onto the front steps, still in her yoga gear. She didn't even flinch in the cold. Jasper was again convinced that his mother must be at least part robot.

"Morning, Victoria," Uncle Fredrick began. "Nice day for it, isn't it?"

"For hockey?" Mrs. Jarvis said, her eyes narrowed.

"No. For walking around in the snow in your short shorts. Yoga again this morning, I see," Uncle Fredrick said and chuckled as Mrs. Jarvis's eyes grew wide and her lips twitched. Jasper didn't know whether to laugh or run. Mrs. Jarvis was most likely to lose her temper right at the moment Uncle Fredrick arrived and today she was in a particularly foul mood.

"Jasper, I think it's best if you come inside with me-" She began, but didn't get far.

"Now, now, Victoria. I was just having a little fun. Jasper's coming with me today," Uncle Fredrick said. There was no question about it. He wasn't asking for permission, which was bound to drive Mrs. Jarvis crazy.

"Well, I've changed my mind. Jasper has a lot of homework he needs to do today and-"

"Please. Victoria. Don't." Three simple words. Mrs. Jarvis's face flushed red as she stood barefoot and barely clothed in the freezing cold morning air.

It was the same story every Sunday Uncle Fredrick came to call. His mother would protest and Uncle Fredrick, cool as could be, would calmly insist that Jasper would be spending the day with him. Unlike every other argument she got into, and she got into a lot of them, Mrs. Jarvis's arguments with Uncle Fredrick never lasted long. She would soon give up and Uncle Fredrick and Jasper could go about their day. It struck Jasper as strange that his mother, who was obsessed with winning everything, would lose arguments again and again to Uncle Fredrick. Although, he didn't think about it too hard. After all, there was no need to question a good thing.

Mrs. Jarvis stared fiercely at Uncle Fredrick for a few moments, her face growing redder and her cheeks puffing out with all the things she wanted to say. Uncle Fredrick just smiled back.

"All right," Uncle Fredrick said, breaking the silence. "We'll be on our way, then." He gave Jasper a pat on the back and Jasper scurried into the front seat of the station wagon.

"Have him home by ten," Mrs. Jarvis said before turning on her heel and going inside, slamming the front door behind her.

"Let's go!" Uncle Fredrick.

As they pulled away from 44 Peter Drive, all thoughts of Mrs. Jarvis left Jasper's mind and he looked forward to a day of outdoor hockey and TV and no homework.

Jake never came to Uncle Fredrick's house on the weekends. Uncle Fredrick never invited him and Jake never asked to go, not that Mrs. Jarvis would have let him, anyway. Jasper figured that since they were going to play hockey the whole day, Jake wouldn't have any fun, so it was probably best he didn't come along. Besides, it was nice to get a break from his brother once in a while.

As far as Jasper knew, Uncle Fredrick was his father's brother, although this had never been confirmed. By anyone. When Jasper asked Uncle Fredrick, he said they had grown up in Toronto. Or on a farm in Alberta. Or in a cabin on Vancouver Island. With Uncle Fredrick, the story tended to change every time and the details were fuzzy. When Jasper asked Mrs. Jarvis, she barked at Jasper to stop asking questions and get back to his homework. When he asked his father, Mr. Jarvis couldn't get a word in before Mrs. Jarvis swooped in and put an end to it. Jasper guessed that maybe his uncle was what they called a "black sheep" and left it at that.

They drove on and Uncle Fredrick let Jasper choose the radio station and turn up the music as loud as he liked. Jasper couldn't keep the smile off his face at the thought of the frozen pond waiting for him at his uncle's farm.

"So, have you been practising your wrist shot?"

"Yes! Lots! I've had ten games and twelve practices since the last time you were here. I've been out in the driveway at night, whenever mom lets me," Jasper said.

"That's great. We'll keep working at it today. Maybe I'll even stand in net for you."

"Awesome!" Jasper loved to take shots against Uncle Fredrick. Not only was it nice to have someone to practice against, but Uncle Fredrick was so big and bulky that Jasper had to work extra hard to score on him. It was almost like he was playing against a real NHL goalie, and Jasper had been known to pretend his uncle was actually Dominic Hasek or Patrick Roy while he stood in net.

Speaking of his late night practising in the driveway reminded Jasper of the woman in the top hat. He had been so worried that his mother wouldn't let him go to Uncle Fredrick's farm that the strange woman had been completely driven from his mind. Now, he could picture her cold, dark eyes staring at him. Watching him. The smile slipped from his face as he thought about the eerie way she had stood completely still in the middle the road and the panic he had felt when he turned his back to her to run into the house.

"Something the matter, Jasper?" Uncle Fredrick asked, turning down the music.

Jasper gave a little yelp.

"Oh, uh, nothing. Not really," Jasper said, suddenly

embarrassed.

"Are you sure? Looked like you were thinking about something pretty important."

Jasper gave a small smile. If he couldn't talk to Uncle Fredrick, who could he talk to? Besides, it was probably no big deal. The woman in the top hat was just a crazy person and Uncle Fredrick was bound to agree there was nothing to get worked up about.

"It's just something that happened at my last game. Someone in the stands. It was weird," Jasper said, not really knowing how to explain what happened.

"Okay. Go on."

"There was this woman," Jasper began, and Uncle Fredrick's shoulders tensed. Uncle Fredrick wasn't often at Jasper's games, but he was well aware of how cruel some of the parents could be.

"One of the other parents?" Uncle Fredrick asked.

"No," Jasper said, quickly. He didn't want to worry his uncle with that, too. Besides, he felt like it was better to ignore the bullies than spend time worrying about them.

"No, there was this woman there. She was really strange. She kept staring at me," Jasper continued and Uncle Fredrick relaxed.

"Ah, Jasper, it's something you'll just have to get used to. People will want to watch you play hockey for the rest of your life." Uncle Fredrick chuckled and ruffled Jasper's hair.

"I know," Jasper said, feeling himself blush at the praise. "But this woman, she was different. She was wearing these really weird clothes and all she did was stare at me." Jasper felt better already for having told his uncle. It sounded so silly when he heard himself say it

out loud.

"Well, it takes all sorts, doesn't it? You'll meet some strange people in your time, I'm sure. Best to just smile and be polite and go about your day."

"Yeah. I think you're right."

Jasper was happy to forget all about the woman in the top hat and was glad his uncle seemed to be of the same mind. If only he had taken a second to mention the top hat, things might have turned out differently for Jasper Jarvis and Fredrick Featherstone that day. Nevertheless, as it was, Jasper didn't think it was important and of course, Uncle Fredrick didn't ask.

Jasper couldn't wait to lace up his skates and spend the afternoon gliding around the ice, spraying snow as he practised stopping and feeling the wind rush through his hair as he sprinted from one end of the pond to the other.

Nothing, it seemed, could spoil this day.

They drove onwards, out towards Paris and Featherstone Farm with the huge grain silo, the red wooden barn, and the old-fashioned farmhouse. It would only be for the day, but Jasper was content to make the most of it and spend as much time as he possibly could out on the ice with his uncle, playing the game he loved.

Little did Jasper know, he would be gone for much longer than just a day.

Chapter 4

Featherstone Farm

Driving up to the farm never got old. Jasper loved watching the large fields unfold as they drove down the tree-lined, twisting laneway leading to the farmhouse. Patches of snowy grass peeked through the trees as the car rounded each turn and Jasper recognized every dip in the field, every cluster of bushes, and every fencepost. Every inch of Uncle Fredrick's farm held its own happy memory. In short, Featherstone Farm felt like home.

The station wagon pulled up beside the farmhouse, gravel clinking in the tires and the engine sputtering to a stop.

"Welcome back!" Uncle Fredrick said. He got out of the car and popped the trunk to unload Jasper's gear. Jasper rolled out of the car and headed straight for the tire swing hanging from the large oak tree next to the farmhouse.

"Have you had breakfast?" Uncle Fredrick called across the yard.

"Not yet!" Jasper spun in a tight circle on the tire swing.

"How does sausages and bacon and French toast sound?" Uncle Fredrick was a big, stocky man and much to Jasper's delight, his ability to cook matched his ability to eat. On more than one occasion, Jasper had been full to bursting after a meal at his uncle's farm. There were no strange vegetables, green muck, or mushy starches here.

"Really good! Will I come and help?" Jasper asked, dragging his feet as the tire swing came to a stop.

"No, no. Enjoy yourself," Uncle Fredrick began, and after a moment's pause, said "Why don't you go check on the animals? I've been busy the last few days and they probably need to be fed. Oh, and bring some eggs along for the French toast."

At the mention of the animals, Uncle Fredrick looked a little concerned. He was never very good at remembering to feed the chickens.

"Sure. I can do that. I'll be back soon," Jasper said.

With that, Uncle Fredrick went inside to get breakfast started and Jasper made his way down towards the barn.

The barn was a cluttered and confused mess of animal feed, hay, and rusted farm equipment. When he was younger, and smaller,

Jasper had spent hours playing here, weaving in and out of the piles of ropes, burlap sacks, garden hoses, saddles, harnesses, rakes, tractor wheels, and broken carts. Back then, the barn had been like a giant maze for Jasper to get lost in, but now that he was older, and taller, the barn felt too full, and Jasper wondered why his uncle didn't get rid of some of the junk.

Jasper walked up to the barn. The red paint was cracked and the wooden boards creaked in the wind. As he swung the heavy door aside, a gob of sticky cobwebs caught him square in the face. A cloud of dust puffed into his eyes and nose, and Jasper coughed. It seemed that no one, not even Uncle Fredrick, had been inside for quite some time. As he took a few steps inside, Jasper heard scurrying and crackling as the resident rats scampered away over the dry straw lining the floor.

Jasper flicked the light switch and for a moment he stood in darkness, waiting. Something brushed against his pant leg and he nearly screamed. The lamps lazily glowed to life, resenting their return to work after such a long vacation. The pools of yellow light revealed a lanky white cat curled around Jasper's leg.

"Hi Hercules," Jasper said, releasing the breath he had been holding. Better a cat than a rat. Hercules stood on his back legs and propped himself against Jasper's thigh, purring and kneading furiously.

"Happy to see me?" Jasper said, scratching behind the cat's ears. Hercules was the resident mouser and unlike most cats Jasper had known, Hercules loved attention. Hercules was pawing and purring and kneading Jasper's leg with so much enthusiasm that Jasper thought the cat might be lonely.

"Want to come feed the chickens with me, eh?" Jasper asked. "Does someone wanna help me feed the chickens? I bet he does." Jasper gave the cat a pat on the head and after thinking for a moment, added, "But you have to promise not to eat of any of them."

Hercules immediately sat down, neatly curled his tail around himself and looked up at Jasper with his big amber eyes. The cat, it seemed, would behave himself.

Not knowing what sort of wild animal might be lurking in the shadows, Jasper moved quickly through the barn. He hoped the chicken feed was still in the same spot and after climbing over a pile of broken wagon wheels, tripping over a coil of rope, and pushing a huge bail of hay out of the way, he arrived at the bulging burlap sack.

He filled a pail, the rushing of dried corn and seed ringing loudly in the quiet. The pail heavy with feed, Jasper closed the burlap sack tightly and turned back towards the barn doors. Hercules following dutifully behind.

The barn doors creaked and squeaked as Jasper pulled them to. He carefully latched them in place. Hercules had fallen behind, needing to sniff at a particularly interesting piece of wood, but he darted out the cat door in the barn's wall and was soon at Jasper's heels again.

The chicken coop wasn't far from the barn. A small, stone building housed the nests where the chickens slept and laid their eggs, and attached to this was a fenced in area for the chickens to feed and walk around.

"Stay here, Hercules," Jasper said. The white cat promptly sat down, watching the chickens intently and flicking his oddly stubby tail.

Jasper slowly opened the door to the coop, careful not to let any of the chickens escape. He was hit with a wall of rancid odour so foul he could taste it on his tongue. If Uncle Fredrick didn't go into his barn very often, it would seem he spent even less time in the chicken coop. Jasper was no expert on chickens and their care, but it smelled like it hadn't been cleaned out in weeks. Feeling sorry for the chickens, and a little sorry for himself, Jasper set the pail down, grabbed the broom leaning in the corner, and proceeded to sweep out the smelly coop.

The nests were all labeled, with names like Henrietta and Maybelle, although Jasper doubted very much the chickens knew their names or could read the name tags. It was a large coop for so few chickens and as Jasper swept the floor, covering his nose with the cuff of his jersey, they squawked and pecked around his feet.

With the floor swept, Jasper grabbed the pail of feed and went into the enclosure. Uncle Fredrick might not be the tidiest of men, but he was definitely one of the cleverest. Since he could never remember to feed his chickens on time, he had rigged up a large metal machine that dispensed food at the same time every day. It kept the chickens happy, and it kept Uncle Fredrick happy too, since he didn't have to go into the chicken coop except to refill the machine. At the moment, judging by the metre on the side, the machine was about half full, maybe a little less. The chickens pecked at the feed dish as he removed the lid and emptied the pail inside. That done, he went back into the coop to collect some eggs.

Each and every chicken nest was piled high with eggs. The nests were so full the chickens had taken to laying their eggs one on top of another. There were only eight chickens, but all twenty nests in the coop were overflowing with white, brown, and speckled shelled eggs.

Jasper carefully filled the pail to the brim with eggs and leaving the still egg-ridden coop behind, he and Hercules returned to the farmhouse.

"Uncle Fredrick? I've got the eggs," Jasper said.

"*Egg-cellent*!" Uncle Fredrick said and roared with laughter.

Jasper set the pail down on the kitchen table. The bacon and sausages sizzled in the pan. Jasper's stomach grumbled.

"Eat up, m'boy," Uncle Fredrick said, placing a plate in front of Jasper. "We've got lots of practising to do today. Wow, that is a lot of eggs."

Uncle Fredrick took the pail and began work on the French toast while Jasper ate.

"The coop is completely full. Those chickens lay a lot of eggs. When was the last time you emptied it out?"

"Uhh....two days ago? Three days ago! I've been busy. I guess those chickens just like to lay eggs."

"I refilled the machine," Jasper said, chewing on his second piece of bacon. "Is the pond frozen?"

"It is, indeed. I was testing it out last night. Completely solid."

"Awesome! I want to work on my backhand today. It's always so hard to do that in the driveway and mom gets mad when I scuff the garage door," Jasper said.

"Well, you needn't worry about that today. We'll practice your backhand shot until it's perfect, but for now, how many slices of French toast do you think you can handle?"

Jasper, fizzing with delight at the prospect of practising hockey all day with his uncle, happily answered, "Three!"

With breakfast finished, Jasper raced upstairs to wash his hands and face and change into warmer clothes. The farmhouse had three bedrooms, although none of them, even Uncle Fredrick's, looked like it was used often. They each had a settled and stiff feeling, like the beds hadn't been slept in for months. The dressers and bedside tables were layered in a thick coat of dust. Nothing moved. There was a stillness and quiet in this part of the farmhouse that Jasper never liked.

Jasper clicked on the lights in the bathroom. They sluggishly flickered to life, glowing deep yellow and humming softly. Jasper took a step and dust swirled up from the floor and into his mouth and nose. He coughed and closed his eyes and swatted his hand in front of his face.

Jasper turned on the taps, which were covered in a murky rust, and out came a sickly gurgling. Brown water spewed out in globs. Jasper let the water run for a few minutes, waiting for it to clear. He was no stranger to the gurgling, rust-coloured water, having dealt with it on every trip to the farm. Not minding at all that the water had been brown only a few moments before, Jasper washed his hands and face and then turned off the taps. Only whiners were grossed out by things like that. Jasper was a hockey player, and that made him tough.

Jasper changed into some thick, fleecy jogging pants and a huge, wool sweater his uncle had given him a few years ago. It came from The Bay and had large, colourful stripes running across the chest. Of course, he pulled on two pairs of thick socks. He knew what his feet were in for and he wanted to avoid the stinging toes of cold weather for as long as possible.

Jasper went back downstairs to find his uncle clearing the breakfast plates.

"All set?" he asked.

"Ready," Jasper said, pulling on his favourite blue toque with the red pom-pom on top. He pulled his heavy winter jacket over his sweater, eager to get outside as he was already feeling warm with in his heavy clothes.

Jasper picked up his skates, tied together by their laces, and hung them over his hockey stick. Uncle Fredrick did the same, his ancient brown leather skates hanging from his solid wood stick, along with a pail full of rubber hockey pucks. Jasper had always liked the gear his uncle used. Of course, he liked his own CCM skates and composite stick, but there was something about his uncle's old-fashioned skates and heavy wood stick that made Jasper think of the days of the first hockey stars, when the NHL was still young. All the adults that liked hockey seemed to like this time the best.

They left the farmhouse and Uncle Fredrick, as always, didn't bother to lock the door. They made their way down the gentle slope of the farmhouse's hilltop, through the empty cornfield, and out towards the frozen pond.

When they reached the pond, they both sat down at the edge to lace up their skates. The ice was smooth and flat. Here and there, the yellowed husks of frozen cattails poked through. Uncle Fredrick had brought a battered goal net down, and it stood at one end of the makeshift rink.

Jasper looked up at his uncle.

"Well, off you go," Uncle Fredrick said, and gave Jasper a soft pat on the back.

Jasper grinned and stepped out on to the ice.

He glided around the rink in large circles, scraping his blades across the ice, shifting his weight between the edges of his skates blades. He loved the feeling of a wide open rink. No one to bump in to or skate around, no one to watch if he made a mistake. Here, anything could happen. He could try any move he wanted, any shot he could think of, and it was all safe. He spun in little circles then weaved down the centre of the rink, drifting from side to side as he warmed up. Uncle Fredrick was busy getting the net in place and Jasper sprayed snow as he came to a quick stop. He grabbed his stick, dumped the pucks onto the ice, and the practice began.

Hours passed. Uncle Fredrick never complained about the time, like Mrs. Jarvis certainly would have done, and Jasper never said a word about his numb nose and frozen toes. Uncle Fredrick waited patiently while Jasper skated up and down the rink, practising stopping, weaving in wide strides from side to side. Uncle Fredrick was a good skater and a good hockey player, and sometimes, he would skate along with Jasper, but mostly, he was happy to watch. Whenever a puck would glide down to his end, he'd easily shoot it back out to Jasper. Uncle Fredrick would call out advice to Jasper, giving him pointers and ideas to try, but it was never mean or angry like Mrs. Jarvis would do during Jasper's games. Uncle Fredrick just wanted Jasper to be the best hockey player he could be.

Jasper started out working on his backhand, then moved on to his wrap-around shot, then on to his slap shot, and then went back to working on his backhand.

"That's great!" called Uncle Fredrick. "Just remember to keep your head up. Try and get your shot off a little quicker."

"Okay," Jasper said, scooping up the puck again. He rounded, heading for the goal.

One, two, three passes from side to side. Head up. Angle to

the right. Get the puck in position and *whack!* he fired off another shot. If there had been a goalie in net, the puck would've flown perfectly over his left shoulder.

"Very nice," Uncle Fredrick said.

Jasper answered him with a huge grin.

It was getting late now. The sun was sinking in the sky and darkness loomed. Jasper's fingers and toes felt frozen solid, his cheeks burned, and his nose ran with a truly gross amount of snot. Uncle Fredrick had long since changed back into his boots, his feet no longer able to withstand the pinch of his skates. All signs pointed to calling it a day.

It was then, out of the quiet of Featherstone Farm, Jasper heard a woman's voice.

"Is *this* him?" It was a lofty, accented voice.

Jasper whirled around, looking for the source, but before he could put the brakes on, he slammed into Uncle Fredrick and collapsed to the ice, smacking his head smartly. It wasn't a particularly impressive way to begin the unbelievable journey that he would undertake that day, but there you have it. This is where it really starts. Jasper began his journey by smacking his head against the ice of the frozen pond on Uncle Fredrick's farm.

Chapter 5

The Door in the Floor

Jasper's head swam and his cheek throbbed as a pair of ridiculously tall high-heels came into view, followed by the tip of a shiny metal cane. He only had a moment to think how odd a get-up it was before he scrambled back onto his skates, rubbing his cheek where it had smashed against the ice.

It was the woman in the top hat. The woman who had been at his game the day before and had been on Peter Drive the night before. The woman who stared with her blank, dark eyes and made him nervous. Here she was, up close and in the flesh.

She wore the same old-fashioned grey dress with the enormous skirt and the same shiny black top hat. The umbrella was gone and the cane was new, but she still carried her yellow briefcase. Her clothes looked too thin to keep her warm in this weather. She looked harsh and hard, like she didn't feel the cold. Up close, she also looked a bit like a business woman, but one that dealt in something nasty, like hunting endangered animals or closing down hospitals. Her bony hand, covered in a bright yellow leather glove, rested atop her chrome cane. Jewel encrusted brass knuckles adorned her gloved fingers. She was fairly young, and so Jasper doubted she needed the cane to walk, and judging by the look on her face, he guessed she used it to hit people when they said something she didn't like. Despite wearing high-heeled shoes on an ice rink, she looked completely stable. Ferocious, really. As though she could break into a run at any moment, brandishing her cane above her head and screaming out a war cry. Jasper chanced a glance up to her eyes, which were as dark as an open closet in the middle of the night, and he had the sudden notion that should the cane fail, her shoes could definitely double as weapons. Overall, she looked annoyed and rather angry just to be there.

"Well?" the woman said, her brow creasing. She was pretty, but the expression she wore made her look bored and angry all at once. Jasper backed toward Uncle Fredrick, edging himself out of the reach of her cane.

"Him? What? No," Uncle Fredrick said in a rush. His face was flushed and he was looking frantically between Jasper and the woman in the top hat. He had his hand splayed out, weakly trying to shield Jasper from view. Jasper was getting nervous. Something was wrong. Uncle Fredrick knew this woman, that much was clear, and he was surprised to see her. Jasper wished he had mentioned her

during the car ride to the farm. Uncle Fredrick was afraid. Jasper's

stomach gave an unsettling clench and he no longer noticed his

frozen fingers and toes.

"But, my dear Fredrick, you have regaled us for months of

tales of a new player. One the likes of which none of us had ever

seen. Surely, you would not be wasting your time with any other.

This must be him." She spoke with such confidence and surety,

Jasper would hate to ever have to disagree with this woman. She

turned her large, black eyes to Jasper and considered him for a

moment. Jasper's mouth went dry. "What's your name, boy?"

"J-".

"*Hush*. He's not the one I told you about. He's not that good.

It would be more trouble than it's worth to take him back," Uncle

Fredrick said, giving a shaky laugh.

In spite of the scary woman standing only a few feet away,

and the worry that if he put one toe out of line he might get a smack

in the face with her cane, Jasper had a moment to feel hurt. Not that

good? Why would Uncle Fredrick say that? He'd always been so

supportive before. All the hours he had spent helping Jasper, had he secretly been laughing at him? Or thinking it was all a waste of time? Jasper's stomach gave another lurch, but this time it had nothing to do with the woman in the top hat.

"I'm pretty good, Uncle. You even said so," Jasper said into the collar of his sweater. He absently tapped his stick on the ice, eyes downcast.

Uncle Fredrick sighed and made a strangled noise in his throat.

"Jasper, you know that's not what -"

"Jasper, is it? Right. Let's see what you can do," the woman in the top hat said.

Jasper didn't move.

"*Now.*"

Jasper was off like a shot. His stiff legs jerked and shook as he glided along the ice. His breathing was fast and heavy as he skated over to the puck. His uncle stood sheepishly next to the woman, wringing his hands and looking nervously at Jasper. As for the woman, she gathered her many skirts, took two graceful steps forward, steady as could be in her enormous heels, and let the fabric fall to the ice in a heavy curtain. She piled both her hands atop her cane and arched her eyebrows slightly, as if to say, "I'm waiting".

Jasper had always felt confident and comfortable while playing hockey, but he was at a loss. What should he do? He had never been put on the spot to impress a terrifying stranger before. Sure, lots scouts came to watch him play, but this was different. He had no idea what this woman wanted. He thought about doing his slap shot, which was pretty hard, but from the way this lady was acting, a backflip followed by a triple axel seemed more appropriate.

Against his better judgement, Jasper skated back over to his uncle and the woman, spraying up a puff of snow as he came to a smooth stop.

"Any requests?"

Before he knew what had happened, Jasper was flat on his back, the chrome cane digging into his chest.

"What did you say?" the woman yelled, voice booming and eyes bulging.

Uncle Fredrick spluttered and made to reach for Jasper, but the woman in the top hat kept him at bay with one bony arm.

"Just trying to be a crowd pleaser," Jasper said, coughing and wincing at the pain in his chest. He should have just gone with a slapshot.

"Do you know who I am, boy?" the woman asked, digging her cane farther into his chest. Jasper squirmed.

"No. How could I? We've only just met." Jasper said.

It was the wrong answer. The cane was joined by the pointed heel of the woman's shoe.

"I'm Ms. Fearce, and make no mistake, I am as fierce as they come. I don't waste my time, I always get what I want, and I have a very short temper. Do not make me angry, boy," Ms. Fearce said in a low voice. "Now," she continued, removing her cane and giving Jasper a kick with her shoe, "Off you go."

Jasper scrambled back onto to his skates. For the next ten minutes, he skated here and there, doing ever shot, trick, and skill he could think of. Adrenaline pumped through his veins. He had been exhausted only moments before, but he was wide awake now. Hearing Uncle Fredrick say that he wasn't that good still stung, and Jasper was determined to do the best he could. Jasper couldn't be sure exactly why, but he wanted to impress Ms. Fearce. She had arrived thinking Jasper was a great hockey player, and even though she had been horrendously mean thus far, Jasper didn't want her to leave thinking otherwise.

Abruptly, Ms. Fearce said, "That will be enough." Her voice carried, crisp and clear, and Jasper came to an immediate stop. Across the frozen pond stood the proud form of Ms. Fearce and the slumped shape of his uncle. Something didn't feel right. Jasper glanced behind him and considered making a run for it, but he knew he wouldn't get far. It was nearly impossibly to run with skates on and besides, he didn't want to leave Uncle Fredrick on his own. Reluctantly, slowly, Jasper made his way across the ice.

"Congratulations, Fredrick. He passes. We'll be off at once. Black is expecting him for the day after tomorrow. We have no time to waste," Ms. Fearce said. At this, Uncle Fredrick went completely pale.

"Are you sure you want him? Perhaps, give me a few more weeks. I could find someone really good," Uncle Fredrick said, his voice trembling, avoiding Jasper's eye. Jasper sniffed, but said nothing.

"Nonsense. The hockey season is already underway. I think

he will do nicely," Ms. Fearce said.

"But..."

Ms. Fearce spun to face Uncle Fredrick. "Is there something you're not telling me?" Uncle Fredrick looked on the verge of speaking, but lost his nerve, crumbling under her gaze.

"No," he whispered.

That seemed to settle the matter. Ms. Fearce grabbed Jasper by the elbow and pulled him from the ice. Tripping and struggling to keep up, Ms. Fearce marched Jasper toward the large grain silo in the corner of Feartherstone Farm. Jasper's ankles ached and he craned his neck to check if Uncle Fredrick followed behind. Questions swirled in his mind, foremost among them, "*Where am I going?!*". For just a moment, Jasper considered asking Ms. Fearce that very question, but when he glanced up and saw the razor-sharp line of her jaw and the angry look in her eyes, he quickly lost his nerve.

Uncle Fredrick hurried along behind them. Jasper glanced back, hoping his uncle might give him a hint as to what was happening, but Uncle Fredrick's eyes were fixed on the ground. Shoulders slumped and his feet shuffling along, he looked on the verge of tears. Jasper only had a moment to realize he was being kidnapped before he was staring up at the towering grain silo.

"Here we are," Ms. Fearce said. She dropped Jasper's elbow, straightened her gloves, and gave her dress a quick primping. She was a prim and proper woman, to be sure. Despite their trudge across the snow-covered field, not a hair was out of place. Her cheeks remained pale and the hem of her dress was dry.

She crisply popped open the large yellow briefcase she carried and began roughly rummaging through its contents, her arm disappearing up to her shoulder as she searched. Jasper edged closer to Uncle Fredrick.

"What's going on?" Jasper asked, trying to speak without moving his lips.

Uncle Fredrick's brow creased and he cast a nervous glance at Ms. Fearce, who still hadn't found what she was looking for in her briefcase. He sighed, giving Jasper a sad smile.

"I promise," he said. "Everything will be okay. I'll explain later."

Ms. Fearce snapped her head around to face them, eyes narrowed.

"Quiet," she said.

Jasper and Uncle Fredrick said no more as Ms. Fearce continued her search.

There were so many questions Jasper wanted to ask. This was all so peculiar. None of it made any sense. He felt nervous and nauseated, and he was sweating like crazy. He was scared. Terrified, really. Ms. Fearce seemed unhinged, with a bad temper besides, and now, clearly, she was in charge. Worst of all, Uncle Fredrick wasn't making much of an effort to stop her. Jasper felt like there was nothing for it but to follow her to wherever it was she wanted to take him.

Jasper thought of his parents and his brother, Jake. What would they say if he didn't come home that evening? Would they know where to look for him? Jasper plucked up his courage and cleared his throat.

"Um, excuse, Miss?" Jasper said, his voice sounding especially meek.

Ms. Fearce dropped whatever she had been holding back into her briefcase and snapped her head around. Her features were set in menacing grimace, like a lion about to pounce.

Jasper couldn't stop his nervous laugh.

"Sorry to interrupt Miss, but, where are you taking me?"

Before the words were even out of his mouth, Jasper regretted speaking them.

Ms. Fearce shoved her briefcase into Uncle Fredrick's hands and stalked over to tower above Jasper. Her eyes bulged and her mouth was a thin line. Jasper scrambled backward, but before he got very far, Ms. Fearce had stretched out one of her long, bony arms. Her grip was surprisingly, and painfully, strong. She grasped him by the collar and lifted him clear off the ground.

Jasper's skates swung back and forth as he choked for air. Uncle Fredrick hurried over, trying to wedge himself between them, but Ms. Fearce used her other, surely just as powerful arm, to hold him back.

"Interrupt me again, waste another second of my precious time, and it will be the last thing you do. Understood?" Ms. Fearce said.

Not understanding was not an option. Jasper made up his mind right then and there not to cross this woman again or to ask her anymore questions. He would have to wait until he was alone with his uncle to figure out what was going on. That, or run away home when the dainty, angry woman with the strength of a caveman wasn't looking.

"Yes, Miss. Sorry, Miss," Jasper said. The collar of his jersey dug painfully into his neck. Ms. Fearce gave him a shake, then tossed him to the ground like a ragdoll.

In a pile on the cold ground, Jasper rubbed his neck and gulped at the fresh air. Ms. Fearce resumed her search in her briefcase. Uncle Fredrick looked nervously at Jasper, but did not approach him. It wasn't long before Ms. Fearce found what she was looking for.

"Here we are," She said, smiling.

She held a semi-circle of rusted iron. There were strange markings cut deep into the metal. The muscles of Ms. Fearce's arm worked under the weight of it and strained against her thin dress, but she did not struggle. Jasper had just a moment to wonder at just how large the inside of Ms. Fearce's briefcase must be if it took her that long to find something that large, but he quickly stopped. Even when he was scared, he really didn't want to be thinking about women's briefcases, or how big the insides of them were.

"Come along," Ms. Fearce said.

She strode through the silo's open door and Uncle Fredrick and Jasper fell in step behind her.

It was dark and dank and smelled of decay. The only light to be had came through the doorway in a murky beam. Specks of dust swirled through the air and Jasper began to cough. The floor was covered in dirt, and straw, and dried grain. Just like everything else on Featherstone Farm, the silo hadn't been used in ages.

Without a second glance to Jasper or Uncle Fredrick, for she was probably quite confident she could catch them if they made a run for it, Ms. Fearce strode to the centre of the silo floor. She kicked a small patch clear and placed the iron semi -circle on the ground. It made a heavy *thunk* as it connected to the dirt with magnetic precision.

Ms. Fearce daintily placed both her gloved hands on the iron and pulled. A perfect square of ground rose away with the metal. In a moment, it was clear. Ms. Fearce had just opened a door in the floor and she had been carrying the handle in her briefcase.

Jasper assumed the door must lead to some underground storage room. Maybe Ms. Fearce planned to tie them up and keep them hostage in there. Maybe they would starve to death or be eaten alive by rats. Maybe Ms. Fearce would return, weeks later, to check on her handiwork, and when she saw the skeletons of her captives, she would cackle at the moon in victory because doing this sort of thing made her very happy indeed.

Jasper's imagination tended to run wild at times.

Jasper shook the images from his head. On second thought, his eaten-alive-by-rats theory didn't really make sense. Hadn't she said something about a hockey season already underway? He would need to be alive to play, he reasoned.

Jasper crept closer for a better look. It was completely black. The light from the door faltered before it could fall upon the opening. Rather than send out sounds of whatever might be hidden within the darkness below, the dark square in the ground gave off silence. The sounds of the silo withered and died as Jasper drew near.

"Let's have a bit of fun, shall we?" Ms. Fearce said.

Jasper didn't say anything, and neither did Uncle Fredrick. This couldn't be good. Whatever this woman considered fun was bound be dangerous or evil. Or both.

Ms. Fearce walked back outside and disappeared from view.

"Come along!" she said.

Jasper and Uncle Fredrick did as they were told.

Ms. Fearce had rounded the wall of the silo and came to a stop in front of a metal ladder. The ladder was rusty and rickety and ran the length of the silo's wall, from ground to roof.

"After you," Ms. Fearce said, smiling her bone-chilling smile at Jasper.

Jasper's stomach gave an uncomfortable lurch. He was not a fan of heights.

"Is this really necessary?" Uncle Fredrick asked, his voice shaking but his face stern.

Ms. Fearce's smile fell immediately.

"No," she said. "But it will be highly entertaining, I'm sure."

"But what if he gets hurt?" Uncle Fredrick said, placing one of his big hands on Jasper's shoulder.

Ms. Fearce let out a loud sigh. Questions, just like everything else, seemed to annoy her.

"If he's as good at getting pucks in the net as you say he is, then surely he'll have no problem getting himself into that door. It's quite large, wouldn't you say?"

Again, Jasper and Uncle Fredrick said nothing.

Ms. Fearce gave another loud sigh, turned to Uncle Fredrick and said, "You first."

Uncle Fredrick hesitated. Ms. Fearce's leather gloves squeaked as she tightened her grip on her cane. Uncle Fredrick checked the distance to the top of the silo and then began to carefully climb the ladder, his boots making a dull *plunk* with every step.

Ms. Fearce watched him climb and the smile reappeared on her face.

"Off you go," she said, turning to Jasper. She flicked her head in the direction of the ladder and her hat didn't budge an inch.

Jasper didn't move.

"I won't. I don't want to. I don't like heights," he said. Things had gone from bad to worse to dangerous. Once again, the thought of making a run for it crossed his mind, but Jasper couldn't, and wouldn't, leave Uncle Fredrick alone with Ms. Fearce.

Ms. Fearce narrowed her dark eyes, but never looked away

from Jasper's face. She reached out a long arm and grabbed the cuff

of Uncle Fredrick's jeans. His uncle had climbed six steps by now,

and was a considerable way up from the ground.

Uncle Fredrick froze.

"Do it, or I'll pull him to the ground," Ms. Fearce said, her grip

tightening on Uncle Fredrick's cuff. "He's not as young as he once

was. He's bound to be hurt. Maybe crack his skull."

Jasper ignored her.

"Uncle!" Jasper said, craning his neck to where Uncle

Fredrick clung to the ladder. "Won't you just come down? *Please?*"

Uncle Fredrick said nothing, however, only hunched his

shoulders and looked away. Jasper stood his ground and Ms. Fearce

gave a sharp tug at the hem of Uncle Fredrick's jeans. His footing

faltered and he scrambled to hold the ladder tighter.

Jasper wouldn't see Uncle Fredrick hurt, and so his mind was

made up. Giving Ms. Fearce the meanest look he could muster,

narrowed eyes and angry eyebrows included, Jasper pushed past her

and began to climb the ladder. Ms. Fearce followed him.

Their progress to the top of the silo was slow. It was getting dark and the wind made the already cold evening unbearable. It was the chilliest of wind chills. The metal of the ladder's rungs stung against Jasper's bare hands, sticking at times and tearing off bits of skin. With every step, he hoped snow would shake loose from his skate blades and land in Ms. Fearce's eyes.

When they finally reached the top, they stood around a small opening in the roof of the silo. Jasper looked down and his vision swam. The door Ms. Fearce had opened in the silo floor looked miles away. Jasper had a sinking feeling that he knew what was surely coming next.

"Here we are," Ms. Fearce said, again giving her clothes a quick straightening and tilting her top hat, making it just so. "Jump!"

Ms. Fearce laughed and pushed Jasper nearer to the opening.

Jasper dug in his heels as best he could and squirmed out of her grasp. He *really* didn't like heights, much less jumping from them.

"You first?"

"I don't think so," Ms. Fearce said, giving Jasper a prod with her cane. "Not to worry. Your uncle and I shall be right behind you."

Jasper gave his uncle one more look, hoping against hope that he would manage to get them out of this mess, but Uncle Fredrick looked away, frowning. Clearly, Uncle Fredrick wasn't going to help him. Jasper looked again to the silo floor below, his head swimming. Despite the cold, he was sweating.

"Fine," Jasper said, taking a wobbly step towards the opening.

Jasper was furious with his uncle. How could he be letting this happen? Wasn't he supposed to protect Jasper? Why was he letting Ms. Fearce get away with this?

Numbed by his anger, Jasper forgot his fear of heights. He stepped to the edge of the opening in the silo's roof, squared his shoulders like a diver preparing to take the plunge, gave Uncle Fredrick one last look, and leaped.

The fall didn't last nearly as long as Jasper expected. Jasper had always been led to believe, thanks to watching movies about secret agents, that falling long distances happened in slow motion. Your hair was supposed to flutter gracefully across your face, your eyes growing wide with fear as a single bead of sweat dripped down your forehead and you screamed "*Noooo!*", arms flailing and hands grasping.

Instead, one second Jasper was on the roof of the silo, the next he felt like he might be sick as blurs of colour flashed by his eyes, and the next he was in complete darkness, staring up at a perfectly square, shrinking patch of light. He had successfully jumped through the door in the silo floor.

Jasper wasn't sure how long he was in the darkness before he was no longer falling. He had landed in a smooth, cold, slanted tunnel and immediately began sliding downwards, the patch of light from the silo door shrinking away until it became a speck and then disappeared all together. His skates collided with an earthy flatness and he came to a stop. There were bumps and bangs as Ms. Fearce and Uncle Fredrick slid down behind him, coming to a heavy stop with a muffled *thud*. Jasper tried to stand, but he was knocked to the ground when his head collided with the hard roof of the tunnel. He blindly reached outward and felt the moist dirt surrounding them.

"Keep moving!" Ms. Fearce said, giving Jasper's ankles a whack with her cane.

"*Ouch!*"

Jasper jumped away and took the opportunity to kick some

dirt at Ms. Fearce. Her cane was more painful than it looked. Jasper decided he would double his efforts to avoid the business end of it from now on.

The ceiling was too low to stand and so Jasper crawled slowly forward, his hands and knees sinking into the earthen floor. The air was musty and smelled of worms. There was no light to speak of and it made no difference whether Jasper opened his eyes as wide as he could or closed them shut. It was pitch black. Jasper carefully felt his way forward into the unknown darkness, not knowing what horrible, slimy, mean little creatures with sharp teeth must surely be waiting for him. Every so often, Ms. Fearce would give the back of Jasper's legs a swift jab with her cane to hurry him along.

They carried on like this, for what felt like hours, in near silence. The only sounds were Jasper's coughing on the thick air and Uncle Fredrick's laboured breathing. Jasper felt light headed, his back ached, his hands were cut and bleeding, and his feet stung in his tightly laced hockey skates. His face dripped with sweat and he was sure the foul smell filling his nose was coming from him. Without a second thought, he shrugged out of his winter jacket and abandoned it there. His one consolation in this misery was picturing

Ms. Fearce, prim and proper as you please, crawling along on all fours through the dirt, tearing her dress, mucking up her shoes, and ruining her perfectly slicked back hairdo. With any luck, Jasper thought, that silly hat of hers will have been crushed as well.

At long, long last, a small light appeared ahead, far off down the tunnel.

"Move along, boy," Ms. Fearce said, giving Jasper another whack with her cane. "We're nearly there."

Jasper obeyed. Not because he cared what Ms. Fearce said, but because he was sure that if he didn't get out of that tunnel and into some fresh air soon, he would go crazy.

Jasper crawled faster, sweat dripping into his eyes, knees smarting, and arms shaking with pain. The way forward began to rise. The incline of the tunnel became steeper and steeper until Jasper was almost completely upright, pulling at roots and rocks to hoist himself farther onwards and upwards.

The light up ahead was close now. It was painful to look at straight on after the complete darkness of the tunnel. Jasper's eyes ached to close themselves against the brilliant white. The opening ahead was perfectly square, just like the door Ms. Fearce had opened in the silo floor.

Jasper was climbing now, grabbing frantically at the clods of earth, the square door growing larger. As he reached the opening, Jasper flung his arm through, his hand grasping wildly. He was surprised to close his fist around a clump of long, frozen grass.

Jasper threw out his other hand and dug his fingers into the solid ground, pulling himself out of the tunnel. He flopped onto his back, breathing hard, staring up into the bluest sky he'd ever seen. The snow on the ground soaked his sweater and he regretted leaving his jacket behind. Wind blew softly, and somewhere not far off, birds chirped and trees creaked in the breeze.

Jasper closed his eyes and gulped down the fresh air, sweat cooling on his brow. His heart was hammering in his chest. All too quickly, he was joined by Ms. Fearce and Uncle Fredrick. They climbed out of the tunnel, Ms. Fearce first, then Uncle Fredrick. Uncle Fredrick looked as filthy as Jasper felt, his sweaty face covered in dirt and his clothes torn, but Ms. Fearce didn't have a spot on her. Jasper's jaw nearly hit the ground. Ms. Fearce's hat was still perched perfectly atop her head, her dress was as neat and tidy as ever, and her gloves were the same nauseatingly bright shade of yellow. Her shoes shone and her hair gleamed.

There was a scratching and rustling from the tunnel. Two pink, pointed ears popped above the edge, followed by the lanky body of Hercules, Uncle Fredrick's streetwise white cat.

"*Hercules!*" Jasper said, and the cat ran to him. "What are you doing here? Did you follow us?"

Hercules gave Jasper a friendly headbutt and purred, curling himself on Jasper's lap.

Ms. Fearce ignored Hercules and gave herself a quick once over, dusting away dirt that wasn't there. Then she turned on her heel and strode over to this new door, and in one heave, closed it shut with a loud *clonk!* This door had a matching handle to the first, which Ms. Fearce neatly plucked from the ground and popped into her briefcase. Metal clanged against metal and Jasper guessed Ms. Fearce had somehow managed to close the door in Uncle Fredrick's silo and bring the handle with her.

A sinking feeling swept over Jasper as he looked back to the spot where this new door had just been. At least, he looked to where he thought it had been, because now it was impossible to tell. The entire area appeared as just a simple patch of frozen grass. Just like,

Jasper was sure, the floor of the silo back on Uncle Fredrick's farm would appear to be just that and nothing more.

Just as Jasper was beginning to feel the stirrings of panic, realizing that no one knew he was here, no one would be able to get here to help him, and he had no way of getting home, Ms. Fearce, stretching out her arms and flashing Jasper a smile that chilled him to his bones, said, "Welcome to Magmelland."

Chapter 6

Magmelland

"I'm sorry, where?" Jasper asked. He'd never heard the name before and it sounded awfully silly.

"Magmelland."

"What's that?"

"*Here*."

"And where's '*here*?'"

"Idiot boy!" Ms. Fearce swung her cane at Jasper's head, but he leapt out of the way.

Ms. Fearce growled in her throat.

"I do not have the patience nor time to deal with this child's insolence. Fredrick, you explain to him what he must know. I will lead us to the city. Move!"

Without another word, Ms. Fearce sped off, ploughing through the field. Her many skirts and high-heels gave her no trouble as she swung her cane ferociously from side to side, cutting a path in the tall, frozen grass.

Jasper and Uncle Fredrick plodded along behind her, keeping a safe distance. Ms. Fearce had proven herself to be something of a loose cannon and Jasper, nor his uncle, wanted anything else to do with her antics.

Jasper's ankles ached. He was fed up with wobbling along in his skates over the uneven grassy field, so plunked down to free his feet. He pried off his skates and flexed his sore soles. His feet were warm and sweaty but already, Jasper felt the cold. Without a word, Uncle Fredrick unlaced his boots and handed them to Jasper.

"Come along, Jasper," Uncle Fredrick said.

Jasper gave him an ugly look.

"What's going on?" Jasper asked. He didn't want to make a scene, but he would, if he didn't get some answers.

"Come along, and I'll do my best to explain," Uncle Fredrick said, pulling Jasper to his feet.

Jasper tried to hand the boots back to his uncle, but Uncle Fredrick would not have it. A moment later, Jasper was flopping along in his uncle's boots, which were at least eight sizes too large, feeling like a clown.

Jasper fought the impulse to ask a hundred questions at once and waited for Uncle Fredrick to explain. With the laces of his skates knotted together over his shoulder, Jasper trotted along beside his uncle and listened.

"This is Magmelland," Uncle Fredrick said, echoing Ms. Fearce. His uncle shot him a sideways, cautious glance.

Jasper held his tongue and waited for more.

"It's a small country that's part of another world. Far away from the one we just left."

Jasper blinked in disbelief and was silent for a few moments.

"How far away?"

To Jasper, it didn't seem like they had travelled that far. True, they had crawled along in that tunnel for what felt like hours, but it could have only been a few kilometres at most.

Uncle Fredrick considered this for a moment while they walked on, Hercules weaving in and out about their ankles and purring loudly.

"It's difficult to say," Uncle Fredrick said, and pulled his jean jacket tighter around him. Magmelland was cold. "Have you ever wondered what's on the other side of the mirror, or what's down in the deepest, darkest parts of the ocean, or way up high above the clouds?"

"I guess..." Jasper answered slowly. Uncle Fredrick wasn't making much sense.

"It's sort of like that. It's a world that's way out of reach, except for the odd lucky glimpse."

"But then how did *we* get here?"

Shivering in the cold and exhausted, Jasper didn't feel particularly lucky.

To Jasper's surprise, Uncle Fredrick chuckled.

"Magic, of course!"

"You must be joking," Jasper said, and laughed too.

"Nope."

"Really?"

"Really."

"I don't believe you," Jasper said. Jasper had always known

Uncle Fredrick was a bit strange, but now he wondered if he might not be full-on crazy. Magic? Everyone knows there's no such thing as magic.

"But, wait." Jasper had a thought. "Why do you know about Magmelland? Have you been here before?"

"Of course! I live here. There's a big city, just up the way. Lived there my whole life."

"But what about Featherstone Farm? I thought you lived there. Didn't you grow up in Toronto? Or Alberta? No, Vancouver! Does my dad know about Magmelland too, since you're brothers? And what were you doing in the other world? The one with your farm in it?"

Jasper couldn't hold back the flood of questions any longer.

"I was in the other world, the one with the farm it, to look after you. I promised I would," Uncle Fredrick said, slowly, ignoring Jasper's other questions.

Jasper's head was beginning to ache with trying to figure this all out.

"Promised to who?"

A nervous twinge twisted Jasper's stomach. He didn't know why, but he desperately wanted to know just who his uncle had made that promise to.

"I promised -"

"*What are you saying?*"

The piercing voice of Ms. Fearce halted Jasper and his uncle in their tracks. She whipped her head around and glared at the pair of them. They had fallen behind her breakneck pace while they talked. Her left eye twitched and if Jasper didn't know better, he would say that the crunching sound he heard was Ms. Fearce grinding her perfect white teeth.

"Nothing, Ms. Fearce!" Uncle Fredrick grabbed Jasper by the elbow and pulled him quickly along. "Just letting the boy know about his training schedule." Uncle Fredrick's voice was calm, but the grip he had on Jasper's elbow was painfully tight.

Ms. Fearce looked them up and down and twirled her cane smoothly through her gloved fingers. It looked to Jasper like she was considering whose kneecaps would be easier to break, his or his uncle's, and how fun it might be to find out.

"Very well," Ms. Fearce said. "The boy knows what he must.

No more of this idle chatter. We've wasted enough time. Keep up."

Ms. Fearce turned on her heel and sped off at an even quicker pace. Jasper and Uncle Fredrick followed, struggling to keep up. When Ms. Fearce had widened the space between them by just enough, Jasper glanced up at his uncle.

"So, who did you-"

"*Shhhhh.*" Uncle Fredrick hushed Jasper, quietly and fiercely. "We can't talk about this now. Not when she might hear. I forgot myself. I will tell you when I can, but please, do this for me now." Jasper strained to hear each slowly spoken word.

Uncle Fredrick looked nervous and scared. Finding out who Uncle Fredrick made his promise to would have to wait. Jasper gave one nod of his head and that settled the matter.

They walked along in silence awhile. The frozen grass crunched beneath their feet and from up ahead came the *whoosh!* of Ms. Fearce's cane as she whacked it from side to side, cutting through the tall grass and sending up puffs of powdery snow with every swing.

"Why am I here?" Jasper asked, keeping his voice low.

Uncle Fredrick's face relaxed and he flashed Jasper a wide grin.

"To play hockey!" Uncle Fredrick said, clapping Jasper on the back.

Jasper couldn't believe his ears, or his luck. If being kidnapped and taken to an unknown world, far away from his family and friends, by an angry and violent stranger was a bitter pill to swallow, knowing he would still get to play hockey was nice way to wash it down.

"Awesome!" Jasper said, grinning back at his uncle.

"Not a moment too soon, either. The team needs you, Jasper. They've been struggling for a long time. They need someone with your talent," Uncle Fredrick said.

Relief and happiness rushed through Jasper and he silently, and completely, forgave Uncle Fredrick for what he had said earlier about Jasper not being a good hockey player.

Once again, Jasper's mind was full of questions, but these were much happier ones. What would his teammates be like? Where was the arena? How early in the morning would he have to get up to go to practice? Could he keep number 93 as his jersey number?

Jasper walked faster, brimming with excitement. He wanted to get to the city as soon as he could.

"Why me, uncle? Aren't there enough hockey players here? It seems like an awful lot of work to cross between two worlds just to pick up a new player." Jasper's happiness at the thought of playing hockey dulled for a moment. Something just didn't add up.

Uncle Fredrick sighed.

"Yes and no. There's so much to tell you....." he trailed off, his brow creased. Uncle Fredrick gave Jasper an uneasy glance, a worried look passing over his face. In that moment Jasper knew there was something his uncle wasn't telling him.

Uncle Fredrick cleared his throat and began again.

"There are lots of hockey players here, but Magmelland doesn't have a tradition of playing hockey. Hockey's new for us. Not like in Canada. Not like in the world we just left. Our hockey players don't have the same skill or love of the game, like you have," Uncle Fredrick said proudly and ruffled Jasper's hair.

They walked on. Uncle Fredrick's thick wool socks were soaked through, but he would not accept his boots back from Jasper. Every now and then, Ms. Fearce would snap her head around, top hat glued firmly to her head, to glare at Jasper and Uncle Fredrick.

Each time she did, Jasper and his uncle would immediately stop

talking and look away. Ms. Fearce was certainly the sort of person

you'd want to keep secrets from.

The landscape was filled with rolling hills hidden beneath a

thick blanket of snow. Little farms dotted the countryside, their

thatched roofs and puffing chimneys popping out against the

whiteness. The sun crept higher in the sky and despite it being late

in the evening back in Paris (Ontario....not Paris, France) on Uncle

Fredrick's farm, it was early afternoon in Magmelland.

Jasper tried prying more information from his uncle.

"Uncle Fredrick."

"Mmm?"

"You said hockey was new to Magmelland." The word felt

strange and unfamiliar on Jasper's tongue.

"Right. We've only had hockey in Magmelland for about thirty

years, I think. The history's a bit murky, but Lord Tan's a huge fan."

"Really? Who's his favourite team?" Jasper asking, laughing.

"The Montreal Canadiens."

"What? But, how?"

"He saw a game years ago on a visit to the other world. Boston at Montreal. He's loved hockey, and the Habs, ever since."

Jasper was stunned.

"Wow," he said. "The Habs really do have fans everywhere."

"Indeed."

"Wait, wait. Who's Lord Tan? And what was he doing in -" Jasper paused a moment, saying it in his head before he said it out loud. "The other world."

Uncle Fredrick said nothing for a few moments. He seemed to be thinking hard, considering each word of his reply carefully. He gave Jasper a long look before he finally answered.

"Lord Tan is the ruler of Magmelland. He has been for years. He's-" Uncle Fredrick dropped his voice. "He's not a nice.....person. But! He loves hockey, and that's where you come in. As for Lord Tan visiting the other world, well, to be honest, there's a lot of coming and going between the two worlds. People just don't tend to notice it. They're much too busy working and shopping and rushing from one thing to the next to notice anything magical. It's unfortunate, really."

Jasper considered this for a moment. Then, he had a thought.

"If Lord Tan is a Canadiens fan, why doesn't he want adults to play hockey for him? Why is he getting kids to play? Unless, I mean, are the other players kids too?" For a terrifying moment, Jasper thought all the other players on his team would be adults and full body-checking would be allowed. He was only 12, but had played with kids as old as 15 before. He knew he could handle that, even if it was a little tricky at times. 15-year-olds were one thing, but adults were quite another.

"Ah, there's so still so much to tell you," Uncle Fredrick said again. "Yes, the other players will be around your age and no, adults don't play hockey in Magmelland. Adults don't play anything here. Adults work. That's the way Lord Tan wants it."

"I like that he likes hockey, but I don't like that he's no fun," Jasper said.

"No fun is right. Lord Tan is quite a character," Uncle Fredrick said.

The sun rose higher in the sky and the air warmed. They walked past empty fields filled with stiff, frozen ridges of hard earth, across ice-covered brooks, through prickly patches of evergreen berry bushes, and down snow-swept, lonely dirt roads. Hercules chased bushy brown squirrels at every chance, his white coat hiding him against the snow until he was ready to pounce. They passed more farms, both big and small, as they continued on their way. Some farms were surrounded by fenced in, empty white fields, while others were home to small herds of cows or horses. Every farm they passed was certainly better taken care of than Featherstone Farm. Jasper gasped, smiling.

"You don't spend much time in the other world, do you, uncle?" Jasper asked, but he already knew the answer. Why else would the chicken coop always be so full of eggs? Or the farmhouse so full of dust? Uncle Fredrick was rarely there.

"No. Not much. Just to check in on you, mostly," Uncle Fredrick said. He was watching the back of Ms. Fearce's head intently and said no more. Ms. Fearce had slowed her breakneck pace and she was quite near now.

They had come to a dell full of thick, thorny bushes coated in frost. A large hill was straight ahead, a dark and tangled forest to the right, and a frozen solid, perfectly round pond to the left. In the exact centre of the dell stood a wrought iron signpost with three arms, each pointing towards either the hill, the forest, or the pond.

Ms. Fearce stopped in front of the signpost and waited for Uncle Fredrick and Jasper to catch up. She clicked her long fingernails on the shiny head of her cane impatiently and turned her head over her shoulder to glare at them. Jasper couldn't be sure, but he thought he saw Ms. Fearce's head turn a little too far over her shoulder to be natural. Just like an owl would do.

As Jasper and his uncle closed the distance between themselves and Ms. Fearce, her crisp voice filled the dell.

"This is where I leave you. Fredrick, I suspect you can handle things from here. Take the boy to the Pavilion at once. He starts tonight," Ms. Fearce said. Uncle Fredrick nodded.

Ms. Fearce turned to Jasper, looking like she might say something. Her neck was again twisted painfully far over her shoulder. Jasper had the sudden urge to run.

Thankfully, there was no need. Ms. Fearce only narrowed her eyes, flared her nostrils, and then snapped her head around. She tossed her briefcase on the ground and it connected with magnetic precision. She daintily bent to open it. Rather than packed to the brim with odds and ends, including the metal handles from earlier, the open briefcase revealed a set of splintering wooden stairs that disappeared down into darkness. It was peculiar, but Jasper found he was not surprised. It was the most magical briefcase he'd ever seen.

The yawning mouth of the briefcase was black against the snow. Ms. Fearce gathered her skirts in one hand. Her heels made a hollow knocking as she stepped down each stair. Just as her head was disappearing into the darkness, her yellow-gloved hand shot upwards and pulled the sides of the briefcase together. She tugged downward. The ground rippled and with a faint *pop!* Ms. Fearce, her hand, and her briefcase snapped out of sight. Where ever she now was, Jasper was sure Ms. Fearce had managed to bring her magic briefcase along.

"Finally!" Uncle Fredrick said, and Jasper laughed.

"There's so many things I want to ask you," Jasper said, speaking quickly. He was glad Ms. Fearce had gone and was hoping to finally get some answers.

Uncle Fredrick looked left and right, then listened for a moment. He fixed Jasper with a serious look.

"I know, Jasper, I know. I promise, all will be explained," He said, before dropping his voice to a whisper. "But now is not the time. It's not safe. We don't know who's listening. We need to be careful."

Uncle Fredrick's face was so serious that any questions Jasper had would have to wait. He trusted his uncle and if Uncle Fredrick said it wasn't safe, then it wasn't safe and that was that. Jasper would wait.

Jasper glanced around them, almost expecting to see hooded figures watching from the trees, but there were only birds up in the branches, and they weren't interested in Jasper and his uncle.

Uncle Fredrick walked over to the sign post. The arrow pointing towards the hill read "TARA", the arrow pointing towards the pond read "PETRIFIED POND", and the arrow pointing towards the tangled, dark forest read "HAROLDWOOD FOREST".

"This way," Uncle Fredrick said, nodding towards the hill. Jasper was relieved they were walking away from the forest.

They walked up the hill, Jasper and Uncle Fredrick slipping on the snow-covered fallen leaves, while Hercules made short work of the climb. Seagulls cawed and the air smelled of salt. There was water nearby. With every trudging step up the large hill, the sounds of waves breaking on a shore grew clearer. The wind blew harder and the wooden creak of boats echoed.

As they came to the top of the hill, Jasper saw Tara for the first time, and it was beautiful. The sprawling city stretched as far as he could see, glinting and sparkling in the late afternoon sun. Surrounded by a high stone wall, with endless turrets and spires dotted along its ledge, the city looked to be bursting at the seams. Buildings of every shape, colour, and size were packed into the walls, with some soaring high above the already high stone walls, and others just peeking above the ledge. Silvery-blue and bubblegum pink, roofs covered with grass and others with beaded glass, houses that shimmered as if made of liquid and others that were built into trees, silky flags of purple and gold, and columns of orange and turquoise smoke. Poles striped like candy canes and beams of light filled with floating sparkles. Tinkling music and shouts of laughter. Every stone and brick and splash of colour was buzzing with energy. Tara was a city that begged to be explored, and Jasper couldn't wait to start.

The land came to a point beyond the far wall of Tara. Deep blue waves were crashing upon a frozen, rocky shore. A pearly white lighthouse stood on an outcropping of rocks on the eastern side of the city. It was a beautiful lighthouse, but cold and lonely as well.

Across the water, another mass of land was visible on this clear afternoon. It was dark and gray, refusing the light and warmth of the sun, and so remained in shadow.

"What do you think?" Uncle Fredrick asked. He was clearly very proud of his hometown.

"It's amazing," Jasper said, and he meant it.

Jasper led the way down the hill, eager to reach Tara. His skates swung from side to side, still knotted over his shoulder, as his walk soon turned into a run. The sounds of Tara grew louder. Shouts of laughter and rhythmic music, snatches of sentences in a language Jasper didn't know, and sharp spices that tickled his nose. Tara seemed to breathe, expanding and shrinking with the life that filled it.

The entrance to the walled city of Tara was marked by a pair of enormous wooden doors in the stone walls. They were wide open, welcoming all those who would enter. Jasper and Uncle Fredrick, with Hercules in tow, passed through the doors. A wall of sound and colour and music and magic hit Jasper all at once. The city whirred under its heavy blanket of crisp snow.

There were people milling about inside, and their clothing matched the city. Some wore wide dresses like Ms. Fearce, but theirs were alive with colour and shining jewellery. Some wore lose fitting smocks over sweaters, with baggy pants and heavy shoes. Hats and scarves of every colour, shape, and size imaginable adorned the passersby. Some had short, neat hair, while others looked wild with beads hanging from tangled dreadlocks. Pointed ears and oddly slanted eyes on some with skin so pale, it seemed to glow with reflected light. Some were short and squat, only as tall as Jasper's waist, while others towered above Uncle Fredrick by a wide margin. Jasper realized he was seeing dwarves and giants for the first time.

Uncle Fredrick took Jasper by the hand, leading him down narrow alleyways and wide cobblestone streets. Everywhere, there were people and things Jasper had never see before. Brightly coloured, exotic fruit being sold by a woman with faintly green skin. An enormous man, who Jasper was sure must certainly be a giant, washing the windows on the third story of slanting red brick house. A group of children using their hands and feet to cling to the side of a sandstone building, flinging a ball back and forth to each other, far overhead. Everywhere, there were sounds and colours and languages and smells Jasper had never experienced before. It was incredible.

Warm laughter tinkled on the air and Jasper looked up to see the prettiest woman he'd ever seen in his entire life. She was walking on the opposite side of the alleyway, carrying a wicker basket overflowing with strange fruits. Her hair was a golden yellow and her eyes were large and blue and when she smiled at Jasper, he felt his entire face flush and he had to look away.

"Careful now," Uncle Fredrick said, chuckling. "That's one of the sirens."

"What's a siren?" Jasper asked, hoping the flush in his face would fade fast.

"They live in the lighthouse, down by the water. They take care of Somnia," Uncle Fredrick said, pulling Jasper through the crowded street, past carts full of food and furniture and animals.

"Somnia?" Jasper asked, confused. Was that her real name?

"She lives in the lighthouse, but she never leaves. They say she's even prettier than the sirens."

Uncle Fredrick stopped. He looked from left to right, and then left again. He had never been very good with directions, and apparently that went for any world he found himself in.

Jasper didn't want to think about anyone prettier than the siren he had seen, for fear he would blush again, and so instead said, "Why doesn't she leave?"

"She can't," Uncle Fredrick said without looking at Jasper. "I think we might be a little lost. Let's try this way."

Uncle Fredrick pulled Jasper by the arm through another throng of people, and Jasper, still enthralled by the sights and sounds of Tara, did not see the frazzled woman until it was too late. The woman was thin and mousy and Jasper knocked her to the ground as they collided. Brown paper packages spilled from her arms and landed with soft *plops* in the snow. The woman adjusted her bulky glasses and looked up at Jasper.

"Sorry," she said.

"Sorry," Jasper said back.

Without another word the woman pulled herself to her feet and began collecting the packages. She had a distracting amount of curly red hair sprouting from her head and with each reach for a package, her hair bobbed and fluttered.

Jasper and Uncle Fredrick made to help the woman, but she said, "No, no. It's quite all right. These are very delicate. Artefacts, you know. It takes a skilled hand."

Jasper and Uncle Fredrick instead stood and watched and waited, not feeling it was right to leave until the woman had righted herself.

At last, she had rebuilt her teetering tower of brown paper and rested her chin upon the top to steady it. She turned to leave and had only made it a few steps before Jasper called out to her.

"Miss! Wait! You forgot one."

A small package sat nearly hidden in the snow. Jasper grabbed it. It was heavy for its size, and there was a metallic clink as the paper shifted in his hand.

"Oh! Thank you. Um," the woman's hands were clinging precariously around the stack of packages. "Just in my pocket, please."

Jasper pushed the heavy little package into the woman's pocket, past a metal ring packed full with keys. With that, she nodded and Jasper waved and they parted company.

Uncle Fredrick and Jasper continued on their way, trudging through the snow, past a never ending stream of twisting staircases, windows set deep into sloping brick walls, and doors painted red and purple and blue and gold. Down wide streets and narrow alleys, with laundry hanging on ropes high overhead and sidewalks crowded with people. All around there were shouts and laughter, squeals of children playing, and the chit chat of everyday life. All the while, Hercules had followed dutifully behind, stopping here and there to investigate interesting odds and ends, but never losing pace with Jasper and his uncle. When they reached the junction of four woefully worn and twisted streets, Hercules rose on his hind legs, gave Jasper's knees a quick knead with his front paws, and then took off down the nearest alleyway.

"Hercules!" Jasper called after the cat, his stubby tail disappearing in the gloom of the alley. "Get back here!"

"Not to worry," Uncle Fredrick said. "He's gone to Hag Hill."

Uncle Fredrick pointed to a weatherworn wooden street sign.

"He'll be fine. Hag Hill's where all the cats live, and Hercules likes it there. I'm sure you'll see him around."

Jasper had always known Hercules to be a cat capable of taking care of himself, and so didn't put up a fight. Uncle Fredrick continued walking, and Jasper hurried along behind him.

After what felt like an hour, they rounded one last corner. Jasper looked up at a swirling, pyramid shaped building, made of smooth sandstone. Water spouted from the very top and poured into a wide trench that spiralled around the outside of the building, and then flowed into a large moat at the base. Trees and shrubs and hanging vines sprouted from the water channel and snaked their way up and down the sides of the building. Uniform rectangular windows dotted the walls, with bright green shutters hanging on either side. From here, it looked like all the floors inside must spiral upwards as well. A set of large, rectangular doors opened onto a drawbridge spanning the width of the moat.

"This," Uncle Fredrick said, clapping Jasper on the shoulder, "Is the Players Pavilion. Welcome home!"

Chapter 7

The Players Pavilion

"Players Pavilion?" Jasper repeated, looking the building up and down once more. The water swirling around the outside of the Pavilion looked like it would make for a perfect waterslide. Jasper liked the place immediately.

"This is where all the hockey players live. Your teammates are inside," Uncle Fredrick said. He pulled a pocket watch from his jeans. "They've finished their lessons for the day. It'll be dinner time soon."

At the mention of dinner, Jasper's stomach grumbled loud enough for Uncle Fredrick to hear. They hadn't eaten since breakfast. Uncle Fredrick ruffled Jasper's hair.

"Sorry about missing lunch. We'll get you settled in, then you'll have your dinner."

Uncle Fredrick led the way across the drawbridge. It creaked with every step and swayed as they walked. There were no railings or ropes to hold on to. Falling over the edge would be easy. The water below flowed smoothly, and it was so clear Jasper could see the speckled rocks lining the moat. Rainbow-scaled fish lazily swam by. A few stopped to stare at Jasper, and he stared back. Then, the fish flicked their tails in a flash of rainbow light and were on their way again.

Jasper and Uncle Fredrick passed through the large set of doors at the end of the drawbridge. They were made of a thick, bumpy glass with hundreds of bubbles trapped inside. Wrought iron branches and leaves climbed up the sides, forming two handles in the centre. The doors hummed with an electric buzz. Jasper reached out his hand. As his skin touched the glass, a biting shock shot up his arm and he jumped back.

"*Ow!*"

Jasper's hand was red and already starting to swell.

"You want to be careful with those," a wheezy voice said.

A short old man was limping his way over. The leathery skin of his face was crinkled with wrinkles and his eyelids drooped. Frizzy brown hair flecked with grey poked out from under a sloppily made red woolen toque. He wore layers of mismatched, bulky clothing which made him look larger than his skinny wrists suggested. On his hands, different from the rest, he wore gloves woven of a silky, dark metal.

"You need these to touch them doors," he said, giving the gloves a shake. "Magic needs magic, you know."

The old man barked out a laugh and then limped over to Uncle Fredrick.

"Fredrick! Wasn't expecting to see you here. You haven't been 'round to see us in ages."

The old man's breathing was heavy now. Each breath whistled past his teeth.

"I've been busy. Bogg, meet Jasper." Uncle Fredrick nodded to Jasper, who smiled politely. "He'll be joining the team."

"Ahhhh, really?" Bogg said, scratching his lumpy chin, looking Jasper up and down. "I wasn't expecting you to bring in a new player so suddenly. Hadn't heard anything about it. Quite the surprise, this."

Bogg stared at Jasper. Jasper gave an awkward smile and became suddenly incredibly interested in the shoes Uncle Fredrick had leant him.

"Yes, this was a little...unexpected," Uncle Fredrick said.

"He looks young. How old are you, boy?"

"Twelve."

"Twelve? That's too young for us, innit?" Bogg said looking up at Uncle Fredrick. The old man looked surprised, and maybe even a little angry.

"I know he's young but he's absolutely the best we could find."

Jasper swelled with pride at this, but Uncle Fredrick was frowning.

"All right, all right. Take your word for it. He's got skates, anyhow. Strange looking skates, but I s'pose that don't matter. I guess we'll get him settled into the dorms, eh?"

Bogg barked another laugh. Uncle Fredrick nodded and Bogg hobbled inside the building. Jasper followed them.

Strange skates? Jasper glanced down at the skates tied over his shoulder. They were brand new CCM skates, and he'd just had them sharpened. They were the best pair he'd ever owned. How could they be strange?

"Come on, come on," Bogg called in a sing-song voice.

"Follow me. P'raps we'll find that no good brother of mine and see what he's been up to."

Bogg limped ahead, leading the way. The humming glass doors opened onto a large, high-ceilinged room with the same sand coloured stone walls as the outside of the Pavilion. To the right of the doors stood a small wooden booth with a chair and some books inside. It looked like a sort of guard post. Lanterns hung down from chains on the ceiling and dark green vines of ivy climbed the walls. The tinkle of water trickling filled the room. There was a wide, curving flagstone ramp at the far side that slowly climbed upward. Bogg started up the ramp ahead of them.

"That's Bogg," Uncle Fredrick said, low enough so that the old man didn't hear. "He and his brother Ding are the caretakers of the Pavilion. They'll look after you, but they're not especially nice. Be sure to stay on their good side."

"What about those doors? When I touched them I got a shock up my arm."

"They're enchanted. Bogg and Ding have the magic gloves that allow them to touch the doors without getting hurt. They open the doors in the morning and close them at night. It's the only way in

and out. Be sure you don't get locked out at night. And Jasper,"
Uncle Fredrick sounded very serious.

"Yes?"

"No sneaking out after dark. It's not safe."

What had only been the whisper of an idea the moment
before was now a fully formed To-Do List item, but Jasper gave his
uncle a smile and said, "I won't."

They walked on. The ramp continued to slope upwards and
became a corridor, growing narrower with each step. The tall
rectangular windows let in the late afternoon light, bathing the
sandstone walls in a warm glow. On their left, they passed several
doors, some of which were closed and quiet and others which were
thrown open, spilling loud laughter and chatter into the hallway. The
smell of baking potatoes and frying steak and roasting chicken filled
the air and Jasper's stomach gave another loud grumble.

"Is it dinner time?" Jasper asked.

"Aye, through there," Bogg said, pointing toward a round
green door. The room was filled with an odd mix of tables and chairs.
About twenty other kids, mostly boys, were sat around the tables
and chowing down on a hearty dinner of steak and potatoes and

chicken and pasta. Jasper wanted to stop right then and there, his stomach growling, but Bogg limped onwards and upwards. Just as Jasper was giving the plates piled high with steaks one last, longing look, he locked eyes with a girl sitting on the far side of the dining hall. She sat alone. Wide eyes stared out from under a mess of tangled hair. She was watching Jasper. None of the other kids had noticed him, but she certainly had. She stared. Jasper gave a small wave and awkward smile. The girl narrowed her eyes and frowned, but did not look away. Jasper hurried after his uncle and Bogg.

The corridor grew narrower still. They were turning in a tighter circle now, passing fewer doors on their left. Finally, Bogg stopped.

"Well, well, here we are! Home, sweet home," Bogg said and pushed open the door.

The smell hit Jasper first. Sweaty socks and laziness, if he wasn't mistaken. Jasper was no stranger to messy bedrooms. Despite Mrs. Jarvis's constant scolding, Jasper's room at home was in a constant state of chaos. Mrs. Jarvis often told him that his could win the award for messiest room on the planet, to which Jasper would reply that he would add the medal or ribbon to his collection, but the bedroom Jasper now found himself in was, without a doubt, the Grand Supreme Ultimate winner of messiest bedroom ever to exist. On a scale of one to ten, one being pristinely clean and ten being a disaster zone, this room ranked a solid 37. There were clothes strewn here and there, some hanging from the posts of the bunk beds, some piled high enough to touch the ceiling. There were two small desks squeezed into either corner of the room, but they were so laden with books, scraps of paper, dirty clothes, mugs, candy wrappers, unidentifiable gooey blobs, and – Jasper did a double take- a toilet seat cover, that the desks themselves were barely visible.

There were shelves at random all over the room, and they were dripping with this and that. Books, plates of half-eaten food, leather soccer balls, and what looked like animal droppings. There were a few hockey sticks propped against an old wardrobe, and some equipment as well, which made the room smell even worse than it looked. The floor was so covered in crumpled paper, dirty socks, wet towels, hockey pucks, and, Jasper was curious as to the reason for these, what seemed like hundreds of little sparkly beads, that he couldn't even tell what colour the carpet was underneath. There were two windows on the far wall, and like the windows lining the corridor, they were tall and rectangular. Below the windows sat a heating stove, with a chimney pipe extending up into the ceiling. A twisted, twiggy bird's nest sat in one window, and a small stack of firewood in the other. To top it all off, thanks to the spiralling floors of the Players Pavilion, much of the room's clutter had managed to slide to one side of the floor in a massive mountain of mayhem. Thankfully, the bunk beds were on the other.

Jasper only had a moment to take in the disaster of room before Bogg and Uncle Fredrick were saying goodbye.

"You'll be in with Mullans. I'll leave you to it, then."

Bogg nodded to Uncle Fredrick and then left to begin his slow and careful trek back down the corridor.

Uncle Fredrick gave Jasper a warm smile.

"I know it's a little overwhelming, but you'll get settled in soon," Uncle Fredrick said and ruffled Jasper's hair. "I've got to head out. There's a few things I need to take care of. A few people I need to speak with. I'll be by to see you in a few days. I think you'll have practice tonight."

"Practice? Uncle, I haven't got any of my equipment. Just my skates," Jasper said, suddenly worried. Come to think of it, he didn't have anything. No pyjamas, no toothbrush, not even a pair of shoes that fit.

"Don't worry about it. I'm sure the team has some extra gear you can use. Mullans will help you out with the rest. He's a real great kid. He's just not the best at keeping his room tidy, but I'm sure you won't mind that!"

"I'm sure I'll get used to it," Jasper said.

The room was quiet for a moment. Uncle Fredrick was looking at the sandy stone ceiling, thinking. Jasper pulled off the shoes his uncle had leant him and handed them back. Uncle Fredrick gave Jasper's shoulders a squeeze.

"I'm really proud of you, Jasper. I know you'll do well here."

"Thanks."

Uncle Fredrick waved goodbye and pulled the door closed behind him. Jasper was left alone. He plopped down on the lower bunk and was just beginning to wonder if he could find his way back to the dining hall, which really shouldn't be that hard as every room opened off the same corridor, when the bedroom door banged open and Jasper found himself face to face with his new roommate.

"Oh, hi!" his new roommate said, a wide smile spreading across his handsome face.

Jasper really had no authority on the subject, but even so, he could tell straight away his new roommate turned heads. He was tall, but looked to be no older than fourteen, with dark hair and strong features. In fact, his black hair seemed to be blowing in an unseen wind, like he was a model posing at a photo shoot. He had sparkling blue eyes and perfectly square, bright white teeth. He had his surprisingly-muscular-arms-for-a-boy-his-age slung around a couple of hockey sticks. He wore a navy blue vest over a loose white tunic and his pants were light brown and neatly pressed. His clothes were messy, but not too messy. In fact, they were just messy enough to make him look exceedingly cool. Jasper looked around the chaotic, wind-free room.

"Where's that wind coming from?"

"What wind?" his new roommate replied. His voice was deep, yet clueless.

"...the wind that's blowing through your hair."

"Oh. Ha, ha."

As the other boy laughed, Jasper swore he heard girls giggle and sigh off in the distance.

"It's like that all the time. Good genes, I guess."

The other boy flashed his perfect smile again. This was getting a little weird.

"Right," Jasper said. They stared at each other and Jasper cringed at the awkwardness of it all. The other boy didn't seem to notice, or care, and so shifted poses. Jasper was now being treated to a view of his perfect profile and strong jawline.

Jasper stood and extended his hand.

"I'm Jasper Jarvis."

The other boy extended both of his hands, the hockey sticks clattering to the floor.

"Mullan Mullan."

"Sorry?"

"Don't be sorry. It's easier to remember when you've only got one name," Jasper's new roommate said, shaking Jasper's hand with both of his. The tinkling of girls giggling and sighing sounded once more. "My family's last name is Mullan. My parents couldn't agree on a first name for me because they can't agree on anything. The only name they could agree on was Mullan, so they gave it to me twice. People call me Mullans, for short," Mullans said.

Jasper had the sense to feel sorry for Mullans.

"That's a bit strange, isn't it?" Jasper asked, trying to be polite.

Mullans considered this for a moment, as if the thought that his name was strange had never occurred to him before.

"....yes. It is," Mullans answered, after a long pause. He stared blankly at Jasper and Jasper found he was suddenly very interested in his own fingernails. "Anyway, welcome to the room. What's mine is yours, and what's yours I'm going to borrow without asking. I hope you don't mind."

"Not at all," Jasper said. "You wouldn't happen to have a pair of shoes I could borrow? Just until I get a new pair of my own, you see." Jasper wriggled his toes hopefully.

"Ummm." A look of hard concentration crossed Mullans's face.

From where he stood, Jasper could see a pile of mismatched shoes under one of the desks. He looked from Mullans, to the shoes, then to back Mullans.

"Shoes...shoes...." Mullans said, lowly and slowly, his brows knitted together and his mouth a frown.

"They're for feet and they look good with socks," Jasper said, meaning to be helpful.

Mullans snapped his fingers.

"Oh, right! Under the desk. Help yourself. Might be a little big for you, but with a good strong effort, you could grow into them. I believe in you!"

Mullans clapped Jasper hard on the back.

Jasper didn't bother mentioning that growing into a pair of shoes had very little to do with how hard you tried. Instead, he rummaged through the pile until he found a matching pair of canvas shoes that looked like they were about the right size. As it turned out, they were also quite comfortable.

Jasper sat to do up the laces. Mullans weaved his way through the mountains of clothes piled on the floor with practised ease, stopping in front of the bird's nest perched in the far window. He dropped his hand into the mess of twigs and carefully pulled out a sleepy-eyed grey pigeon.

"Hey Ikarus, how are you?"

Mullans did a spot on imitation of a pigeon's coo and offered the bird a piece of bread from his pocket.

"Why have you got a pigeon?" Jasper asked.

"For company," Mullans said. "Pigeons are smarter than most people think. Ikarus can always find his way back to his nest."

Jasper had never been terribly fond of pigeons and he had never known anyone to feel differently until now. They were rats with wings, as Mrs. Jarvis often said. However, Jasper thought it best to keep this general dislike of pigeons to himself for the moment.

"Is there any chance of some dinner? I'm really hungry," Jasper said, his stomach once again making its emptiness known.

"Yes. Yes, there *is* a chance of some dinner. In fact, more than just a chance. Dinner is for sure. Follow me!"

Mullans gently placed Ikarus back into his nest and in three long strides, he had crossed the room. He made to leave, but stopped short in the doorway and Jasper banged into him.

"Oh, but wait. If anyone asks, I was with you all afternoon, reading up on how to fix a broken hourglass and those skate laces were tied together when we got there."

Mullans smiled at Jasper and flipped his hair. The dark strands of hair seemed to sparkle and shine and move in slow motion and Mullans's smile was so toothy and perfect, Jasper couldn't help but agree. That, and he would say anything to get down to the dining hall quicker.

"Sure. I can do that," Jasper said, and the pair were off down the corridor.

Chapter 8

Erin Wickenheiser

Mullans led the way down the winding corridor, now bathed in fat squares of orangey light streaming in from the tall windows. They passed other boys in the corridor, most of them returning to their own dorm rooms after a satisfying supper. Jasper gave a small smile or a wave each time they passed someone new, which some of the boys returned. Others just watched him curiously from their doorways and bunk beds. Jasper was no stranger to people whispering and watching as he walked past, and the familiar feeling was oddly comforting.

"So, you're the new player they've been telling us about," Mullans said. It wasn't a question, and he didn't seem at all surprised to suddenly have a new roommate.

"Yeah, I guess so."

"They've said on and off for ages that they were going to bring in someone new. Black and Tan love a good hockey game and we're always on the lookout for promising new players. Are you from across the water?"

"Sort of, I think. I'm from Brantford," Jasper said.

"Brantford? I've never heard of that country," Mullans said, looking up at the lamps hanging from the ceiling, his hair once again ruffling in an unseen breeze.

"Oh, it's not a country. It's near Hamilton. Not too far from Toronto. In Ontario. Canada."

"I don't know what those are," Mullans said, flashing another toothy grin. He looked like he had no intention of finding out, either.

"Sorry. It's okay. Don't worry about it," Jasper said.

They arrived at the dining hall, stepping through the huge circular green door. The room had emptied out considerably and many of the mismatched chairs and tables sat empty. The unfriendly, frowning girl was still there, however. She sat alone at a small rectangular table, a half-eaten dinner gone cold in front of her. She returned Jasper's gaze, following him across the room with unblinking eyes.

Mullans plopped down at a table raised only a few inches off the ground, surrounded by an assortment of plush pillows. Despite the hungry crowd of hockey players the dining hall had just played host to, Jasper was pleased to see the table was still piled high with piping hot bowls of pasta and platters of crispy roasted chicken.

Mullans began to scarf down the food immediately and Jasper didn't need inviting. They ate in silence at first and the food was good. The grumbling in Jasper's stomach soon disappeared as he chomped his way through two pieces of chicken and a mountain of pasta covered in a rich tomato sauce, helped along by a handful of crispy bread rolls. Jasper was so focused on his dinner, feeling his stomach grow fuller and fuller, he did not notice the girl rise from her table and cross the room. It wasn't until she was standing right over him, arms crossed and scowling, that Jasper looked up, saw her, and stopped chewing.

She was tall and pale, with lean long legs and wiry arms. She looked to be about Jasper's age, if not slightly older. She had a splash of freckles across each of her cheeks that stood out violently against her pale skin. She had the hair of a crazy person. Long and tangled, with a few braids here and a couple dreadlocks there, it at one point must have been brown, but now it was a confused mix of tinted purples and blues and reds, with painfully bright bleached blonde accents. To finish the ensemble, wooden beads and bits of colourful cloth adorned each clumsy chunk of bushy hair. She wore a purple smock that hung down to her knees and was cinched together with a thick, brown leather belt. Red and white striped socks poked out from under the smock's hem and chunky black boots covered her feet. She had what looked like a hundred brightly coloured bracelets adorning each of her forearms and they clinked and clanked as she uncrossed her arms and clamped her hands on her hips.

"Who are you?" the girl said, narrowing her eyes at Jasper.

Jasper looked to Mullans, but Mullans was lost to a daydream. Gazing off in the distance and his hair glistening in sunlight that wasn't there, his eyes were unfocused and a small smile played at his lips. No help there, apparently.

Jasper stood up and looked the girl in the eye. Jasper was tall for his age, but this girl was just as tall, and maybe even a centimetre taller.

"I'm Jasper Jarvis. Pleased to meet you."

The girl scowled down at his hand and did not shake it.

"Why are you here?"

"To eat dinner."

Jasper nervously laughed and tried to smile. The girl was not impressed.

"I know *that,*" the girl said, crossing her arms again in a huff. "Why are you here in the Players Pavilion?"

"Oh! To play hockey. I'm the new player for the team."

The girl didn't say anything, only looked Jasper up and down.

"Are you any good?"

Jasper hated this question because he never knew how to answer it. Yes, he was good, but no, he didn't like to brag. Fortunately, Mullans came to his rescue.

"Oh, Erin! I didn't see you there!" Mullans said, snapping out of the daze during which his eyes had been resting on Erin.

Erin rolled her eyes. "Daydreaming again, Mullans?"

"I can't get through a day without it. This is Jasper. He's my new roomie and the new player on the team. Jasper, meet Erin Wickenheiser."

Mullans looked from Jasper to Erin and back to Jasper, smiling and oblivious.

"Yeah," Erin said. "We've met."

Jasper didn't know what he had done to make Erin so angry, but he had dealt with mean and competitive teammates before. He would grin and bear it for now. On the rink is where it really mattered, not here.

"I hope you're as good as they say," Erin said. "Wouldn't want you to let us all down. You're here to save the team, after all."

Erin walked away, but not before jabbing Jasper sharply with her shoulder as she passed.

Jasper took a deep breath. On the rink, he thought. Save it for the rink. With his stomach full, his nerves crept back to bother him. Here to save the team? Is that why they brought him here? Endless questions sprouted in Jasper's mind. He didn't know if he was up to this challenge and now he worried he'd let his new team down.

Mullans stood and gave Jasper's shoulder a squeeze.

"Don't worry about it, son. Women are complicated."

"What? No, that's not..." Jasper tried to explain, but the dazed look had returned to Mullans's eyes.

"So complicated. A girl once threw a boot at me after I asked her for the time," Mullans said, nodding sagely.

There was shuffling and coughing as Bogg limped into the

dining hall.

"Come on, you two!" Bogg said, wheezing for breath. "You've got practice tonight!"

After a quick trip back to the dorm to grab his skates, Jasper met Mullans in the front hall. The sun had nearly set. Bogg was there, using a long metal rod to light the lanterns hanging from the ceiling. Bogg perched precariously on a rickety wooden stool, and Mullans held onto the legs just as precariously, dazing off at the drawbridge beyond the entrance.

"Ready?" Jasper asked. The metal gloves Bogg had used earlier on the entrance doors now hung from a peg in the small guard station, glinting in the gloom.

"Yup!" Mullans said, instantly letting go of the stool, despite Bogg's outstretched pose to reach the last lantern.

The stool overbalanced and Bogg tumbled to the floor in a heap, coughing furiously.

"What are you doing on the floor?"

"You let go of the stool," Jasper said.

"I....what? Oops," Mullans said. "I get distracted easily."

"It's okay," Jasper said. He offered his hand to Bogg and pulled the old man to his feet. "Are you okay, Mr. Bogg?"

Bogg coughed and gave Mullans a sour look, but only said, "Yes, fine. I'll finish these lanterns on my own. You two better be off, now. Coach doesn't like to be kept waiting. And make sure you're back before Somnia starts in with her howling."

"Yes, yes, yes, sir!" Mullans said, waving to Bogg and jogging out the entrance doors.

"Sorry about the stool!" Jasper said, and ran after Mullans.

Walking across the creaking, swaying drawbridge, Jasper again wished there were a railing to hold. Mullans wasn't bothered. He waved to the fish in the water and told them how much he liked the underwater rainbows their tails made.

"Why does Somnia howl?" Jasper asked once they had safely crossed the drawbridge. Mullans turned down a narrow laneway lined with tall houses. Jasper followed.

"Maybe because that's *howl* she likes it." Mullans stopped to see if Jasper got the joke. He didn't.

"Right," Jasper said. Somnia could wait. What was important

now was his new team. "Where are we going now?"

"Trillium Gardens. It's where we play hockey."

Mullans was taller than Jasper and walked quickly. Jasper jogged to keep up. Their path took them down alleyways and through wide, cobblestone squares, under stone archways and over worrisome wooden bridges, and past glassy shop windows and brightly coloured painted doors. Everywhere, frosted vines climbed the stone walls and shrubs sprouted out of window boxes. Several large trees poked through the fabric of the city, having been allowed to grow where they pleased, in the middle of laneways and through the roofs of houses.

"Is it a nice arena?"

"It's the nicest one I've seen. Come to think of it," Mullans said, slowing his pace, "It's the only one I've seen."

Strange. So, they always played home games? Didn't they ever have road trips? Jasper had never liked the long bus rides out to Sarnia and Windsor, but playing games away from your home arena was part of hockey.

"So, all the other teams always come to your arena? They always come to Trillium Gardens?" Jasper said, a small smile playing at his lips. Just saying the name of his new barn gave him a tickle of excitement.

"Other *teams*? You mean other team. There's just one," Mullans said.

"You play all your games against the same team? That doesn't sound very fun," Jasper said, following Mullans as he scaled a low wall and then quickly turned a corner.

"It's not," Mullans said.

Jasper rounded the last corner and set his eyes on the towering structure that was Trillium Gardens. He stopped and stared. Up and up it went, with level upon level of stadium seats. The nearby buildings shrank away, cowering in its shadow. Jasper craned his neck to see all the way to the top. Trillium Gardens didn't have a roof. Jasper had never seen any arena reach so high into the sky. Surely, he thought, it must hold thousands and thousands of people. It might even be bigger than every NHL arena. Combined.

It was an enormous, oval-shaped building made of glittering, dark purple bricks. There were neat rows of square windows cut into the walls of every level. Jasper took a deep breath and swallowed hard. An arena this big meant big crowds.

"This way!" Mullans said, heading toward what must be the main entrance. It was a row of shiny glass doors with rounded tops. Jasper gave the massive building one last look and then followed behind Mullans.

"We'll let Coach know you're here. Then, we'll gear-up," Mullans said, looking from left to right. Jasper worried Mullans might be lost, and it wouldn't have surprised him. Mullans looked from left to right once more, made up his mind, and took off to the right.

The concourse turned gently, matching the oval curve of the Gardens. On their left, the seat sections were written with purple paint in spindly, tall numbers above rounded doors placed at even intervals. There were staircases leading in every direction: up, down, across, and around. An ever changing, and increasingly confusing, combination of letters and numbers were written above the staircases and on their steps. Jasper was glad he wouldn't have to find a seat in this place, as it might take a while.

At last, Mullans came to a stop and passed through a door labelled "C 3". Jasper could smell the ice before he could see it. The cold, crisp air stung his nose as he breathed deeply, cooling his face and hands.

Mullans walked down a sloping aisle towards the looming boards lining the edge of the rink, his footsteps echoing in the empty arena.

Jasper looked again to the very top row of seats. He had to squint to see them. His hands shook ever so slightly as he followed after Mullans. The ice surface itself was larger than any rink Jasper had ever played on before. It was smooth and perfect, ready for that evening's practice. The boards were made of solid, dark wood and rose high above the first five rows of seats. Slits had been cut into the wood so those sitting near the ice could still watch the game.

"*COACH!*" Mullans said, his voice booming in the empty space, making Jasper jump.

On the ice, a pair on skates scraped to life and with each stride, the cut of the skates grew louder. The telltale *wshhhhh* and spray of snow as Coach came to a stop on the other side of the boards. The shift and clunk of a bolt, and the heavy wooden boards creaked apart to reveal a short, heavyset man with a bushy black beard. He had a round red nose and a shiny bald head, with a ring of dark hair circling from ear to ear. He wore three heavy sweaters and dark leather gloves. His skates were leather as well, brown and well-used and he carried a worn, wooden hockey stick in his hand.

"*COACH!*" Mullans said, again.

"Mullans, not so loud. I'm right here," Coach said, kindly.

"This is the new player, Coach. He arrived today. He's here for practice tonight," Mullans said.

Coach wrinkled his brow.

"I wasn't expecting any new players," he said. "This is a surprise."

"I wasn't expecting to have a new roommate, but we're all in this together," Mullans said, slinging his arm around Jasper and giving his shoulders a squeeze.

Coach nodded at Mullans, a small smile playing at his mouth.

"All right. Thanks, Mullans. You can head over to the locker room and get your gear on and I'll get-- sorry, what was your name?"

"Jasper Jarvis," Jasper said, and stuck out his hand. Mrs. Jarvis had always told him this was the polite and proper thing to do when meeting important people for the first time.

Coach's eyebrows shot upward, the smile falling from his face.

"Jasper?" he said, quietly. "That's a good name, and a rare one in Magmelland. I knew someone with that name, once."

"People always tell me it'll suit me by the time I'm very old. I like it." Jasper smiled. Mullans saluted Coach before disappearing back up the aisle.

"Do I just call you Coach, Coach?" Jasper said.

"My name is Gregory Sparkenfalupalants."

"Sparken....what?"

The stout man gave a jolly laugh that made his belly jiggle.

"Most people around here call me Coach Sparkle Pants. I don't like it, but it's stuck, so if you shorten it down to just 'Coach', I won't mind."

Coach Sparkle Pants gave another hearty laugh. Jasper liked him already.

"When did you get in?"

"This afternoon. My Uncle Fredrick and Ms. Fearce brought me."

Jasper tried to keep his voice even, but Coach Sparkle Pants noticed the sour note at the mention of that awful woman's name.

"She's not particularly nice, is she?" Coach chuckled. "Your uncle is a good friend of mine. Now that you mention him, I suppose I have been expecting you. He's been telling us about you for months. He's says you're a really great hockey player."

Jasper swelled with pride and smiled.

"Coach, I haven't got any gear," Jasper said suddenly, glancing down at his borrowed shoes. "Ms. Fearce made us leave in such a rush. I've only got my skates with me."

Just then, the entirety of Jasper's new team came hurtling onto the ice, with skate blades flashing, hockey pucks whizzing and snow spraying. Their equipment was strange and to Jasper's eyes, they looked a little like medieval knights. Their leather and steal gear squeaked and clanked as they moved, and they wore scarlet jerseys with silver stripes at the collar and elbows.

These hockey players were tall and strong and fast, and with a clench of his stomach, Jasper realized they were likely much older than him. With a heart beating faster than was strictly necessary, Jasper hoped he wouldn't let Uncle Fredrick and Coach Sparkle Pants down.

"All right, folks!" Coach Sparkle Pants said, his loud voice carrying easily across the rink. "Let's get warmed up!"

The team dutifully began skating from one end of the rink to the other, passing pucks back and forth and taking shots on goal.

"Jasper, you can head up to the equipment room. Go out that door, take a right and it'll be the third door on your left, past the locker room. Bring a lantern with you. You should be able to find everything you need. Get back here as soon as you can. I want to see what you can do."

Coach left Jasper by the edge of the rink and skated into the midst of practice, shouting instructions and blowing a shrill note from the whistle around his neck every so often.

Jasper followed Coach's directions, plucking the first lantern he saw off the wall. It took longer than he had expected, although his progress was slowed by gazing at the vaulted ceiling of the entrance hall and the heavy gold lanterns hanging there. Eventually, he found the door with "Equipment Room" carved into it. One, two, three heavy pulls and the door reluctantly swung back. It smelled of stale sweat and old hockey equipment, which, in Jasper's opinion, was one of the worst smells there was. He coughed and gagged. The equipment room was absolutely packed full. Pile after pile of wooden hockey sticks and leather-made protective pads were crammed almost to the rafters. Jasper swung the lantern in front of him and gazed into the gloom.

Holding his breath, Jasper took the plunge and set about finding some gear. Elbow pads and gloves and shin guards he found easily enough, but shoulder pads and shorts proved more difficult. Jasper was big for his age, but he was on the small side for most of this equipment.

He found a metal helmet with a wrought iron cage on the front that fit well enough and he put it with the gear he had set aside. A solid wooden stick that was just a bit too long for him soon joined the pile. He found a set of shoulder pads that were made of a tight, brown leather and looked like the sort of the thing Maurice Richard would have worn. They were loose, but they would have to do. He added a tattered, numberless scarlet and silver sweater with a frayed collar to his stash. The first pair of shorts he tried on fell right to the floor around his ankles, as did the next, and the next. Jasper waded farther and farther into the fully packed room, trying on every pair of shorts he came across. With every step forward, the splintered wooden floor was harder to see. At last, in the very back of the room, he spied a pair of shorts that looked small enough, wedged at the bottom of a teetering pile of tattered goalie pads. Sweating now, Jasper shoved and heaved his way through and grabbed the shorts. Equipment rained down around him. Cowering and covering his eyes, Jasper waited for the heavy heaps of gear to finish shifting. He cracked one eye open, then the other.

On the floor in front of him lay a round brass ring.

He knew he should hurry. Coach was waiting and practice had begun, but Jasper's mind flicked back to Ms. Fearce and the metal handles she had carried with her and used to make a door appear from nowhere. Jasper set the shorts down and took a closer look.

Perhaps it was just a strange piece of equipment he wasn't familiar with. Jasper tried to lift it from the ground, but it did not budge. He cleared a small patch of the floor and found a trap door hiding there.

Knowing he should hurry back to practice, Jasper couldn't help wanting to see what was beyond the door.

He redoubled his grip on the brass ring and pulled. Nothing. Jasper braced his back against the wall and heaved, sweat running into his eyes. The door popped open and stale air spilled out. He coughed as he let the trap door fall back against a pile of nearby equipment.

Jasper stared into the pitch black square in the floor, and the yawning darkness stared back. Jasper scrambled down onto his stomach and rather bravely, or rather stupidly, depending on the type of person you are, stuck his head down into the darkness to have a look around.

At first, solid blackness. The air was dry and the space felt small. Jasper guessed that if he were to jump down, the fall wouldn't be very long. Thankfully, he was smarter than that. He had no ladder to get back up into the equipment room. His eyes adjusted to the darkness and for the second time that day, Jasper saw a prick of light at the end of a long tunnel.

Jasper stared at the speck of light for a moment longer, wondering where it might lead. Then, he stood and closed the trapdoor. He had to get back to practice now, or he might miss the whole thing. He paused, thought a moment, and then piled equipment back over the trapdoor, hiding it once more.

Jasper grabbed his equipment, small enough shorts included, and stuffed it all into one of the large canvas sacks piled near the door.

He found the locker room just down the hall. Sitting down in front of an empty locker, he quickly changed into his gear.

He grabbed his stick that really was just a little bit too big, took a deep breath, and passed through the door that opened onto the arena. The cold air hit his face and his mind was immediately focused. It was time to show his new teammates what he could do.

Chapter 9

Practising to Lose

The aisle running from the locker room to the rink was lined with a spongey, green material that looked like moss but bounced like rubber. Jasper reached the huge wooden boards, pulled the bolt aside and let the doors swing back. Now that he was level with it, Jasper was certain this was the largest ice rink he'd ever seen. A smile spread across his face, despite the nervous quake in his stomach. This was going to be fun.

Jasper skated out on to the Magmelland ice for the first time and he felt at home. His skate blades scraped across the ice and the cold arena air was on his face and he felt calm.

Jasper skated to Coach Sparkle Pants and came to a neat stop, spraying just a little snow. Coach blew his whistle.

"Okay lads and lasses, over here!" Coach said, his voice booming.

The rest of the team, some of whom had been stretching against the boards or passing pucks to and fro, dutifully skated over.

There were about twenty of them in all. Some were tall and broad shouldered, while others were shorter and wider. There were two goalies. Each of them wore hulking leather padding on their legs, covered in straps and laces, and huge metal chest protectors. Both had metal masks covering their faces, with only a small slit for their eyes to see out. The larger of the two goalies had metal spikes sticking out the top of his helmet, while the other had a mohawk of red bristles on his. If Jasper had to guess, he would say the one with the spikes was the goalie they went with for shoot-outs.

Every single player was bigger and taller than Jasper. All except for one. The thick cage on the front of her helmet hid her face, but Jasper recognized the twisted mess of hair. Erin was the only one on the team even close to his size and as she skated up, she made sure to spray Jasper with a hearty helping of snow before coming to a stop. She crossed her arms, and then made a show of looking unimpressed, rolling her eyes and huffing.

Jasper smiled his widest smile and brushed the snow from his equipment. *Save it for practice*, he thought.

Jasper glanced around at his new team. They looked serious and sad, with tight mouths and intense eyes. Everyone's eyes flicked between Coach and Jasper, sizing up the new arrival. The question on their minds was clear.

Only Mullans, who had taken his helmet off and flipped his hair in a swish of sparkle and floral scent, waved at Jasper, grinning. Jasper returned the wave.

"As you can see, we've got a new player. Everyone, say 'hello' to Jasper Jarvis," Coach Sparkle Pants said and clapped his hands.

No one joined in the applause, or even made a sound, except for Mullans, who clapped loudly and tried to whistle.

Coach stopped clapping and heaved a heavy sigh.

"Look, I know this isn't easy, but we need to make the best of it. I've been told Jasper is a great hockey player. He can really help the team."

"Help us do what, exactly?" said a tall boy with a fringe of red hair poking out from under his helmet. The rest of the team murmured in agreement, some even tapping their sticks on the ice.

Coach Sparkle Pants laid a hand on Jasper's shoulder and gave it a squeeze.

"He'll help us play the best hockey we can play. Keep that in mind, lads and lasses. Always remember, that's why we do it."

"It's not fair," said another boy, nearly as tall as the first, but leaner. A few sweaty brown curls were plastered to his forehead. Next to him, a shorter, rounder boy jerkily nodded once. A swirling tattoo ran across the tanned skin of the shorter boy's face.

Jasper shifted uncomfortably. Did he mean it wasn't fair for Jasper to just walk on to the team? Was there usually a try-out? Jasper looked from face to face, surveying the rest of the team, hoping he wouldn't see agreement there. What he found were downcast eyes and set jaws. Jasper was ready to prove himself, but the team wasn't asking.

"I know, I know," Coach said, his hand slipping from Jasper's shoulder and his voice softening. "But this is the only way. We play because we love the game, not because we need to win."

At this, some of the players jerked their heads to glare at Coach and there were rumblings of dissent and barks of laughter.

"We don't need to win?" Jasper said, confused. Everything Mrs. Jarvis had every said to him rushed to his mind. Jasper, like any hockey player, loved to win games. He had never before met a team that didn't want to win.

Coach Sparkle Pants shifted uneasily. There was a moment of quiet.

"Jasper, we aren't *allowed* to win. We have to lose every game. Those are the rules."

"Why do we even bother to practice?" a loud voice shouted from within the group players.

"We should play hooky next time Black's in town," came another voice.

There were calls of agreement and sarcastic cheers, in amongst which Jasper distinctly heard Mullans helpfully say, "We play hockey. Not hooky."

"*HEY!* That's enough!" Coach said. His booming voice was immediately followed by silence. "I've said we're going to play the best hockey we can, whether we win or lose, and that's exactly what we're going to do. Jasper, Mullans will help you get settled. Everyone else, let's practice. Clean passes! Finish your checks! Let's go."

With a few muted grumbles here and there, the team got moving. Jasper skated over to Mullans, his mind buzzing with questions.

Mullans's hair was once again blowing in a soft breeze that wasn't actually there.

"What does he mean, we aren't *allowed* to win?" Jasper said, coming to a quick stop, his stick dangling weakly in his hand.

"We aren't allowed to win. Emperor Black doesn't want to see his team lose. Ever. So they don't. They always win, we always lose, not matter how well we play. In the whole history of Magmelland, we've never won a game."

"But that's not fair! Who wants to play hockey just so they can lose?"

Jasper had never even seen this Emperor Black, but already, he hated him.

"We do, I guess."

Jasper skated smoothly in a circle around Mullans, thinking.

"Who is this Emperor Black, anyway?" Jasper said.

"Did you see the water on your way into the city?"

Jasper nodded.

"That's the Breakwater Channel. He is Emperor Black of Eridares. That's the land across the water. He travels across the

Channel in a huge boat. It's shaped like a dragon. He brings his team with him. That's the team we play against. The only team we ever play against. Emperor Black loves hockey, but he hates to lose. Even if we're winning we have to let them score enough to win the game before the match is over."

Jasper had played a lot of hockey games in his short life. Sometimes his team won, sometimes they lost. Sometimes the score was close and sometimes it was miles apart. Sometimes he hated the other team while the game was on and he'd work hard every second to keep them for scoring. Sometimes, he would skate until he could hardly breathe, trying desperately to get another goal and get his team ahead. Other times, the opposing team was pitifully bad and if they managed to score a goal, Jasper wouldn't hold it against them. The thing was, Jasper never just gave up. A hockey game could turn around in a second, so long as you worked hard and kept competing. Jasper had never, ever considered just letting the other team win. That wasn't how he played hockey, and that wasn't the game he loved. Just the idea of it made Jasper want to slap pucks at the net and throw his stick on the ice all at once.

"But can our team beat Emperor Black's? I mean, are we better than they are?" Jasper said.

Mullans was trying to check his reflection in the blade of his hockey stick. It wasn't a reflective surface, but Mullans hadn't noticed.

"Oh yes," Mullans said, as if it were the most obvious thing. "We're a very good team. You see that guy, over there?" Mullans pointed to a tall player with bulky shoulders and huge calves. "That's McGee. Troy McGee. He's team captain. He'll break your shins if you get in the way of his slap shot."

To prove the point, McGee wound-up and let a puck rip. It flew through the air and hurtled into the boards, leaving a black dent in the wood.

"Wow." It was all Jasper could say.

"And rumour has it, he can grow a full beard," Mullans said.

"*Wow.*" Jasper was doubly impressed.

"Guilherme Morenz over there," Mullans said, pointing his gloved finger to a lean player not much taller than Jasper, stretching against the boards, "He can out-skate anything on.....skates. The fastest on the team."

Jasper nodded and silently made a point of checking his

speed against Morenz's as soon as he got a chance.

"Of course, your girlfriend isn't bad either." Mullans slapped Jasper on the back. Erin's bushy hair jerked as she turned to glare at the two of them. She narrowed her eyes at Jasper, but Jasper didn't look away. With a flip of her hair, Erin returned to the pucks she was craftily stickhandling in figure eights before shooting them into the upper corners of the net.

"She's not my girlfriend," Jasper said, giving Mullans a little shove.

Mullans glided away from Jasper and started trying to whistle again, but only ended up making rather rude noises. Jasper skated along beside him.

"How do you stand it? If you know you can win but you always have to lose?"

Mullans came to a stop and for the first time since Jasper had known him, he had a serious look on his face.

"It's what we have to do. We love to play this game and if we just pretend that there's a chance we could win, if we keep it alive in our minds, it's not so bad. Once we give up, we'll start hating the game. I don't ever want that to happen." Mullans finished speaking and blinked slowly. His mouth was a little line and his eyes were cast downwards toward the ice, thinking.

Then, he jerked his head up, smiled, flicked his hair (a girly giggle sounded somewhere far off in the arena), and Mullans slammed his helmet onto his head.

"Time for practice, Jarvis!"

Mullans skated off, legs pumping, head up, and stick on the ice. Jasper followed behind and they joined the rest of the team in the skating and passing drill that Coach had just whistled into play.

The practice had been a long one. Jasper was used to practising daily, but this team was bigger and stronger and faster than any team he had played on, and so they worked harder and longer. By the end, after endless passing, shooting, and skating skills, and a rather intense scrimmage to top it off, Jasper's toes were frozen and his wrists and forearms ached. Coach called an end to the practice and Jasper's legs wobbled as he followed his teammates to the locker room. Before he stepped off the ice, Jasper gave Trillium Gardens one last look, all the way up to the very last row in the stands. He was going to like playing in this barn. He smiled a small smile as he realized he was the last person to leave the ice after his first practice.

"Good work today," Coach Sparkle Pants said, slapping Jasper on the back. Jasper sat at his locker, exhausted.

"Thanks."

The locker room was quiet except for the snap of laces being undone and the thud of gear tossed to the floor. There were mumbles here and there, but most of the team kept their eyes down and their mouths shut. Jasper wondered what it would be like after a game if the team was this down after a practice.

Jasper changed out of his gear, carefully hanging everything in his locker. Someone had carved a trio of stars and a set of moose antlers into the wooden bench in front of his stall. He ran his fingers over the gouged groves, thinking it was a bizarre bit of graffiti. He missed his old equipment but this leather stuff wasn't so bad. He hung his skates from two hooks in the wall and slid his feet back into the canvas shoes Mullans had leant him. Jasper loved the wobbly, cool feeling that came with taking off a tight pair of hockey skates and changing back into street shoes. It felt like walking in a strange new world, but for the first time, it was actually true.

Jasper took his time changing out of his gear. The rest of the team filed out of the locker room in twos and threes. Casually as could be, Jasper took the opportunity to size up his new team.

All around, they were bigger and taller than Jasper. Some of them looked like they could be sixteen or seventeen years old, with broad shoulders and massive forearms. Some had short hair or shaved heads, while others had long hair that now hung in funny, bunched shapes. Even in Magmelland, the curse of helmet hair was real. Some wore long tunics like Erin's, with heavy belts around the middle, and others wore neat shirts and vests paired with suspenders and pants rolled up to the knees over wooly socks. Jasper recognized the boy with the tattooed face and was surprised to see the ink continued down his entire body. Dark swirls and sharp lines circled his neck and ran the length of his arms, all the way to his wrists, and his entire chest was covered in bold, black shapes.

"What are you staring at?" Mullans said, his face suddenly right next to Jasper's, a broad smile on his face.

"What? Nothing!" Jasper jumped a little ways down the bench and looked away.

Jasper finished changing and left the locker room with the last of the team.

"I like Howe's tattoos. I think they make him look dangerous, but actually, he's very friendly," Mullans said.

"Is he?"

The rest of the team was disappearing down the arena concourse. They remained strangely quiet for such a large group of young hockey players.

"He is, when you get to know him. It's actually really surprising, considering what happened to his family," Mullans said, frowning.

Jasper was just about to ask what had happened to Howe's family when a loud *creeeeeak* sounded behind them. Erin pushed open a heavy wooden door. She had changed back into her purple smock and her messy hair stuck out in all directions. A tall girl, with darkly tanned skin and long, whitish blonde hair, was helping to push the door. This girl had arms that looked too long for her body and legs that reached nearly to Erin's neck. Another girl, with pale skin and black hair, dressed from head to toe in deep red robes, stepped out behind them. Jasper looked away and hurried along the corridor. Mullans quickened his pace.

"Is that the girls locker room?" Jasper said as they reached the main entrance doors of Trillium Gardens.

Mullans stopped. "Why? Do you want to go tie their skate laces together? Or put frogs in their helmets? Or fill their locker room with squirrels?" Mullans was smiling and looked ready to turn right around.

"What? No. No, pranks. I just --" But Jasper had answered his own question. Of course the girls had a separate locker room. "So, there's three girls on the team?"

"Erin Wickenheiser, Saffron Hoffman, and Jade Lapensée. I hope you don't have a problem with that." Mullans narrowed his eyes at Jasper. "They're my friends, and they're great hockey players."

"No. No problem. There just weren't a lot of girls on the teams I played on, but if they can play hockey, that's all the matters."

Right then, Erin, Saffron, and Jade hurried past. Briefly, Jasper felt a hand on his shoulder. The wrist was stacked with brightly coloured bracelets. It was Erin. Jasper was sure she was going to shove him again, bracelets clanking and her female teammates giggling, but she didn't. Her hand rested there for the smallest moment, and then it was gone. The three girls walked out the doors, quickly and quietly.

When the girls were out of earshot, it was Mullans who started to giggle.

"*Ohhhhhh*, Jasper has a *girlfriend.*"

"I do not. Stop it." It was getting dark now, and Jasper hoped that Mullans couldn't see him blushing.

"We need to hurry. Ding and Bogg will close the gates soon. I don't want to get locked out. I had to sleep outside once. It was awful," Mullans said taking off at a jog.

Jasper did his best to memorize the route from Trillium Gardens back to the Players Pavilion, but in the growing darkness, his mental map became a murky mess. Mullans turned corners and pushed through gates and hopped over stone walls so quickly, that soon enough, Jasper was having a hard time just keeping the flapping arms of Mullans's tunic in view. Despite the cold evening air, Jasper broke out in a sweat. The moon was rising and the snow lined streets were draped in a blueish glow.

All around them, Tara was readying for sleep. Shutters drawn and doors locked, candles blown out and cats let out for the evening. Calls of G*oodnight!* and *Until morning!* sounded here and there above the noise of doors clonking shut and gates clanging closed.

One after another, the warm squares of light were snuffed out. The darkness of the evening closed in around the boys.

What had looked friendly and colourful during the day now looked sharp and shadowy and uninviting. The jagged, irregular buildings cast strange shadows upon the cobblestones and the crooked streets were full of unexpected turns.

After what must have been the most indirect route possible, the drawbridge spanning the moat around the Players Pavilion was in view. Mullans, pointing frantically to a figure near the enchanted doors, picked up the pace and Jasper hurried behind.

Their footsteps thudded on the draw bridge as it swayed sickly from side to side, the absence of a hand rail made worse in the darkness. Jasper caught a flash of his reflection in the water below. His eyes were wide and his skin was pale in the moonlight.

"Cutting it close, aren't we?" said the man standing next to the doors.

This must be Ding. He was taller and rounder than Bogg, with blond hair and a round, almost friendly face. He wore a toque just like his brother's, but Ding's was blue and even more sloppily made. The brother's shared a sense of style. Ding wore the same mismatched, bulky layers as his brother, and the finely-woven metal gloves on his hands. The boys scooted past, just as Ding was reached for the first door. He gave the boys a big toothy grin.

"*Coo-roo-coo-coo-coo-coo-coo-coo*!" he sang. "Almost got stuck out there, eh?" He laughed as if it were the most entertaining thought he'd had all day.

"Almost!" Mullans said, continuing his quick pace across the entrance hall and towards the ramp.

"Who's your friend?" Ding said. "I don't recognize him!"

"Jasper Jarvis!" Mullans said, not looking back, still running.

Jasper flipped his hand in a wave as he followed behind Mullans, still running.

"I heard about you!" Ding said, but he and his voice faded away and out of sight.

Jasper wondered just what it was Ding had heard as he and Mullans jogged all the way up the winding corridor, past closed doors hiding muffled murmurs, and through the swaying circles of light cast by the overhead lanterns until, finally, they reached their own door. Mullans pushed it open and fell face first onto the lower bunk.

The room was blue with shadow, with only a few streaks of pale moonlight filtering in through the windows. Ikarus popped up and cooed softly from his nest, welcoming them home, before nestling back down and out of sight.

"There's some pyjamas that are almost clean somewhere over there," Mullans said, pointing towards the corner next to the door, his voice muffled by the pillow in his face. "Toss me those striped pants, will you?"

Jasper grabbed the pants in question, which crunched in a sickeningly stiff sort of way under his grasp, and tossed them to Mullans. It made Jasper wonder just what "almost clean" meant to Mullans.

Mullans changed into his pyjamas and set about lighting the heating stove and shuttering the windows, while Jasper gingerly sorted through the heaping pile of clothes next to the door. He had never been one to worry himself about the general cleanliness of his clothes, especially because his mother used to do all that worrying for him, but as he sniffed cautiously at the different garments he managed to pull out of the pile, he found himself missing his mother's endless piles of perfectly cleaned, neatly pressed, fresh laundry.

At last Jasper found a pair of blue cotton drawstring pants that smelled something like soap. They would have to do. He changed quickly, noticing for the first time the cool night air as it hit his skin. He climbed up the narrow wooden ladder at the edge of the bunk beds and wasn't surprised to find his bed covered in clutter. Notebooks, more hockey pucks, piles of yarn, empty wooden boxes, and, strangely, a green top hat littered the mattress. Jasper scrambled forward on his hands and knees. The mattress rustled and crunched and bowed under his weight. It was being held up with a net of ropes from underneath.

"You don't mind if I clear some of this, do you?" Jasper hung his head upside down over the edge of the bunk bed to see Mullans contentedly wrapped up in a patchwork quilt.

"Go right ahead. Anywhere on the floor is fine."

"I thought so."

Jasper tossed everything down, except a lumpy pillow and a heavy knitted blanket that had definitely seen better days. The junk made soft *plops* and *clunks* as it collided with the rest of the mess littering the floor. Clutter and mess aside, once he was snuggled under his blanket and curled into the centre of the mattress, Jasper

found that he was very comfortable, and quite sleepy.

Just as Jasper was tossing his head from side to side, trying

to beat his pillow into a comfortable position, he heard the first soft

notes of a song. For a second, he thought it might just be Mullans

humming himself to sleep, but no, there was no way Mullans could

sing that well. The voice was quiet at first, and echoed in through the

open windows from far off. The song ebbed and rose with the

breeze. The voice grew louder and louder and it was beautiful. The

woman was singing a lullaby that Jasper thought he knew, but

couldn't remember the words.

"What is that? Who's singing?" Jasper said, keeping his voice

low. He didn't want to interrupt the song.

"It's Somnia," Mullans said, yawning. "Every night she sings

Tara to sleep. I like this song. It's a good one." Mullans's mattress

ruffled softly as he turned onto his side.

"That's who Uncle Fredrick was talking about. The woman,

who lives in the lighthouse. Is she really prettier than the sirens?"

"I've never seen her myself, but McGee says he has. He says

she's definitely the prettiest woman alive. He said she has nicer hair than me, so she must be really pretty, then."

Jasper tried to imagine a woman prettier than the siren he had seen earlier, with hair shinier and better smelling than Mullans's. It made him want to venture down to the lighthouse to try and sneak a peek.

Jasper's eyes drooped and he fought to hold them open. He squirmed over to the edge of his bed and looked down at Mullans again.

In a whisper, Jasper asked, "What happened to Howe's family?"

Mullans was quiet, eyes closed, breathing softly. Thinking him asleep, Jasper made to pull his head back up, but Mullans answered in a hushed voice.

"Theo, that's his first name. Theo Howe. His family came from one of the countries across the Breakwater Channel. I don't know which one, but it's gone now. It became part of Eridares. Emperor Black and his army swallowed up their country. Howe was lucky enough to escape to Magmelland. His family wasn't."

Mullans turned onto his other side and said no more. Within a few minutes, he was softly snoring.

Jasper curled back into the centre of his mattress and felt sorry for Theo Howe. Even though Jasper didn't miss his mother nagging him or Jake being a brat, he still had Uncle Fredrick. Jasper wondered if Howe had anyone like Uncle Fredrick, or if he was just alone.

The more Jasper learned about this Emperor Black, the more he hated him.

Chapter 10

A Glimpse of an Imp

On the brink between wakefulness and sleep, Jasper was sure it had all been a dream. Trillium Gardens, the Players Pavilion, Mullans and Erin. Everything. An elaborate, yet oddly convincing, dream. At any moment, Mrs. Jarvis would burst through his bedroom door, hollering at him to get out of bed and get ready for school. It wasn't until Mullans swam into view, stretching and yawning in the middle of the messy room, that Jasper was convinced it was all real.

Jasper rubbed the sleep from his eyes and threw back his blanket.

"Sleep well?" Mullans asked, scratching his head and blinking in the morning light.

"Yes."

"Hungry?"

"Yes."

"Breakfast."

Without another word, Mullans shuffled out of the room,

barefoot and bare chested, his eyes half closed and his hair immaculate.

Jasper rummaged through the mountain of clothes near the door and pulled a wooly red sweater over his head before following Mullans. The lanterns had lost their light some time in the night, but the soft morning glow poured through the windows, glinting on the puffs of powdery snow swirling along the corridor. It was chilly and Jasper was glad of the sweater.

Most of the doors they passed were closed. Apparently, the team liked to sleep in. Jasper found himself glad, and not for the last time, that his mother and her rigid schedule were far, far away. He was looking forward to sleeping in.

Mullans picked up his pace.

"I'm hungry. Let's hustle." Mullans grabbed Jasper by the arm and rushed them down the twisting, turning corridor.

Jasper allowed himself to be pulled along. As they ran, a door creaked open to reveal two sleepy eyed hockey players dragging their feet into the daylight. Jasper made a mental note to start learning everyone's names as soon as he could.

The dining hall was warm and cluttered. Filled with a

mismatched collection of tables and chairs of every design imaginable, it matched the style of Tara perfectly. There were squat, round tables that barely rose off the floor and long banquet tables with thick legs. One-piece, sturdy tables carved out of thick tree trunks, and delicate, dainty tables made of glass. There were plump, cushioned sofas, and tall, thin chairs with spindly metal backs. Powerful wooden thrones were mixed in with puffy pillows and cushioned benches. Stained glass windows high up on the walls bathed the round room in a reddish glow. The dining hall was warm and welcoming, full of nooks and corners perfect for sitting and chatting and eating.

Mullans led the way to a high-top table surrounded by four bar stools. Jasper climbed into one of the chairs. His feet dangled far off the ground and he swung them back and forth, wishing he were taller.

"I like breakfast. It's one of my top three favourite meals of the day," Mullans said.

"That sounds about right," Jasper said, surveying the breakfast laid out on the table. There were eggs done every which way, piles of buttered toast and bacon, bowls full of hash browns, and stacks of waffles and pancakes. The boys helped themselves and heaped food onto their plates.

"You boys just tell Christoph if you need any more things."

Jasper looked up and his mouth fell open in surprise. Before him stood what looked like a cross between a man and an octopus. Christoph, as seemed to be his name, had purplish brown skin and enormous, watery black eyes. The corners of his mouth curled high on either side of his face and his upper lip hung out hugely over his lower lip. A few course black hairs stuck out from under his chef's cap and he wore a white jacket stained down the front with splats of food. Most surprising were the extra arms he had at his sides, making for eight in total. Each arm was long and loose, without any solid joints, and ended in a dark, clammy hand finished with stubby fingers. A few hands held plates laden with food and others a spatula or a whisk.

Jasper realized he was staring and looked quickly at Mullans.

"We will. Thanks Christoph," Mullans said, not looking up from his pancakes.

Christoph was still looking at Jasper. One of his lengthy arms swooped inwards and the plump, bumpy fingers scratched at his forehead.

"Who is you?" Christoph asked. He narrowed his eyes at Jasper, drips of water running from the corners and down the side of his scaly face.

"I'm-" Jasper's voice came out in a whisper. He cleared his throat and tried again. "I'm Jasper Jarvis. I'm new to the team."

Jasper stood and extended his hand. Christoph stared at it for a moment, then bent down and sniffed at Jasper's palm. His bulgy nose left a smear of wet goop.

"I is Christoph. I cook for you. And the rest. Is nice meeting you," Christoph said, using one of his empty hands, which was just as sloppy and wet as his nose, to pat Jasper on the head.

Not wanting to be rude, Jasper ignored the slime sliding down his face, which was inching dangerously close to his mouth, and did his best to smile.

"Nice to meet you, too."

Christoph added a bowl of steaming hot home fries to their table.

"If you want something special, you let Christoph know. I

cook everything. Anytime. Anything for my hockey guys." Christoph flashed Jasper a smile full of blackened teeth.

"Thanks!" Jasper said, taking his seat again. He would ask Christoph to cook him some poutine just as soon as he had the nerve.

"He's an interesting guy," Jasper said, doing his best to wipe his face on the cuff of his sweater without a fuss.

"He has eight arms and his mother is an octopus. Definitely an interesting guy."

Across the room, the two sleepy eyed hockey players they had seen in the corridor ambled into the dining hall. Mullans's hand shot into the air, froze there for a moment, and then beckoned to them.

"Well, well, *well*," said the taller of the two, taking a seat of the table. "We are in the presence of greatness this fine morning."

"Oh, stop."

"Not you, Mullans. Your new roomie."

"He is pretty great, isn't he?"

Mullans's toothy grin sparkled in the dimly lit hall.

"Mullans, talking to you makes me feel like kid again. You make my weary heart feel *young*." The tall boy laughed and gave Mullans a punch on the arm.

"Anytime, McGee," Mullans said and flipped his hair. He tried to wink as well, but only managed to look like he had something in his eye.

Jasper recognized the tall boy from their practice the day before. He was the bulky boy with the huge calves. His forearms were massive and his tunic was stretched tight across his broad shoulders and wide chest. He had a dark complexion and sturdy look to him, with a set of the strangest eyes Jasper had ever seen. One was a golden brown, the other a deep green, and both of them were now trained on Jasper.

McGee extended his hand.

"Troy McGee," he said in a deep voice.

McGee squeezed Jasper's hand painfully hard.

"Guilherme Morenz," said the other boy, extending his hand as well. He was smaller and leaner, and closer to Jasper in age. Whereas McGee was dark and gruff, Morenz was light and almost delicate. He had soft features and light brown hair and a friendly, round face. His grip was soft and his skin smooth, and his pale blue

eyes and bushy eyebrows gave him a boyish look.

"Everyone calls him Gui," Mullans said, reaching for more

toast. "Guilherme is too long."

"I hear you're here to save the team," McGee said to Jasper

giving him another hard stare.

Jasper thought for a moment. He had to say the right thing.

"I'm going to try. I hope I can help."

McGee continued to look at Jasper with that same hard

stare, his mismatched eyes watching Jasper's face. Jasper would not

look away. A few moments passed, then McGee spoke again.

"I hope so, too."

Morenz looked between the two of them.

"Don't let McGee scare you," Morenz said, his voice soft and

reassuring. "You're part of the team now. We know you'll do your

best."

"Thanks," Jasper said, relief flooding through him.

McGee began piling food onto his plate, while Morenz

nibbled at a piece of toast. The foursome fell into a comfortable silence, enjoying their breakfast as they shook off the cobwebs of sleep. More team members drifted into the dining hall in twos and threes, taking seats at the mismatched tables and helping themselves to the sizeable breakfast Christoph had set out for them. Quiet conversation murmured around the room as the sun rose higher in the sky, washing the dining hall in warm hues of brown and red and gold. Feeling full and content, Jasper knew he could get used to mornings like this.

Breakfast finished, the boys bussed their table. Christof waved goodbye, promising them a delicious lunch, while balancing their empty plates in his many hands.

Back in the corridor, Morenz and McGee headed back up to their room.

"See you in class," McGee said before they were completely out of sight.

"Class?" Jasper said, turning to Mullans. "Do we have to go to school?"

He wasn't surprised, just disappointed.

Mullans stretched his arms above his head and gave his stomach a pat. It was a good breakfast, after all.

"We do, but we don't go to school with everyone else. We have a teacher who tutors us. His name is Mr. Brock."

"I haven't got any notebooks with me," Jasper said as they made their way slowly back up the corridor. Mrs. Jarvis's words came back to him, reminding him just how important it was to make a good first impression.

"I've got you covered," Mullans said, trying to wink again. He almost managed it this time, but his eye still gave a funny twitch, making him look more menacing than helpful.

"I owe you one," Jasper said.

After passing several more bedroom doors, most of which were open and displaying a varying degree of messiness (with an odd sense of pride Jasper noted that he and Mullans most definitely had the messiest room), they arrived back at their own door.

Jasper leapt over the pile of clothes blocking the doorway and tumbled to the floor, laughing. Paper crunched and skittered across the room in a flash of green. Some unknown thing moved across the floor.

"Heads up," Mullans whispered, grabbing Jasper by the shoulder.

Mullans was staring intently at the corner of the room. He bent smoothly to gaze under one of the desks piled high with papers and books.

"I know you're here!" Mullans said loudly and Jasper jumped.

Jasper squinted his eyes and pushed himself flat against the floor to get a better look. Standing there was a little creature no more than a foot tall. Covered in green scales from head to toe, its bony little chest rose and fell in heaving breaths as its bulging eyes looked frantically between the boys and the nearest window. The tiny muscles in its arms and legs strained against its scaly skin as it tensed in its pose. The little green creature flattened its pointy ears back against its bumpy head and hissed at the boys, showing off a mouth crammed with jagged teeth. Its fingers were long and bony and in its hands, it clasped one of the colourful beads Mullans had strewn about the floor. It took Jasper a moment to realize they had just caught a thief in the act.

"Hey, put that down!" Jasper said, scrambling across the floor on his hands and knees.

"Get him, Jasper!" Mullans said, leaping across the room to try and block the window.

In a green flash of jerky, swift movements, the creature was on the window ledge.

Jasper flung out his arms, reaching for it, but the thing took off out the window, frantically flapping two wispy wings of leathery skin. Just for good measure, it turned and gave the boys another hiss before rising into the clouds, the stolen bead glinting in his hands as he disappeared from sight.

"What was that?"

Jasper leaned out the window, staring at the spot in the sky where the thief had just disappeared.

"An imp. They're nasty little things. Real unfriendly, and they'll steal anything they can get their hands on. That's why I leave out all the beads. They like shiny things the best," Mullans said with some authority.

"But why leave the beads out if they're only going to steal them? Doesn't that just bring more of them here? What if they take something important next time?"

"I don't like having them here any more than you do, but if you can catch one, they'll give you a wish."

"A wish?"

"You got it."

Jasper looked again at the spot in the sky where the imp had disappeared. You'd have to be pretty quick to catch one of them.

"Have you ever caught one?"

"Not me, but my mom did, once. She wished for me to have great hair." Mullans gave his head a shake and his hair sparkled as it swished in a wide arc and landed in a perfectly coiffed wave that fell handsomely around his face.

"That's some strong magic," Jasper said.

Japer wasn't sure what he would wish for, but immediately he knew he wanted to catch an imp.

"We've got to get to class. Mr. Brock hates it when we're late. He makes you tell the whole class why you're late and then apologize. I don't mind the apology, it's the explaining what I've been up to that gets out of hand."

Jasper gave no argument and soon the boys were dressed for the day. Mullans even managed to find an extra notebook, bound with splintering twine and filled with thick, cream coloured paper for

Jasper to use. Mullans piled everything into his book bag and they were on their way.

Ding and Bogg were in their guard booth next to the main doors, their feet propped up and their toques pulled low over their eyes. Each of them snoring softly with forgotten books resting in their laps.

"All right, Ding!" Mullans laughed as he gave the wooden frame of the guard booth a rap with his knuckles. "Up and at 'em, Bogg!"

Ding and Bogg started awake, jolting upright on their stools and knocking several books and mugs to the floor as arms and legs flailed.

"Working! Working! Always working!" Bogg shoved his toque out of his eyes and blinked into the morning light, frantically picking the books up from the floor. He opened one of them to a random page and began to read intently.

"*Coo-roo-coo-coo-coo-coo-coo-coo!*" Ding sang, shaking his head from side to side, like a dog shaking water from its fur. He stood up, sat down, stood up again and straightened out his many layers of clothing.

Mullans hurried out the front doors before Ding and Bogg could realize they'd been caught sleeping on the job. Mullans crossed the drawbridge at a jog, and Jasper did his best to keep his eyes focused ahead, ignoring the sickening lurch his stomach gave as the bridge clattered from side to side.

"This way," Mullans called over his shoulder, ducking under a painted archway and turning sharply.

They passed under countless lines of laundry swaying in the morning breeze, squeezed down bustling alleyways, leapt over low brick walls, and hopped across some of the narrow streams dotting the city. None of the streets ran in straight lines or turned at square angles. Everything was mashed together and piled on top of everything else. The houses were crammed in and squashed against one another. There were windows blocked by neighbouring buildings, staircases that led nowhere, and doorways that opened onto dead ends. The buildings of Tara climbed high into the sky and leaned dangerously out of kilter as they rose. Jasper and Mullans passed by towering square doors scaling high above their heads and tiny rounded doors no more than a foot high from the cobblestone street. It was as if giants and dwarves and everything between were living right on top of each other. Confusing and congested to be sure, yet Jasper loved the look of Tara. There was an excitement and an energy that only comes from having so much diversity packed into one place.

After passing down a wide alleyway lined with wooden carts filled with colourful fruits and flowers the likes of which Jasper had never seen, Mullans came to an abrupt stop.

He nodded towards a narrow set of stairs clinging to the side of the alleyway, leading up to circular tower at the end of the lane. "We're here."

Mullans led the way and Jasper followed closely behind, keeping a hand against the wall. The steps were as shallow as they were narrow and for the second time that day, Jasper had to remind himself to keep his eyes ahead and not look down.

They arrived at a polished wooden door, sunk deep into the brick wall. Mullans grasped the handle and pushed gently, peeking behind the door before motioning for Jasper to follow. Jasper closed the door as softly as he could behind them. He followed Mullans to the nearest row of desks and they quietly took their seats.

It smelt of dust and damp and old books. It was a large, circular room that dipped downward. Each new row of benches and desks were a step below the outer ring that came before, like the

arena seating in any hockey rink. There were only a few small

windows set high in the smooth brick walls, giving the room a dim,

gloomy feel. Shafts of light cut through the dark room, illuminating a

simple wooden desk standing at the classroom's centre. A black

slate board was nailed to the wall behind it.

A man stood next to desk. He had been speaking when they

came in and he continued on without pause. Jasper hoped they had

gone unnoticed. The man wore a loose tunic with wide sleeves under

suspenders and trousers rolled up to the knees. His woolly socks

could not hide the athletic curve of his calves. He was tall and

handsome. His shaggy auburn hair was swept carelessly back from

his face. He looked old enough to be a real adult, but not so old as to

be unfriendly, mean, or boring. Jasper guessed that this man must be

what they called "middle-aged". His face was angular and lean, with

cheekbones jutting out sharply, and his crisp jawline was dotted in

stubble. His blue eyes were bright behind the rounded glasses he

wore. This, Jasper thought, must be Mr. Brock.

Mr. Brock finished what he was saying, something about the

difference between poisonous and non-poisonous plants that could

be found in a place called Haroldwood Forest, and smiled to the class. Jasper could see the rest of the team comfortably spread out around the room. Down in front, but not in the first row, he even recognized Erin's shaggy, tatty hair. It looked even worse from the back. Some of the team lazily scribbled notes in their books, while others longingly stared up at the sunshine poking through the little windows. Morenz was the only one who seemed genuinely interested in what Mr. Brock was saying.

Mr. Brock looked around the room, the smile never leaving his face as he called up, "Mullans! So nice of you to join us."

"Eek," Mullans said quietly. "He's on to us. I'll handle this."

Jasper hoped he and Mullans weren't going to get into too much trouble. It was only his first class, after all.

The rest of the team turned to look at them. Jasper's face flushed. Their looks ranged from bored and sleepy to bored and slightly annoyed.

"Aw, sir, I'm sorry. Really, I am," Mullans said, standing up and clasping his hands in front of his chest. "But Jasper nearly caught an imp just before we left and he needed me there to play defence."

"There's a first time for everything!" someone shouted and

the room exploded in laughter.

"The best defense is a good offense, Lapensée!" Mullans said, before grabbing Jasper by the collar and pulling him his feet. Jasper gave an embarrassed little wave. Erin rolled her eyes and turned away, furiously writing in her notebook.

Mr. Brock gave Jasper a long look. Then, he clapped his hands and jogged up the steep steps, which ran down the centre of the room, and stopped in front of Jasper's desk. He bent down, meeting Jasper eye to eye.

"Jasper, is it?" Mr. Brock asked, narrowing his eyes again and giving Jasper another long look.

"Yes, sir. Jasper Jarvis. I'm new to the team. My Uncle Fredrick just brought me here yesterday."

"Ahhh," Mr. Brock said, closing his eyes and nodding his head. "Yes. I've heard about you. I've heard a lot about you, actually."

Erin sighed loudly and began tapping her pencil against her desk.

Jasper wanted to tell Erin to quit being so annoying, but he didn't dare say so just now. Hoping Mr. Brock would allow him and Mullans to sit down soon, Jasper just smiled at his new teacher. Mullans was also smiling, probably hoping for the same thing. Jasper was sure they must look fairly foolish.

"Enjoying yourself so far?"

"Yes."

Mr. Brock waited for a better answer, so Jasper added, "Trillium Gardens is really nice and Christoph makes good pancakes."

"I'm sure he does," Mr. Brock said, extending his hand. "My name is Nathan Brock, Jasper, but you may call me Mr. Brock. It's very nice to finally meet you. Very nice indeed."

Erin's pencil tapping had changed to fist pounding. Her desk shook as the bumps banged through the quiet classroom.

"Well, we shan't keep Miss Wickenheiser waiting any longer, shall we?" Mr. Brock dropped Jasper's hand and Jasper sank back into his seat.

Mullans was just about to sit down in his seat next to Jasper when Mr. Brock called out, "Oh no, not you, Mullans. Come on down.

You're going to help me with the next lesson."

Mullans flung back his head.

"*Aaaaaooooohhhhhh.*"

Mullans slowly and dramatically pulled himself back to his feet. He followed Mr. Brock down the aisle stairs, his heavy, plodding steps dragging behind Mr. Brock's long, quick stride.

Mr. Brock reached his desk and turned to wait patiently for Mullans, watching him with the faintest of smiles.

"Thank you for your enthusiasm, Mr. Mullan."

Mullans gave a little salute before going to stand next to the slate board.

"What's the next lesson, sir?" someone called out. Jasper craned his next to see who had spoken. It was the tall boy with the red hair.

"Excellent question, Renato. It's Mullans's favourite."

At this Mullans covered his face with his hands and doubled over, whimpering.

"Mullans, would you be so kind as to tell Mr. Richard what we'll be studying next?"

Even muffled by his palms, Mullans's voice travelled to the back of the classroom.

"History."

The whole glass groaned.

Chapter 11

A Helping of History

There was a flurry of muffled whines and complaints. Papers shuffled and heavy leather-bound books thudded on desks as the class readied themselves for the history lesson.

Mullans leaned against the slate board, moaning and groaning. He picked up a piece of chalk and began doodling on the slate.

"History is boring," Mullans said as he drew a cartoon cat on the board.

Mr. Brock's chipper attitude would not be dampened.

"Mullans, your enthusiasm is an inspiration to us all."

In the row ahead of Jasper, a boy with the name "ORR" stitched onto the back of his baggy red team sweater turned around.

"Have you got an extra pencil?" the boy asked. Bright green eyes peered out from under a mop of light blond hair. His cheeks stood out brightly red against his otherwise pale skin, giving him the look someone who has just come in from the cold.

"Sure." Jasper ruffled through Mullans's bag, pulling out a pencil and handing it over to the boy. "Orr, right?"

"Yeah. Asher Orr. Nice to meet you."

"Jasper Jar-"

"Yeah," Orr said and smiled. "I know who you are. You like history, Jarvis?"

"Sometimes it's okay," Jasper said, creasing the notebook Mullans had leant him and writing 'History' at the top of the page. The notebook was otherwise blank, but tattered and stained around the edges. Jasper didn't want to think about how long, and under what circumstances, it had been in Mullans's room.

"Mr. Brock loves it. He goes on for *ages,*" Orr said, then turned back around, hunched over his notebook, and began writing. There was a jagged scar on the back of Orr's neck, running from the fringe of his hair and down past the collar of his red sweater. Jasper stared for a moment, realized he was being rude, and then quickly looked away. Where had Orr gotten a scar like that? It was no hockey injury, that was for sure. The cut was far too deep.

"Who's excited to learn?" Mr. Brock asked, stretching his arms outward towards the class, smiling wide.

There were more groans from the class. Erin tried to run her fingers through her bedraggled hair, but when that didn't work, she just hunkered down close to her desk, preparing for the worst.

Mr. Brock laughed and spun in a circle.

"The energy in this room is undeniable!"

Mr. Brock gave his head a shake and a few strands of auburn hair fell into his eyes. He didn't bother to brush them away.

"Last time, we talked about the Hundred Year Treaty. Who can give me a quick review of the main points?"

Silence. Mr. Brock was unfazed. He bounced on his heels, then began pacing from one end of the room to the other.

Jasper had never much enjoyed learning history at school. Usually, he would just doodle all over his notebooks, much like Mullans was doing now on the slate board at the front of the room. Yet, there was something about Mr. Brock's enthusiasm that made Jasper wish he knew the answer to the teacher's question.

Mr. Brock stopped his pacing and came to a stop in front of a dark haired boy with bulky, broad shoulders and huge upper arms. The boy wore a faded black cap over his bristly short hair and his knitted red team sweater, which had "TREMBLAY" stitched onto the back, looked to be at least two sizes too small.

"Ah, Luca. Thank you for volunteering."

Luca Tremblay slumped in his seat and the players on either side of him stifled laughs.

"I'm no good at history," Tremblay said. A blush crept up his thick neck.

"Give it a try. Tell me three things about the Hundred Year Treaty."

There was a pause while Trembly thought hard, the blush creeping from his neck to his ears.

"Um.....it's between Magmelland and Eridares...."

"Good."

"......and it's why Lord Tan is the Protector of Magmelland...."

"Great."

".....and it'll last for a hundred years?"

The room erupted in laughter, which Mr. Brock allowed to carry on for a moment, before gently silencing the class with a wave of his hand.

"Excellent. Thank you, Mr. Tremblay," Mr. Brock said, bouncing on his heels again. "Mullans, if you would be so kind as to write that down on the board?"

Mullans gave another little salute before turning back to the dark slate. Rather than erase the small herd of cats he had drawn by now, Mullans squeezed the three points of the Hundred Year Treaty in around his doodles. Mr. Brock did not complain, only laughed and said, "That's a lot of cats."

"Did you know you a group of cats is called a clowder?" Mullans said.

"I did not."

"Most people don't," Mullans said, and tutted disapprovingly.

Jasper began writing in his own notebook, carefully copying down what Tremblay had said. Now that he thought about it, knowing some of the history of this strange new world might prove useful.

Mr. Brock continued the lesson.

"So, nearly one hundred years ago, Magmelland and Eridares

came to an agreement. They agreed to stop fighting each other for at least one hundred years."

Near the front of the classroom, Erin's face was still pressed close to her desk as she swiftly wrote in her notebook. She didn't bother to look up at what Mullans had written on the slate board. On either side of Erin sat Jade Lapensée and Saffron Hoffman. Lapensée was having a nap, her long black hair falling in a shiny curtain in front of her face. Hoffman was more interested in Mullans and his cat doodles than the lesson and was coaxing him to draw more.

"Let's talk about Luca's second point a little more, shall we?"

Mr. Brock turned his back to the class and looked up towards a large portrait hanging in the centre of the wall. It showed a grossly fat man with blotchy pale skin wearing a ruffled collar and a velvet cap. He gazed out from the portrait with watery grey eyes. His many chins were spotted with a gritty layer of blond fuzz that matched the lank strands of greasy hair hanging limply on either side of his bloated face. The velvet cap couldn't hide that the man was balding. His thin lips were pulled back in an attempt at a smile, but what he really looked like was a man who was about to be sick.

Mr. Brock pointed to the portrait and turned to face the class again.

"Who is this dashing gentleman here?"

Mr. Brock didn't need to wait long for an answer.

A boy with short, curly black hair and deeply tanned skin raised his sinewy arm, splaying his long fingers wide as he reached his hand high. Stitched on the back of his team sweater was the name "GALLANT".

"Felix, go ahead."

"It's Lord Tan, sir. The Lord Protector of Magmelland."

"Indeed, he is. Tell me, Felix, what does Lord Tan protect us from?"

Felix Gallant thought for a moment, scratching his head through his bushy, black curls.

"Well, everything, I guess. Eridares and Emperor Black."

Mr. Brock nodded and signalled to Mullans to write that down on the slate board.

"Do we need protecting from Eridares? Isn't the Treaty enough?" Mr. Brock asked.

This time, there was an immediate answer as a pair of hands slammed down against a desk.

On the far side of the classroom, right under the row of little windows, Gui Morenz sat between Troy McGee and Theo Howe. McGee was leaning far back in his seat, clearly asleep, but Howe was glaring at Mr. Brock, breathing hard. The tattoos running across Howe's face gave him a dark, fierce look. He stared at Mr. Brock, unblinking, hands splayed on his desk. Morenz looked uneasily from Howe to Mr. Brock, then slowly raised his hand.

"Gui, please, go ahead."

"Yes," Morenz said in his soft voice. "Of course we need protecting from Emperor Black. He's not a good man."

Morenz looked back to Howe and gave his shoulder a quick squeeze, but Howe kept his eyes fixed firmly on Mr. Brock, his hands shaking.

"You're right," Mr. Brock said, his voice growing quiet. "He's not a good man."

In the row ahead of Jasper, Orr was running his pale fingers along the scar on his neck. His other hand was clenched into a tight fist on top of the desk, his pencil and notes forgotten.

Mr. Brock took a few slow steps forward, nearing the first row of desks. Mullans had stopped doodling on the slate board, the chalk hanging limply from his hand, and he watched Mr. Brock with a level of concentration Jasper didn't know Mullans was capable of.

"We all have our reasons for disliking Emperor Black," Mr. Brock said, his voice growing even softer. Jasper strained to catch every word.

"Of course we do!" Orr shouted, now gripping his neck tightly, his fingers turning white. "Just look at the map."

There were a few stifled cheers and a wave of restlessness swept through the room.

Mr. Brock gave a quick nod in Orr's direction.

"Excellent idea. Mullans?"

Mullans tossed his chalk onto the ledge of the slate, then stood up on his toes and reached for the large canvas map curled above the board, pulling it down. It unfurled with a *whoosh,* covering the slate board entirely. Jasper leaned forward in his seat to get a better look.

It was actually a series of maps showing the same area of

land, but in each one, the borders and colours of the land changed. The first map showed a little green island surrounded by bright blue water. Across a narrow channel there was a much larger piece of land, speckled with different patches of colour. Jasper guessed that each little patch of colour was a different country. In the next map, a large greyish blob had appeared along the coast, right across from the small island. The colourful little countries that had been there before had disappeared and were now covered in grey. From frame to frame, the grey country grew and grew, spreading outward from the coast and swallowing up more of the little patches of colour. By the last frame, nearly the entire map, save for the bright green island and four larger pieces of land right at the edges of the map, was completely covered in grey.

"This," Mr. Brock said, pointing to the little green island, "Is us. Magmelland."

It was tiny compared with the grey mass across the channel.

"And this," Mr. Brock said, sweeping his hand over the huge grey country, "Is Eridares."

There was quiet again. Asher's hand was still clenched tightly at his neck and Howe still glared at Mr. Brock. Jasper suddenly found himself wondering which of the little colourful countries Howe had lived in with his family before he escaped to Magmelland. He felt another wave of sympathy for the boy he barely knew. No wonder he was angry.

"This map has changed a lot over the last hundred years. Magmelland and Eridares were once equals. Some people still insist we were the stronger country and agreeing to the Hundred Year Treaty was a coward's decision, that we could have defeated Eridares, if only we'd had the courage."

Mr. Brock turned his face away from the class, thinking. Then, his head snapped up and he looked right at Jasper. Jasper straightened in his seat. He felt suddenly hot, despite the chill in the air.

"People just wanted the fighting to end. They could have never known what would become of their decision."

Jasper looked back at Mr. Brock, his notes forgotten. Mr. Brock was speaking directly to him and Jasper struggled to find Mr. Brock's meaning.

"All of these countries," Mr. Brock said, motioning again to the first frame of the map covered in all the patches of brightly coloured countries, "Fell to Eridares. They lost their independence, their culture, their history. Everything. As they fell, Eridares grew stronger."

There was a scrape of wood against stone. Across the room, Howe rose from his seat. Morenz stretched out an arm, making to pull Howe back down, but thought better of it, and drew back his hand.

"Emperor Black is a foul, evil man," Howe said. He was still, but his voice shook with fury. "And Lord Tan is no protector. He's just as bad as his brother."

The class had turned to stare at Howe in awed silence. It was the first time Jasper had heard Howe speak, but for the way everyone was gaping at him, it might have been the first time anyone had heard him speak.

More silence as Mr. Brock considered Howe, a thoughtful look on his face. From above came a ruffling and scratching. A gigantic eagle had perched on the ledge of one of the windows set high into the far wall. The eagle did not flick its legs or peck at his feathers in the way birds often do. It was completely still, its head cocked to the side and its beady eyes fixed on Howe. Jasper had the sudden uncomfortable thought that this bird could understand everything they were saying.

Mr. Brock cleared his throat, glancing nervously up at the eagle.

"Theo, please have a seat," Mr. Brock said, his words coming out in a rushed tumble.

Howe slowly sank his bulky frame down onto the bench, never taking his eyes off the eagle in its high perch.

With a flick of its head, the eagle now watched Mr. Brock with its black eyes.

"I think we can all agree," Mr. Brock said, a nervous tremble in his voice, "That Emperor Black and Lord Tan are the rightful rulers of Magmelland and we are grateful to be under their protection."

Clearly, Mr. Brock didn't mean a word of what he said. Two spots of colour stood out on his high cheekbones as he looked wide-eyed around the room. No one, not even Howe or Orr, said anything to the contrary.

Slowly, Jasper raised his hand. Mr. Brock's mouth fell open in surprise.

"Yes, Jasper, what is it?"

"Mr. Brock, if the Hundred Year Treaty is the only thing protecting Magmelland from Eridares," Jasper began and Mr. Brock gave a curt nod, "How many years are left in the treaty?"

Jasper looked over the maps again. With that many changes, most of those one hundred years must have already passed.

"Five, Jasper. There's five years left in the Treaty."

Jasper's mind worked quickly. The rest of the class had turned to watch him, but he didn't care.

"What happens in five years? What happens when the Treaty is finished?"

Mr. Brock looked slowly around the room, meeting each student in the eye before turning back to look at Jasper.

"No one knows."

Chapter 12

Judith Gleeson

No one knows. The final words of Mr.Brock's history lesson echoed in Jasper's mind at that evening's practice.

Coach Sparkle Pants had the team doing shooting, skating, and passing drills up and down the length of the Trillium Gardens ice.

"Push through! Finish strong!" Coach said, his voice booming and his whistle poised between his fingers. "We've got a big game tomorrow."

Jasper's legs ached and the cold air burned in his throat. They'd been at it for hours.

Coach blew his whistle and the shrill sound echoed throughout the empty arena, careening up and up, bouncing off the endless rows of stadium seats. Jasper looked skyward, once again marvelling at just how high the seats climbed. Trillium Gardens looked large enough to house the entire population of Tara. Tomorrow, those seats would be full. Jasper let out a shaky breath.

Coach split them into two groups and they lined the boards on either side of the goal. Reid Roy, the team's starting goalie, was in net. His padded equipment added to his already considerable bulk and the metal spikes sticking out of the top of his goalie mask made him extra tall. Even bent double, Roy blocked nearly the entire net. Scoring on him was tricky, but Jasper had been able to get a few pucks past him by going low on Roy's blocker side.

The passing drill got underway and Jasper lined up next to Mullans along the boards.

"*Pssst.* Mullans."

"*Ohhh*, are we telling secrets?" Mullans asked, his voice a hissy whisper. The din of hockey sticks slapping against pucks and skate blades scraping across ice made them unlikely to be overheard.

"I was thinking about what we talked about today in class."

"This secret sucks.*"*

Before Jasper could get another word in, it was their turn. Jasper and Mullans shot away from the boards, sticks on the ice and heads up, precisely passing the puck between them as they raced towards the goal. Roy came out of his net to challenge them, keeping his eyes on the puck and defending the goal. Mullans wound-up then deked, passing the puck to Jasper without ever taking his eyes off the net. McGee, playing defence, sped towards Jasper, but the second the puck was on his stick, Jasper angled the blade and redirected the puck up into the air. It flew easily between McGee's skates, then slipped past Roy's parted leg pads and into the back of the net.

"Very nice, Jarvis!" came Coach's voice.

Mullans patted Jasper's helmet as they returned to the line along the boards.

"I was thinking about," Jasper began again, "Orr."

"Orr?" Mullans said, looking to where Asher Orr stood on the other side of the rink.

"He's got this huge scar on his neck and he got really upset when Mr. Brock started talking about Emperor Black and Lord Tan."

Now, Orr and Morenz were streaming down the ice, passing the puck back and forth, and trying to outskate Theo Howe's defence. Despite their quick skating, Howe got the better of them and blocked Orr's shot before it ever reached Roy.

"Orr doesn't really talk about that scar, but I've seen it. It goes all the way down his back."

"How'd he get it?"

"I'm not sure," Mullans said, leaning on his stick while they watched and waited. "He must have gotten it when he and his family escaped. They only came across the Breakwater Channel a few years ago."

Jasper glanced back at Orr, who was smiling and laughing with Morenz. In the cold arena air his cheeks were an even brighter red than usual.

"Hey. Jarvis. Mind your own business."

It was Erin. She stood on Mullans's other side. Jasper hadn't noticed her there, but now, with her face inches from his and her sweaty, knotted mess of hair poking out from her helmet, she was hard to miss.

"I was just-"

Coach cut him off. "Jarvis! Wickenheiser! You're up!"

Erin and Jasper shot away from the boards. Jasper slapped the puck to Erin, hoping she would fumble the pass. She didn't. Jade

Lapensée was playing defence, but Erin and Jasper charged by her. Erin flung the puck back to Jasper, almost bouncing it over his stick. Jasper settled the puck and approached the net, dragging the toe of his skate blade along the ice to decrease his speed. Roy over estimated where Jasper would be, leaving the entire left side of the net open. Jasper fired off a shot and the puck flew neatly into the back of the net. Erin scowled.

"Easy goal," she said, slamming into the boards.

"I'd like to see you do better."

"I could!"

Their faces were inches apart again. Beads of sweat speckled the patch of freckles running across Erin's nose. Her green eyes were wide and wild.

Coach whistled the drill to a stop and Jasper was glad. He didn't want to fight with one of his own teammates, even if it was with a girl as annoying and rude as Erin Wickenheiser.

Coach Sparkle Pants motioned for everyone to join him at centre ice.

"Circle up! Circle up!"

It had been a tough practice and there were red, sweaty faces all around. Steam escaped past the collars of jerseys, rising and curling, then disappearing. Heated, heavy huffs of breath puffed in front of their faces.

"Good work today. We've got a big day tomorrow so I want everyone to get plenty of rest. Mullans, that means no midnight parties or pranks on Bogg and Ding."

"Ah, come on Coach. Bogg and Ding love my pranks. They find it charming. Endearing, even. I'm like the son they never had."

"And never wanted!" Renato Richard laughed, his face nearly as red as his hair.

Coach fixed Mullans with a look.

"Mullans. No." Coach's eyes moved to look at Jasper. "Jarvis, how are you feeling? Are you ready for tomorrow?"

Jasper's stomach had been in knots since the moment he learned his first game in Magmelland was approaching. He had never been more aware of just how tall and strong and fast his teammates were. Even so, he couldn't stop a smile from spreading across his face.

"I'm ready to play some hockey," he said, and a few of his teammates clapped their heavy gloves together or tapped their sticks on the ice.

"Great. You'll be on the second line with Mullans and Wickenheiser."

"But, Coach!" Erin said, skating over and coming to a quick stop, spraying Jasper with snow. "Coach, please, no. Clarke or Dionne would be so much-"

Coach Sparkle Pants raised his hand and Erin fell silent.

"Wickenheiser, my decision is final. I think you three will make a great line," Coach said, and paused, waiting for Erin to say more. She didn't. "All right folks, practice is over."

In twos and threes, the team made their way off the ice and down the mossy green pathway to the locker rooms. Erin grumbled and glared at Jasper, and Jasper did his best to ignore her. He had to focus on tomorrow's game. Even if they weren't allowed to win, Jasper wanted to show Coach Sparkle Pants, his teammates, and the crowd in the stands what a great hockey player he was. Perhaps even the mean and menacing Ms. Fearce would be in attendance, and Jasper wouldn't mind proving to her that he had been worth the trip. In any case, Jasper refused to let Erin Wickenheiser spoil this game for him.

Once they were changed and their gear was stowed in their lockers, Jasper and Mullans made for the Trillium Gardens main doors. Up ahead, Morenz and Howe were standing in one of the nearby alcoves at the foot of the arena's main staircase, speaking quietly. Morenz looked worried but Howe was stony and still, the alcove casting shadows on his tattooed face. Howe noticed them and then he was gone, out the doors without a backward glance and into the darkening evening.

"All right, Morenz?" Mullans asked.

"Fine. Howe's still rattled from class is all," Morenz said, then turned to face Jasper. "Ready for the game tomorrow? Nervous?"

"Yes. A little."

"You'll be fine, m'boy."

Mullans ruffled Jasper's hair and Jasper ducked away.

"Will Howe be okay for the game?" Jasper asked.

"Yeah, he'll be fine," Morenz said, leading the way towards the rounded glass doors of the entrance. He walked softly and smoothly and his footsteps didn't make a sound. "That stuff Brock talked about in today's lesson, it's touchy, you know? It's real personal for some of us. Howe's had a difficult life."

"The history lesson, you mean?"

"Yes, but it's not history for everyone. Some people have seen it firsthand. They lost their homelands to Emperor Black and his armies. It's not something you forget easily."

Orr's whitened fingers clutching at the long scar on his neck flashed in Jasper's mind.

"Emperor Black is not a nice man," Mullans said, kicking a rock down the cobblestone path as they exited Trillium Gardens.

The sun had sunk below the horizon and the night air was cold.

"The last thing we need is to run into a night angel. Boys, let's hurry," Morenz said, and set off at a jog.

The largest stray cats Jasper had ever seen prowled the walkways and window sills lining the first street they jogged down. Uncle Fredrick's mouser, Hercules, was not among them, but Jasper suddenly missed the stubby tailed cat with a sharp pang. He hoped

Hag Hill was treating him well.

"I have a question," Jasper said, his breath coming in quick gasps. He remembered something from the lesson.

"I bet Morenz has the answer," Mullans said.

The darkness of the night was closing in around them and Morenz's light footsteps fell faster and faster.

"Orr said something today in class about Black and Tan being brothers. Is that true?"

"Yes. Unfortunately, yes."

Jasper thought back to what Mr. Brock had said about the Hundred Year Treaty.

"But if Magmelland and Eridares were enemies, why would Magmelland ever agree to be ruled like that?"

Morenz gave a soft laugh and Mullans joined in after a moment, although Jasper was fairly certain Mullans didn't know why he was meant to be laughing.

"You're not the first person to ask that question. It doesn't make sense now, but it was part of the Treaty when it was written. That was the only way Eridares would stop fighting, if the Emperor of

Eridares got to choose who was in control of Magmelland."

"Sort of like 'keep your enemies close'?" Jasper asked.

They jogged in silence, their feet sinking into the snow, leaving a trail of hurried steps behind them.

"Yes. Something like that. Anyway, for the past 95 years the ruler of Magmelland has been chosen by the Emperor of Eridares."

Jasper thought of the elections he learned about in school and he found it strange that a country wouldn't be able to choose it's own leader by voting.

"Then, that must mean Lord Tan does whatever Emperor Black tells him to do."

"Mullans, your roommate is a genius."

Mullans beamed proudly and thumped Jasper on the back before they all broke into a run, hurrying against the cold of the night.

The rest of the team had returned to the Players Pavilion by the time they arrived. Ding stood by the entrance, and the huge glass doors hummed loudly as Jasper passed through. Ding made a show of putting on his woven metal gloves.

"Time for sleep, time for sleep," he sang. "I'm going to lock you in!"

His bark of laughter bounced around the entranceway.

A few players dotted the hallways, meandering about in their sleep clothes, saying goodnight. Morenz left them when they reached the room he shared with Troy McGee.

"Goodnight and good luck, Jasper. Until tomorrow....." With that, Morenz closed his bedroom door with a soft click.

Mullans and Jasper made their way to their room and they were soon changed and set for sleep.

Just as Jasper was settling into his bed, his sleepy eyes drooping, Somnia's voice crept in through the windows. Soft and soothing, she sang of a world under the waves and a garden in the shade. Jasper had worried that he would be too nervous to sleep that night but within minutes of his head hitting the pillow, both he and Mullans were softly snoring.

Jasper had barely opened his eyes the next morning before the nervous clenching settled back into his stomach. It was game day. Time to show everyone what he could do.

He swung out of the top bunk and landed with a crash on the cluttered floor. Mullans's eyes shot open.

"I thought you might have been an ogre."

Jasper wasn't even surprised. "Are there ogres here, too?"

"Not often, but they have been known to sneak into people's rooms at night and borrow their shoes. Best to stay on your guard."

"Right," Jasper said, filing the information away to the Advice He'd Never Use section of his brain. "It's game day."

"It's game day. Ready?"

"Ready."

The boys threw on some sweaters and made their way quickly down the corridor to the dining hall where breakfast awaited. There was a cold bite to the morning air. Snatches of Tara flashed by through the windows lining the corridor. Sloping roofs piled high with snow and everything else coated in frost. Winter was in full swing.

In the dining hall, Jasper and Mullans sat down to a breakfast of steaming oatmeal, sweetened with brown sugar and honey. There were warm buttered buns of cinnamon bread with raisins, cold glasses of milk, and freshly squeezed orange juice.

Christoph was in fine form this morning, buzzing around his kitchen, pots and pans in all his hands, singing loudly in a language Jasper didn't know. The walls vibrated with each note and some of the other players in the hall whistled or tried to sing along.

Despite the delicious spread, Jasper wasn't hungry. He forced down a spoonful of oatmeal, but it stuck in his throat and he washed it down with a gulp of orange juice. His hand shook as he brought the glass away from his mouth. Mullans noticed.

"Nervous?" Mullans asked, arching his eyebrow so perfectly as to make any girl swoon.

Jasper shook his head, looking away and for a distraction. He would not let his nerves get the better of him. Across the hall, a girl he'd never seen before sat with Erin.

"Who's that?"

Mullans craned around to look, surrendering all subtlety. Jasper sunk lower in his chair as Mullans leaned farther out of his, trying to get a good look.

Mullans swung back around.

"That's Judith Gleeson. She's Erin's cousin. She lives out in

Hobgoblin Town, I think."

While Erin was lanky and lean, her cousin was short and round. Judith struggled to sit comfortably on her tall-legged stool at the small table she shared with her cousin. She was a chubby girl, the round belly resting atop her thighs matching her round cheeks and plump fingers. She wore a woolen dress which looked uncomfortably tight and showed off a pair of dimpled calves and thick ankles. Her hair was bright blonde and tightly curled. She had a shy, timid look about her and she kept her eyes trained on the table in front of her. When she happened to look up, she caught Jasper's eye and quickly looked away, blushing furiously.

"What's she doing here?" Jasper asked.

"She visits Erin a lot. Lapensée and Hoffman don't live in the Players Pavilion anymore, so there aren't any other girls around. I guess she visits so they can talk about girly things."

Judging by the rat's nest of hair, the smudge of dirt down her cheek, and the rumpled purple tunic she was wearing for the third day in a row, "girly things" were not high on Erin's to-do list.

Now it was Erin's turn to catch Jasper staring. She puffed up her chest and flicked her chin in Jasper's direction. Jasper dropped his eyes back to his oatmeal.

"Why does Erin hate me?"

"She doesn't hate you."

Over Mullan's shoulder, Erin was glaring at Jasper, and she pounded her fist into her palm, narrowing her eyes at him.

The rest of the morning and afternoon passed by in a blur, despite Jasper's not having much to actually do. The knot in his stomach grew tighter as the day grew longer and game time approached.

There was a small, comfortable lounge area a few doors up from the dining hall, and most of the team gathered there, whiling away the afternoon.

The door to the lounge was round, like the dining hall's, but in here, the colours were no accident. The room was decked in rich reds and sparkling silvers. Everything from the plush chairs and fat floor cushions to the floor length drapes and stained glass windows matched. Jasper sat next to Mullans and across from team captain Troy McGee. Neither McGee nor Mullans seemed nervous about the approaching game, and Jasper did his best to hide his own nerves.

Judith had apparently left for the afternoon and so Erin sat on her own, reading a book by the large heating stove at the far side of the room.

"It's hard to get excited about a game you can't win," McGee said.

"I wonder what it would feel like to win," Mullans said, gazing at the ceiling, his blue eyes wide.

The floor to ceiling stained glass windows lining the walls had been propped open, letting in a soft breeze and an all-around view of Tara.

The city was full to bursting with buildings crammed together and fighting for space. Some buildings leaned dangerously askew, bending and twisting around each other the way too many teeth will fight for space in a too small mouth. From many windows hung scarlet and silver banners and as Jasper watched, more and more banners unfurled to flap in the wind.

"The city always supports us," McGee said, with a smile that managed to look like a frown.

"Even though they know we're going to lose?" Jasper asked.

"That's dedication for you."

"If hockey stopped after two periods, we'd be winners," Mullans said, snapping out of his daze.

"You're on to something, Mullans," McGee said.

Jasper watched as even more scarlet and silver banners appeared from the mismatched and crooked windows of Tara. They fluttered in the breeze, adding to the already crazy crush of coloured doors, bricks, walls, and bridges.

McGee looked up at the tall grandfather clock at the end of the room. It read four o'clock, exactly.

"It's game time," he said.

Chapter 13

A Great Day for Hockey

A rumble of noise rose as McGee stood to leave. The rest of the team followed his lead and filed out of the lounge, making for the main doors of the Players Pavilion.

Jasper wasn't expecting to make any stops along the way. He was caught off guard, and crashed into Mullans's back, when his teammates began turning off the hallway and into a small alcove near the entrance hall.

Five portraits hung in a neat row along the wall. Three lanterns dangled from chains fixed to the ceiling, their light shifting in lazy circles. Each player took it in turns to walk past the row of portraits, touching each as they went. A gentle touch on the canvas here, and a rap of knuckles against a wooden frame there. To each their own ritual.

Jasper looked at Mullans, his question obvious on his face.

"For luck," Mullans said.

They were portraits of hockey players, that much was clear.

They were decked out in their full equipment, minus their helmets.

Four boys and one girl, all of whom looked to be in their late teens.

They wore jerseys of scarlet with silver stripes at the collar and

sleeves. Below each, a name was engraved into a golden plaque.

"Who are they?" Jasper asked, following Mullans down the

row.

"The Famous Five. They were the best that's ever played for

Magmelland. They're famous," Mullans said, giving the portrait

engraved "GUS FLOWER", which showed a boy with a crooked nose

and a gapped grin missing two teeth, a high-five.

"WILLIAM GREYTONE", "MAURICE M. ROYAL", and "PENNY

GUINEVERE" followed next along the wall. Mullans gave each

portrait a quick high-five and Jasper stared up in awe, wishing he

knew more about these players. The last portrait on the wall was

labeled "EAMONN MORAN".

Eamonn had a friendly, handsome face. He was leaning on

his stick, which had the letters E.R.M. carved into the handle, and his

sandy blond hair fell in shaggy waves around his face. His smile was

small and a little dimple was just visible on his right cheek. The

collar of his jersey hung loosely around his neck, showing the thick silver chain of a necklace.

"Where are they now?" Jasped asked, touching the corner of Eamonn's portrait.

"They're still around. They're retired now, but they still come to watch the games." Mullans's brow creased and he made a sour face.

"Except Eamonn. He's gone."

"Where did he go?"

"No one knows for sure. People say he got into trouble with the people in charge, maybe even did something to make Emperor Black angry. He disappeared years ago without a trace. It's a bit of a Magmelland mystery, really. There's new rumours every year."

Jasper gazed at the smiling portrait of Eamonn Moran. Did Eamonn have any idea what would happen to him when sat and smiled while this portrait was painted? Jasper suddenly felt quite sad and sorry for Eamonn Moran.

"Was he a good hockey player?"

"The best," Mullans said, pointing to the 'C' on Eamonn's jersey. "Captain, too."

Jasper touched Eamonn's portrait again, hoping it might bring him luck, as another wave of nerves washed over him.

They left the alcove and exited the main doors of the Players Pavilion. Bogg and Ding were in their guard booth, both of them wearing scarlet and silver striped scarves that had a distinctly sloppy, homemade look to them.

"Good luck today, boys!" Bogg said, waving a tattered pompom.

"Start a few fights for me, eh?" Ding laughed so hard he began coughing and Bogg thumped him on the back, only making Ding hack harder. "It's the best part of the game."

"The best part, the best part," Bogg said, joining in laughing, and coughing, with his brother. Soon they were thumping each other on the back as they both coughed and gasped for breath.

"They always say that," Mullans said, his bright blue eyes glinting. "But I hate that iron maiden. She's so....prickly. No penalties for me, not if I can help it."

Jasper was just about to ask exactly what the iron maiden was when Mullans took off across the bridge at a jog and Jasper ran to keep up. Jasper was so nervous about the game, he didn't even notice how the bridge swung wildly from side to side as they crossed, footsteps hammering and wooden planks creaking.

The streets of Tara were now heavily decorated in flags and banners hanging from every door and window, and the team made their way easily down the crooked streets with everyone they passed hurrying to make a path for them. The crowds wished them luck and a good game, and some even tossed bits of ribbon or red leaves on the players as they passed.

On the way, they passed a mansion painted a violent shade of pink, covered in carved wooden hearts and flowers, and stinking of sickly sweet perfume. It was full to the roof with shrieking girls. There were girls peering out of every window, girls crowded on the front lawn, and even more girls stuffed into the main entrance way.

Seeing Mullans, the crowd of girls went insane.

"*Eeeeeeeeeeeeee!*" they screamed, tossing paper hearts and flowers. Some of the girls were so excited, they were crying.

Up ahead, Erin covered her ears and ran past the pink mansion without a glance.

"Half Heart Village," Mullans said. "They love game days."

"I can see that."

The team kept walking and soon the shrieks of the Half Heart Village had been replaced by the general bustle and hum of Tara.

All around them, people and creatures of every description went about their daily business. There were tall, pale women with long black hair and dark eyes, hairy men with the legs of goats, green skinned sprites, and wrinkled little men in green and gold suits whom Jasper thought might be leprechauns. They filled Tara's crowded streets, bringing the city to life.

Jasper was so curious about the citizens of Tara that, for a moment, the upcoming game disappeared from his mind. It wasn't until the glittering purple walls of Trillium Gardens swam into view that his nerves returned.

"Hockey time," Mullans said, smiling and taking Jasper by the shoulders and leading him through the rounded glass doors of the entrance.

The arena was quiet. There were still a few hours until puck drop. They walked the wide hallway lined with empty food stalls until they arrived at the entrance to the locker room. The last few hours leading up to the game passed by in a blur. Mullans showed Jasper the ropes, letting him know where and when and how to do the team's pre-game stretch and warm-up exercises. By the time they returned to the locker to change, the walls were humming with excitement. The crowds were arriving in droves, sparking Trillium Gardens to life. Most of the team were inside already, gearing up in their equipment, taping their sticks, and lacing their skates. Jasper and Mullans found their lockers and quickly changed.

The team dressed in their scarlet sweaters with silver stripes at the elbows and collar, just like the jerseys the Famous Five wore in their portraits. They reminded Jasper of Team Canada jerseys and for the first time since arriving in Magmelland, he felt a tinge of homesickness.

Coach Sparkle Pants poked his head through the locker room door.

"Okay lads, are you decent?"

There was a general murmuring in the affirmative.

"Come on in, ladies."

Erin, Lapensée, and Hoffman came in, waddling in their heavy equipment. The boys were all dressed, so no one was scandalized.

"Jarvis, here you go," Coach said, tossing a jersey to Jasper. He unfurled it and smiled when he saw 93.

"Your uncle told me it was your number."

"Thanks," Jasper said, still beaming. He pulled the jersey over his head. It was a little big, but Jasper knew he'd grow into it.

"Listen up!" Coach said, and the room grew quiet. "We know what we're up against tonight. It's what we've always been up against, but don't let it get you down. We're going to go out there and play the best hockey we can. We're going to play the hockey that I know each and every one of you is capable of. I want clean passes and driving to the net and no easing up. What do you say? Are you ready?"

Everyone clapped and cheered and bonked each other on the head with their heavy gloves.

"Let's play some hockey!"

With that, the team hustled out of the locker room, down the springy moss walkway and took to the ice.

Trillium Gardens was something to see even when it was

empty, but now, packed to the rafters, it was nothing short of breathtaking. The rush of sound echoed in waves, bouncing off the curved walls in a roar. The brightly clothed citizens of Tara stood out against the ever-darkening evening sky. Hundreds of fireflies flitted throughout the air, lighting the arena. Brightly burning wooden torches lined the top of the boards, casting an orange glow to the ice below. In every seat, someone waved a scarf or flag, splashing the already colourful crowd with scarlet and silver. Jasper's stick hung limply from his hand as he stared upward. He couldn't believe just how many people there were. His mouth hung open and he could taste the crisp arena air.

Around him, the team was warming-up. Coach dumped a pile of pucks on the ice and players were zooming up and down, stickhandling, passing, and taking shots on net. Roy was in the crease, scuffing the ice and stretching against his goal posts. Hanging above each goal at either end of the rink were two cages. They were held in the air by thick metal chains dangling from sturdy wooden posts protruding from the stands. Their rounded roofs were covered in red stained glass and inside of each curled a dozing creature, steam rising from between their scales.

"Are those *dragons*?" Jasper asked Mullans, who was

stretching on all fours on the ice while a gaggle of girls in the stands giggled.

"Yes, of course. Don't tell me you've never seen one before."

"I haven't."

"How else will we know when someone scores if we don't have a dragon to breathe fire?" Mullans shook his head.

Jasper looked again. The dragon in the cage above the Eridares net flapped its wings irritably and hissed steam from its nostrils. Jasper couldn't wait to see it breathe fire.

Jasper did a few laps around his team's end, taking some shots on Roy, but mostly, he scanned the crowd. Game time neared and the cheers grew to a roar. Behind the Magmelland bench, sitting about ten rows back, was Uncle Fredrick.

Jasper waved.

"Good luck!" Uncle Fredrick shouted, giving Jasper two thumbs up.

Farther back in the stands there was a black box with a golden crest on the front panel. Unlike the rest of the arena seats, which were narrow, wooden, and cramped closely together, the black box was spacious and richly decorated. A row of plump red chairs were evenly spaced between two heavy velvet curtains. The box was empty.

Mullans was at Jasper's side, elbowing him.

"They're coming," he said.

Mullans pointed across the ice, past the Eridares bench. He heard them before he saw them. Low rumbling grew louder and louder and was soon joined by a *thump! thump! thump!* The corridor behind the bench darkened, filled with bulky, shifting shapes. Jasper swallowed hard, his eyes wide. The shapes grew larger and larger, their footsteps falling heavier and faster until all of Trillium Gardens seemed to shake.

The team from Eridares took to the ice.

Jasper's hand slackened and he nearly dropped his stick. Knees shaking, he wobbled on his skates. Mullans wrapped a bracing arm around him.

The Eridares team was huge. Enormous, really. They plodded heavily across the ice, their skates leaving deep gashes in the smooth surface. Their bulky arms and legs were covered in rough, greenish-grey skin, dotted with patches of warts, scars, and hair.

They wore little hockey equipment and no helmets. Their skin looked leathery enough, and their skulls thick enough, to withstand even the heaviest of checks or hardest of slap shots.

"What *are* they?" Jasper asked after a few moments of stunned silence.

"Golems. They're twice as mean as they are ugly."

Jasper looked at the face of a passing golem. Its lower jaw had won the race against the rest of its face and stuck out a full three inches beyond its nose. Its mouth, packed full of crooked teeth and a lolling tongue, hung open. Drool dripped down its chin and neck, past the flimsy chest protector it wore, and came to pool in the creature's navel.

It grunted and blinked its heavy lidded eyes at Jasper before using its hockey stick, which looked like a toothpick in its massive fist, to chop gracelessly at a nearby puck. The stick snapped and the golem howled in dismay.

"This is who we play against?" Jasper asked.

"Every time," Mullans said.

The rest of the golems were sluggishly skating around the

ice, shoving each other, grunting, and slapping their sticks at anything that moved.

The Magmelland team wasn't bothered. Jasper's teammates easily skated around them, avoiding their swinging, bulky arms as the golems struggled to skate.

Jasper did his best to finish warming up, but he couldn't help stopping to stare at the golems across the ice every now and then. He had just fired a shot through Roy's five-hole when a hush fell over the crowd.

Cheers and laughs fell to whispers and murmurs. The quieted crowd watched the black box.

The heavy velvet curtains lining the back of the box ruffled, then parted.

It was the woman in the top hat, Ms. Fearce, looking as severe and angry as ever. Her pleated jacket was crisply pressed and her chrome cane gleamed in her yellow-gloved hand.

She walked to the box railing, moving in polished, graceful steps. If she still wore her impractically high heels, she didn't let on. She rested her hands firmly on the edge of the box on either side of a large, white trillium which bloomed at the centre. The flower's stem split and curled, running the length of the black wood.

She spoke into the flower and Jasper heard every word, even though she was at least twenty rows back from the ice. There were trilliums and stems and vines running along all the stands and boards, acting as speakers.

"The most honourable Protector of Magmelland, Lord Tan," Ms. Fearce said in her clipped, cold voice.

There was a smattering of half-hearted applause. The curtain ruffled again and Lord Tan ballooned into view.

His portrait didn't do him justice, for Lord Tan was fatter, balder, and shorter in the flesh. He waddled heavily forward, his belly swaying and jolting with each laboured lurch. He plopped heavily into the nearest cushioned chair and pulled out a silken handkerchief to mop his brow. Jasper felt sorry for the chair.

Ms. Fearce bent down to the trillium again.

"Her Majesty, the Black Queen."

Even less applause. The curtain ruffled and parted once more. A skeletally thin woman appeared, her pale skin tinged blue and pulled tightly across her bony face. Her black eyes were pits sunk deep into her face and her mouth was a tight, thin line. In place

of hair, wispy, twisted branches sprouted from her head, falling past

her shoulders and down to her waist. She wore a black gown with a

neckline that plunged to her navel, showcasing a shockingly visible

ribcage through the greyish-blue skin of her chest. Her sinewy

muscles rippled and strained as she moved. Despite the cold arena

air, she did not shiver. Next to the Black Queen, Ms. Fearce looked

positively friendly.

The Black Queen delicately sat down next to Lord Tan as Ms.

Fearce moved to speak again.

"His Imperial Majesty, Emperor Black."

The arena was silent. Eyes bulged and stared as the crowd

held their breath.

The curtain ruffled and parted for the fourth time.

A man dressed entirely in black strode forward. His black

hair was slicked harshly back from an angular faced shaped by high

cheekbones and a sharp nose. Atop his head sat a pointed platinum

crown inlaid with massive garnets, rubies, and fiery opals. The collar

of his robe rose all the way to his square chin. Long-fingered hands

stemmed from abnormally long arms. In his left hand, he grasped a long, ebony staff, topped by a glittering sapphire of the deepest cobalt blue. He sat stiffly next to the Black Queen, his spine ramrod straight, his eyes surveying the ice with jerky movements of his head.

Her task complete, Ms. Fearce took a seat on the Emperor's right at the far side of the box. Jasper was sure he'd never seen a less enthusiastic group of people at a hockey game.

A spattering of applause, a few cheers and the rumble of the crowd began to rise again.

Just as Coach Sparkle Pants blew his whistle, signalling for the Magmelland team to head over to their bench, the trilliums dotting the arena barked to life again.

"Welcome, welcome, *WELCOME!* It's another night of hockey in Tara!"

The crowd cheered their approval.

"I'm Tavish Shannahan-"

"And I'm Lorcan LaLonde-"

"But you know us better as-"

"*Shinny and Lickbo!*" the pair finished together.

Jasper scanned the arena for the source of the chatter. Opposite the team benches and about thirty rows up, there was another wooden box built into the stadium seating. This one was plain, natural wood and scuffed and scratched from years of use.

Inside sat two men, each with a large trillium coiled near their mouth.

"Well Lickbo, it's shaping up to be another great game," Shinny said. He was thin and balding and neatly dressed in a vest and cravat.

"You're right about that, I tell you. We're in for another great contest so long as these guys can learn to keep their **sticks on the ice**!" Lickbo banged his fist against the box shelf, rattling the panels. A full head shorter than Shinny, Lickbo was sturdy and broad and dressed in garish shades of orange, yellow, and purple.

"Okay, take it easy, let's-"

"Every year, I tell these guys. '*Keep your head up!*', and how many concussions did we have last year?"

"I'm not sure of an *exact* fig-""

"Seventeen. That's sixteen more than we should've had."

"........."

"One's good for morale."

"Oh."

Shinny and Lickbo bantered on and Jasper skated to the bench. Only the starting lines for each team remained on the ice. Troy McGee, the Magmelland captain, was playing defence, alongside a boy called Aidan Moore, who was almost as big as McGee and whom Jasper had yet to meet properly. Felix Gallant was at the centre dot for the face-off, with Gui Morenz on the left wing and Asher Orr on the right. Reid Roy was poised and ready in net.

A referee, wearing a brown leather vest studded with metal grommets and fastenings, skated out on to the ice. His head was shaved and his face was serious.

The ref slid to a stop at the centre dot and the crowd roared. Across the rink, an official prepared to flip a large hourglass filled with red sand. Gallant bent low, stick poised to strike. The golem opposite him plodded over and came to a clumsy stop, nearly falling to the ice before leaning forward heavily on its stick.

The referee blew his whistle, slammed the puck to the ice, and the game began.

For one shining moment, Jasper was sure playing against the golems would be a challenge. After all, they were big and bulky and outweighed the Magmelland team by at least triple. The first seconds of the period ticked away and it became clear. The golems couldn't play hockey to save their lives.

Magmelland deftly outskated Eridares. Jasper's teammates avoided the lumbering strides and ungainly grasps of the golems with ease. Gallant dumped the puck into the Eridares end, where it was swiftly picked up by Orr, a nice tape-to-tape back to Gallant, and the first goal of the game had been scored.

The scaly green dragon above the Eridares net sprung to life, wings flapping and nostrils flaring, and scorched the bars of its cage with a peal of orange fire. The stained glass roof of its cage burned bright red. The crowd went wild.

From behind Jasper, a troupe of faeries shot into the air above the bench. They glowed red and sliver and formed themselves into a '1'. In a cubby hole dug into the boards behind the Magmelland bench, the faeries had their own bench in miniature, complete with tiny water flasks, minuscule towels, and scaled down versions of the Magmelland Jerseys.

"*GOOOAL for number ten, Felix Gallant!*" Shinny's voiced boomed throughout Trillium Gardens.

"That was a real beauty of a goal and a nice assist from number seventy-seven, Asher Orr," Lickbo said.

"That's one-nothing, Magmelland."

The first line was skating briskly towards the bench and before Jasper was sure that yes, he had just seen a dragon breathe fire, Mullans was pulling him up by the shoulder and hauling him to the ice.

Jasper clattered onto his skates and took off towards the centre dot. His heart pounding in his ears, he took a long, shaky breath. The crowd screamed and waved their scarlet and silver scarves. Jasper had never played in front of a crowd so large.

He came to a neat stop at the centre dot and bent low, ready for the face-off. Jasper met the mismatched eyes of the golem standing opposite him. One was trained lazily on Jasper's face, and the other was looking over Jasper's shoulder. Drool ran down its chin and hung in stringy ropes, dripping onto the ice. A sour, ripe smell wafted off the golem and Jasper held his breath, waiting for the puck to drop.

The referee extended his hand. The golem growled and Jasper squeezed his stick. The puck slammed to the ice and in the blink of an eye, Jasper had won the face-off, shooting the puck to his right wing and onto Erin's stick. She was off in a flash, driving deep into the Eridares end. Mullans and Jasper followed, with the golems lagging behind.

Erin made to circle around the golem playing defence, but the golem jabbed its stick between Erin's blades. As she fell to the ice, Erin passed the puck neatly back to Jasper's tape. Jasper looked to the referee, waiting for a tripping penalty to be called, but the referee said nothing, his stony expression never changing.

Jasper sped forward, showering the golem who had knocked Erin down with a spray of snow before skating to the net, angling his stick and raising the puck right over the goalie's shoulder. Jasper didn't see the puck hit the back of the net, but the cheers of the crowd roared again, the glittering green dragon breathed its flames, and he knew he had scored. The faeries above the Magmelland bench swiftly rearranged themselves to form a '2'. The Eridares goalie turned to stare at the puck in the back of its net, its jaw gaping in surprise.

"Nice one!" Mullans said, giving Jasper a pat on the head.

Jasper skated to Erin, offering his hand to help her back onto her skates. She glared up at him.

"I can manage," she said, ignoring his hand and hauling herself back up.

"The ref should've called tripping-" Jasper began.

"*I know!*" Erin said, skating away before Jasper could say more.

Jasper followed, a smile spreading across his face. His first shot on his first shift in his first game for Magmelland, and he had already scored a goal.

The first period wore on. Scoring against the golems was not particularly difficult. The Magmelland team played with enthusiasm and energy and before long, they were up by five to nothing. With each goal against, the golems grew angrier and angrier, and soon, they took their frustration out on their opponents.

They hooked and slashed, tripped and speared, crushing the much smaller Magmelland players into the boards whenever they could. Yitzhak "Yitzi" Dionne, the third-line centre who, at only 15 years of age, sported a full moustache, took a violent check to the head. It was the worst sort of goon hockey. All down the Magmelland bench, players were bruised and bloodied. The left side of Jasper's face was marked with a deep gash, thanks to a golem who was using its hockey stick like a sword. The referee did not blow his whistle and did not say a word. Play only ground to a halt if one of the Magmelland players was too injured to leave the ice and had to be helped off.

Jasper was just about to ask Mullans if there would be any penalties at all when play was blown dead by the referee. The ref hooked his arms and motioned toward Luca Tremblay, indicating a high-sticking call.

The Magmelland bench groaned.

"What?!"

"His stick never left the ice!"

"Ref, are you *blind*?"

But it was no good. The referee led Luca over to the strangest penalty box Jasper had ever seen. Across the rink from the players benches and behind the wooden boards, stood a tall, bell-shaped metal structure. There was a bust of a woman's face perched on top, her mouth twisted in a silent scream and her eyes

bulging. This must be the iron maiden.

"Magmelland penalty, number 66, Luca Tremblay. Two

minutes for high-sticking," Shinny's voice boomed throughout the

arena.

"First call of the night, but not the first time we've seen it,"

Lickbo said.

The referee opened the gate in the boards and then pulled

on a latch at the side of the iron maiden. The metal panel swung

open, revealing an inner chamber lined with spikes. Luca carefully

climbed inside, struggling to keep his bulky shoulders away from the

spikes. The referee slammed the door closed and the crowd grew

quiet.

Then, someone was laughing. A roaring, choking, gasping

laugh crackled in the air.

It was Emperor Black. His was laughing so hard his pale face

was flushed with colour. He pounded his fist against the arm of his

chair, rocking back and forth with each peal of laughter. His

shimmering crown teetering on his head.

"What's so funny?" Jasper asked.

"Emperor Black loves to see us hurt," McGee said next to Jasper on the bench. "He likes hockey, but he likes seeing the golems beat the tar out of us more."

Emperor Black's barks of laughter filled the uncomfortable quiet. Theo Howe had said Emperor Black was a foul, evil man. Jasper was beginning to understand what he meant.

By the time Luca had served his penalty, emerging from the iron maiden wide-eyed and wobbly with blood dripping from his forehead, the first period was nearly over. The last red grains of sand filtered through the hourglass and a gong sounded, the thrum reverberating throughout the Gardens. The dragons at either end sprang to life once more, spewing flames into the air, calling an end to the first period.

Wide gates at one end of the ice opened and a gigantic octopus slithered on to the ice. Wriggling tentacles shot out as the octopus pulled itself along the boards, it's mottled purple and grey skin leaving a trail of silvery goo behind it.

Jasper looked to Mullans, who answered before Jasper asked.

"Her name is Cherry. She cleans the ice between periods.

Christoph claims she's his distant cousin, on his mother's side. Don't tell me, you don't use an octopus to clean the ice where you come from?"

Jasper shook his head. "Zamboni."

"Ha. That sounds so *weird*," Mullans said.

The teams went to their locker rooms.

The first intermission was brief. Coach Sparkle Pants was happy with their game so far and reminded the team to keep driving hard to the net.

"They don't play fair," Coach Sparkle Pants said as the team filed out of the locker room, back towards the bench. "Remember that."

The second period was just like the first, with Magmelland playing quick, clean hockey. They scored another five goals, making it Magmelland ten, Eridares zero. Jasper even managed a shorthanded goal, with an assist from Mullans, after Howe had been given a penalty for tripping. Howe had gone quietly to the iron maiden. In truth, the golem had tripped him, but Howe did not complain.

Magmelland was playing so well that Jasper was certain they would win the game. There was no way they could lose. It wasn't until the start of the third period, when the cheers from the crowd all but disappeared, that Jasper remembered what Coach Sparkle Pants had said in practice. *We aren't allowed to win. We lose every game. We have to. Those are the rules.*

The Magmelland team's energy and enthusiasm vanished in an instant. Eridares won every face-off. Jasper's teammates glided slowly along the ice, keeping pace with the golems who huffed and growled and drooled their way into the Magmelland end. One of the golems was able to coordinate itself long enough to get a shot off and the puck skittered weakly across the ice, trundling into the goal crease. Reid Roy could have stopped the shot with his eyes closed, but instead, he stepped aside and let the puck slide slowly in.

The crowd groaned.

A team of faeries from behind the Eridares bench shot into air. They glowed deep blue and black, forming themselves into a '1'. The score now read 1 – 10.

Emperor Black's roaring laugh sounded again. He cheered and clapped his hands while Lord Tan slapped his bulbous belly in approval. The noise echoed through the quieted arena.

"Why don't they leave?" Jasper said, watching as Troy McGee let himself be outskated by a lumbering golem with only one eye. "Why do all these people stay and watch the game if they know we're going to lose?"

"They have to," Mullans said, cringing as the one-eyed golem scored and the crowd groaned again. "Emperor Black wants everyone to see his team win."

Jasper watched Emperor Black clap and cheer and shout insults to the Magmelland team. Angry resentment bubbled in his chest. Jasper hadn't played in such an unfair game in his entire life, and it made him angry. This wasn't real hockey. This wasn't the game he loved.

The third period continued on and as the red sand slowly drained through the hourglass, the golems were allowed to score eight more goals. They were tied at ten goals apiece. With the last grains of sand left in the hourglass, Jasper's line took to the ice.

Jasper bent low at the face-off circle, waiting for the puck to drop. He met the eyes of the golem across from him. The golem stared stupidly back, blinking slowly. This golem couldn't play hockey. None of them could. They didn't practice hard, like his team did. They didn't play hard, like his team did. They just had their win handed to them every single time.

It was more than he could bear.

Jasper gripped his stick, clenched his jaw, and made up his mind.

The puck dropped to the ice. Jasper flicked it through the golem's legs, dumping it into the Eridares end. He whipped around the golem, chasing after the puck. Jasper glanced behind him. Erin, Mullans, Lapensée and Howe were glued to the ice in their face-off positions, watching with wide eyes and open mouths. The rest of the team were on their feet at the bench, craning their necks to get a look.

"Jasper! No!" Coach Sparkle Pants yelled, waving his arms furiously. "*NO!*"

Jasper heard him, but he didn't stop. He couldn't stop. He zoomed down the ice, his eyes seeing nothing but the goal. The red sand had nearly gone from the hourglass. He would only have one shot.

All the air seemed to have been sucked out of the arena. In

the stunned silence, Jasper's skate blades scraped loudly along the ice. He felt dizzy as he kept his watering, unblinking eyes trained on the Eridares goal.

"*STOP!*" Coach screamed, but it was too late.

Jasper swooped in towards the goal, faking right, then going low blocker. The golem goalie moved to block the shot. It swung its thick stick wildly, but was too slow and only managed to trip Jasper after he got his shot off.

The last few grains of sand slipped through the hourglass as the puck flew into the back of the net. The glittering green dragon above the goal let out a peel of fire, lighting its lamp. The crowd gasped and held its breath.

Then, there was silence.

Jasper crashed into the boards behind the goal with a bang. Shaking, he pulled himself back to his skates. He filled his lungs with the cold arena air, the panic rising in his chest. He was going to be sick.

Silence.

He looked into the faces of the crowd. They stared back at

him. The darkened sky above Trillium Gardens opened up and let loose a stream of powdery snow. The snowflakes piled silently onto the arena ice in the stunned quiet.

Someone screamed.

"*YESSSSSS*!

A thump on his helmet and a strong pair of arms around his chest. Tatty hair poked from beneath a scratched helmet, and Jasper couldn't believe his eyes.

"We won! *WE WON!*" Erin screamed in Jasper's face, laughing and whooping, tears running down her cheeks. Her laughs bounced through the arena. Jasper's knees wobbled and he held onto Erin. They spun in slow circles, celebrating alone together while both teams and the entire population of Tara watched.

Their cheers dwindled and, still clutching at each other's jerseys, they looked up to where Emperor Black sat. Breathing hard, sweat dripping, they waited.

"What happens now?" Jasper said. His voice sounded strange and small.

"I don't know, I don't know, I don't know....." Erin said again and again, her voice breaking as she held back sobs.

Emperor Black watched them. His dark, glinting eyes did not blink. Lord Tan, the Black Queen, and Ms. Fearce all looked to him and waited.

An eternity seemed to pass in which a million increasingly painful scenarios played out in Jasper's mind.

Emperor Black laughed and clapped his hands slowly, shaking his head.

"A great goal," he said, his voice a deep rumble.

He laughed louder and clapped faster.

"What a game. Fantastic!" the Emperor said, motioning for the others in the black box to join him. Lord Tan slapped his belly and the Black Queen tapped her fingertips together. Ms. Fearce rapped her chrome cane on the ground, looking less than pleased.

A spattering of applause here and there, and soon, Trillium Gardens was roaring. Jasper's teammates poured onto the ice and he and Erin were swallowed in a mass of scarlet and silver jerseys.

"*That was the best goal I've ever seen!*" Erin screamed into Jasper's ear.

" *Thanks!* "

They hugged again, soaking in the exhilaration of celebrating the first win in Magmelland's history. Jasper and Erin emerged from the crush of hockey sweaters as friends.

Chapter 14

Judith's Gift

The celebrations lasted all evening and continued well into the early hours of the morning. After the winning goal was scored, everything was a blur. Jasper's jersey was torn from him and he never saw that particular hockey stick again. His teammates hoisted him on their shoulders and ruffled his hair, cheering and screaming as they left Trillium Gardens on their way back to the Players Pavilion.

All of Tara joined in, waving their scarlet and silver scarves proudly. An unending stream of noise filled the air. No one could hear themselves speak.

The crowd wended its way down a narrow street lined with colourful wooden doors and the noise dipped to a murmur. Smiles slipped from faces and Jasper was hastily set down, his feet meeting the ground with a tingling thump. Two enormously muscular men stood at the end of the lane. Their shoulders were so wide, and the street so narrow, they completely blocked the way. Each man had an eagle perched on his right shoulder, similar in look and size to the one perched in the window during Jasper's first lesson with Mr. Brock. The men were bare chested and wore black breeches and thick leather sandals. Glimmering broadswords hung at their hips. Deeply tanned skin made them nearly invisible in the dark evening air. Long black hair hung in straight shiny curtains around their stern faces.

The quieted crowd neared and shadowy shapes behind the strangers swam into focus. Wings of bristly black feathers sprouted from their backs.

One of the massive men tilted his square jaw to the sky.

"It's late," he said, his deep voice full of gravel.

"It is," said the second man. The eagle on his shoulder rustled its wings.

Troy McGee stepped forward and stretched his arms wide, urging everyone to stay behind him.

"We don't wan't any trouble," McGee said. His voice was steady but his hands shook.

"Who are they?" Jasper said, his voice a whisper.

"Night angels," Mullans mouthed.

One of the night angels drew his sword. A gasp and the crowd lurched back. Asher Orr made a strangled sound in his throat before lunging forward to stand next to McGee. Orr's hand grasped at the scar on his neck.

"Put that away," Orr said, his voice shaking with anger. "We're allowed to be out in the city after dark on game days."

The second night angel growled a laugh before unsheathing his sword as well.

"Aye, but....." he twirled his sword, the blade glinting madly in the moonlight. "The game's over."

The night angels advanced and the crowd hurried backward. McGee and Orr stood their ground.

"Well, we'll be on own way then," McGee said, taking Orr by the shoulder.

"Yes," the first night angel agreed, extending his sword so the point came to rest in the centre of Orr's chest. "We'd hate for you to break curfew. The punishment can quite painful."

"And worse," added the second night angel.

Orr moved to lunge at the night angel, but he was knocked

backward by McGee.

"Okay everyone. On your way. We'll take the Banshee Bridge," McGee said.

The night angels burst into laughter as the crowd dispersed. The Magmelland team walked briskly.

Jasper walked between Mullans and Erin. Erin checked to see if the night angels were following them.

"What did he mean, '*or worse*'?" Jasper asked.

Mullans and Erin shared a look.

"The night angels patrol the city at night, as soon as it gets dark. If they catch you breaking curfew, they're likely to cut you up pretty bad, or worse," Erin pulled her sweater tighter around her shoulders, "Make you disappear entirely."

"Disappear? Do you mean," Jasper took a breath, "*Kill* them?"

"No one knows for sure. Some people think so," Mullans said.

"But some people say it's worse than death. You just disappear and never see your family again and...." Erin's voice failed.

"No one knows," Mullans said again.

Jasper thought of Eamonn Moran. Had he disappeared at the hands of a night angel? Was he dead? Or had he suffered a fate worse than death?

The team wasted no time in returning to the Players Pavilion. Ding and Bogg were waiting for them.

"WE WON!" Ding said, cheering as he and his brother twirled each other around in the worst dancing Jasper had ever seen.

McGee wrangled Jasper around the neck and messed his hair.

"The new kid's a real beauty, no doubt."

"And the way Emperor Black just clapped and cheered! I thought you were in for it for sure, kid," Bogg said, punching Jasper's stomach sharply.

"Look's like things might be changing around here," McGee said.

"You got that right, hoo boy."

The team filed past the enchanted doors and Bogg pulled them closed with a heavy metal *thunk!* Everyone went straight to the lounge and the celebrations continued until the early hours of the morning. Even Ding and Bogg joined in the fun, singing songs off-key and dancing on tables. Dorian Clarke and Luca Tremblay raided the kitchens and came back to the lounge carrying armloads of Christoph's pastries and cakes. Jasper's cheeks were sore from all the smiling and laughing he did, and his hands burned from endless high-fives.

When sleep finally claimed him, Jasper was curled up in a plush armchair near the large heating stove, his head resting on a crumpled sweater and a tattered knitted blanket thrown over him.

It was late morning when Jasper awoke. Sunlight streamed in through the stained glass windows, painting the room red and orange.

Jasper's stomach gave a queasy lurch. He had eaten too many of Christoph's pastries the night before. Mullans was on a nearby sofa, looking as sick as Jasper felt. He made to roll over onto his side, but tipped himself off the edge of the sofa instead. Mullans curled himself into a ball on the plush carpeted floor, groaning.

"My stomach hates me," he said, his eyes shut tightly against the brilliant sunshine.

"I know how you feel."

The lounge was littered with more of Jasper's teammates, some of whom had managed to claim a sofa or squeeze themselves into an armchair, and others who had given up and just slept on the most comfortable bit of floor they could find. The more sensible members of the team, like Morenz and Howe, had gone to sleep in their own rooms.

Mullans hauled himself to a sitting position and raised his arms above his head.

"We won," he said, his voice rasping. Jasper still wasn't tired of hearing it.

Jasper's stomach ache disappeared at the memory of scoring the winning goal.

Across the lounge, Erin emerged from a pile of blankets and stretched like a cat.

"This lounge is filthy," Erin said, her rat's nest of hair looking worse for wear. "I'm going to my room."

"We'll walk you," Mullans said, hopping to his feet and wrapping a sheet around himself like a toga.

Jasper stretched his legs and climbed out of his chair, following Erin and Mullans out of the lounge. As they walked up the winding hallway, Jasper could see scarlet and silver flags dotting the windows and doorways of Tara. He hoped the city had celebrated as much as the team had.

"Where's your room?" Jasper asked.

"All the way at the top. The very last one. I can hear the water rushing through the wall," Erin said.

Jasper thought of the stream of water that erupted from the top of the Players Pavilion and curved around the sloping outer walls, still convinced it would make a great waterslide.

When they reached the room Jasper and Mullans shared, Erin yawned and mumbled a goodbye before shuffling onward up the hall.

Jasper pushed open the bedroom door. There was a gasp and a shriek. It was Judith. Her breath came in shaky puffs and her eyes were wide. She clutched a bulky canvas bundle to her chest.

"What are you doing in here?" Jasper asked.

Judith's face turned a deep shade of red and she looked on

the verge of tears.

"I....he......I was meant to......Ding and Bogg....." She stumbled over her words, her voice rising.

Erin appeared at the door and pushed her way inside, expertly stepping over the piles of clutter.

"Judith, it's okay," Erin said, taking her cousin by the shoulder.

Judith nervously shifted her weight from foot to foot.

"How did you get in here?"

"Ding and Bogg," Judith squeaked, looking apologetically at Jasper. "They know I'm Erin's cousin. I told them I was here to see her."

"Why are you in our room? I mean, it is pretty nice." Mullans spun in a circle, still wearing his toga, admiring his kingdom. "But, I'm confused."

Judith took a small step forward. Her chubby legs struggled to manoeuvre over the mountains of dirty clothes while her chubby arms struggled to hold onto the package.

"Jasper," she said. "This is for you."

"Me?" Jasper asked. Judith took another step towards Jasper, extending the bundle in her arms. "What is it?"

Judith pushed the bundle into Jasper's arms and took a few quick steps back.

"I don't know, I swear. I never looked," Judith said, looking anxiously from Jasper to Erin to Mullans.

"It's okay," Jasper said. "No one thinks you did."

This earned him a small smile from Erin.

"Thank you for delivering the package and welcome to our room," Mullans said, extending his arms and flipping his hair in a shimmer of light. He leaned over and circled his arms around Judith in a giant bear hug. Judith's face flushed a deep crimson and she only managed a small squeak in response.

Jasper sat down on Mullans's bed and pulled at the knotted twine wrapped around the canvas.

A battered wooden hockey stick tumbled to the floor. Inside the wrappings lay a frayed blue and red toque, a scuffed hockey puck, and a small wooden chest.

"What is this stuff?" Jasper asked.

"There's a note. Look," Judith said, pointing a plump finger at the scrap of paper wedged beneath the chest.

It read:

Jasper-

Nice goal. Eamonn would want you to have these.

Jasper passed the note around.

"Who sent it? There's no signature," Mullans said, flipping the note over to check the back.

"Does it mean," Erin began, then gasped and grabbed the hockey stick from the floor.

She frantically looked it over, her eyes growing wide.

"It can't be," she whispered. She stared at Jasper for a moment before running from the room. "Come on!"

Jasper, Mullans, and Judith hurried after her.

Erin was running down the hallway, her tatty hair bouncing with each stride and the hockey stick swinging in her hand.

When she reached the entrance hall, Erin swung into the

alcove and Jasper and Mullans followed. Judith had fallen behind, and arrived a few moments later, out of breath and sweating. She was so light on her feet that Jasper hadn't heard her soft-footed approach. She appeared at his elbow quite silently.

"Look," Erin said, holding the hockey stick up to Eamonn's portrait.

The initials carved into the stick in the portrait, E.R.M., were an exact match for the initials carved into the stick in Erin's hand.

"Is this Eamonn Moran's stick?" Jasper asked, running his fingers over the letters in the handle. The wood felt smooth and worn under his fingers. It had seen a lot of hockey.

"Well, cuff me on the chin and call me flummoxed." Mullans asked. "Looks like it. Who sent it?"

Erin and Jasper turned to look at Judith, who promptly blushed again and stared at her shoes.

"I don't know. I really don't. I was out in the Hobgoblin market, picking up a few things for mom. Pomegranates have just come into season and I thought it might be nice if -"

"Judith, get on with it," Erin said, tapping her foot.

"Oh, right. Well, I was shopping and this man came up to me and asked if I knew where the Players Pavilion was. I started to give him directions, but he stopped and asked if I was Judith Gleeson, Erin Wickenheiser's cousin."

"That's strange. Did you recognize him?" Erin asked.

"No. He had a big black cloak on and the hood covered most of his face and he had scarf wrapped around his chin. He asked me if I'd do him a favour. So, I asked him what it was and he wanted to know if I could get into the Players Pavilion to deliver something. I said I could." Judith looked up sheepishly.

"That wasn't the smartest thing to say, was it?" Erin asked.

"I realized after how stupid I'd been, but at the time I was just so scared. I couldn't think. He handed me the package and made me promise not to open it. He said to just leave it in Jasper's room. Then he gave me this," Judith held up a small leather pouch. "Then, he disappeared into the crowd before I could ask him anything else. I came straight here. I was hoping I'd be able to get in and out without you seeing me," Judith said in a rush, biting her lip and looking timidly at Jasper.

Erin took the leather pouch from Judith and upended it into

her palm. Five silvery green coins rolled out.

Mullans whistled.

"A pretty nice delivery fee," Erin said, flipping the coins over in her palm. "It's too bad you didn't see his face."

"Why's that so important?" Jasper asked.

"Eamonn Moran disappeared twelve years ago because he made Emperor Black angry. No one likes to talk about him because no one wants to cause themselves trouble with Emperor Black. Now, someone with a lot of money sends you his old stick," Erin handed Jasper Eamonn Moran's hockey stick. "I think someone is trying to get you into trouble."

Jasper grasped the stick in his hand. Now, more than ever, he wanted to know what happened twelve years ago.

Chapter 15

Scuttlebutt

The days passed in a blur. Jasper attended his lessons with Mr. Brock and practice with Coach Sparkle Pants, but his mind was always on the package he had received. Was someone really trying to get him into trouble? And why?

Late one evening, two weeks after Judith had made her delivery, Jasper lay awake in bed. Despite Somnia's soothing singing, Jasper was restless. He thought of the game Magmelland had won, his winning goal, and the cheers of the crowd. Emperor Black's cruel laugh echoed in his ears. As Jasper drifted in and out of sleep, he saw Eamonn Moran's portrait, the smile gone from his face and his stick gone from his hands. Eamonn's face was scared and angry. Jasper looked down into his hands and saw the stick there. He tried to give it back, but Eamonn shoved it into Jasper's hands, pushing him to the ground. Jasper's stomach lurched sickly and his legs jerked.

Jasper awoke with a start, sprawled on the messy floor of the room he shared with Mullans. The cool air poured through the window, chilling his sweaty face. His breath came in shallow gasps and he squinted his eyes against the morning light.

"Sometimes I like to sleep on the floor, too. You have better dreams that way," Mullans said, stretching and rubbing his eyes.

Jasper glanced at Mullans and hesitated for a moment. Then, he said, "I had a dream about Eamonn Moran. He was angry I had his stick."

Mullans ruffled his hand through his tangled black hair and thought for a moment.

"Well, it was just a dream, wasn't it? Someone's kept that stick safe for twelve years, and now they want you to have it. Whoever they are, they think Eamonn Moran would want it that way," Mullans said.

"Right. It was just a dream. Someone gave that stick to me. It's not like I stole it."

"Exactly. All's well," Mullans said, swinging his legs out of bed and pulling on a pair of mismatched slippers. "I'm starving. Time for breakfast. Coming?"

"I'll be right down."

Mullans left, pulling the door closed behind him. Jasper went to the window and looked out over Tara. The city was just coming to life in the early morning sunshine. Frost glittered on the rooftops. Red faced citizens pushed teetering wooden carts and led horses down winding streets, their breath puffing in the cold air.

A creak and the door opened again.

"I'm coming, I just --" Jasper stopped short. "Uncle Fredrick!"

Uncle Fredrick stood in the doorway, clad from head to toe in his uniform of denim. His round blue eyes were shining and a wide smile was spread across his jolly face.

"Jasper, m'boy! I meant to come sooner, but I've just been so busy. I've had so much to take care of," Uncle Fredrick said, his long legs easily stepping over a pile of clothes.

Jasper ran to his uncle and hugged him tightly. Uncle Fredrick smelled of grass and hay and grain and life on a farm.

"I saw you at the game," Jasper said.

Uncle Fredrick's smile faded.

"That was very risky, what you did. Very risky. You know that Magmelland has never won a game before?"

"Yes."

"And you know that it's because Emperor Black wanted it that way?"

"Yes," Jasper said, dropping his eyes to the floor.

"Emperor Black is a dangerous man. You do not want to get on his bad side."

"That's what everyone keeps saying, but," Jasper looked up at his uncle. "I just couldn't help it. Those golems don't know the first thing about hockey. They play like goons. They didn't deserve to win."

"I know it's tough to lose, especially to a team like that, but things were like that for a reason. You could've gotten a lot of people, yourself included, into serious trouble."

Jasper looked out the window again, the victory turning sour. Ikarus was snuggled in his nest. Jasper patted his head and the pigeon cooed.

"Will we have to go back to losing?"

Uncle Fredrick didn't answer for a moment. Jasper held his breath and waited.

"No," Uncle Fredrick said. "You won't have to lose. Ms. Fearce has informed me that Magmelland will be permitted to play to the best of their abilities for the time being. Emperor Black feels that it's good fun, and a boost to morale."

Uncle Fredrick's face turned dark and hard. It was only a flicker, but his brows creased together and his mouth flattened to a tight line.

"If that changes, and Coach Sparkenfalupalants tells you not to win anymore, you must listen to him. Is that understood? Jasper?"

Uncle Fredrick's voice was so severe, Jasper couldn't nod his head fast enough. His uncle was always one for laughs and smiles and jokes. Uncle Fredrick hardly ever took anything seriously. If this were that important, Jasper knew he'd have to agree.

Uncle Fredrick heaved a sigh and sat heavily on Mullans's bed.

"I'm getting old," he said. "I can't sit down without making a noise."

Jasper giggled. Uncle Fredrick was back to his old ways.

"It was a great goal," Uncle Fredrick said, his smile crinkling his face.

"Thanks!"

Jasper couldn't stop the grin spreading across his face. He grabbed Eamonn's stick from its place leaning against the wall and handed it to Uncle Fredrick.

"I guess someone else thought so too. They sent me this."

Uncle Fredrick inspected the stick as he might have done with any other, checking that the shaft was straight and testing the flex of the blade. His saw the initials carved into the handle and the smile fell from his face.

"Who sent you this?"

"I don't know. There was a note," Jasper said, grabbing the slip of paper from the shelf.

Uncle Fredrick's eyes skimmed the paper. His breathing was heavy, but he did not speak.

Finally, he said, "Who knows about this?"

"Mullans, and Erin, and her cousin Judith. She's the one who dropped it off."

"And who gave it to her?"

"She said it was a man in a cloak. She couldn't see his face."

Uncle Fredrick exhaled heavily and closed his eyes, rubbing his temples. When he opened them again, he fixed Jasper with stern look.

"You must keep this a secret. No one else can know. Do you understand?"

"But, why?" Jasper said. "Wasn't Eamonn Moran a great hockey player?"

"The greatest."

"Then what's so bad about me having his this?" Jasper asked, reaching for the stick.

Uncle Fredrick made to move the stick out of reach, but instead let his hands fall open, allowing Jasper to take it.

"Jasper, there's a reason no one likes to talk about Eamonn Moran. He disappeared twelve years ago because he made a lot of powerful people very angry. You're already on thin ice after scoring that winning goal. It just won't do to get mixed up in this."

Jasper ran his fingers over the initials carved into the stick end. He wondered what Eamonn had been thinking about when he carved them.

"Can I keep the stick?"

Uncle Fredrick was silent while he thought, his brow creasing again. Jasper tightened his grip.

"Yes," Uncle Fredrick, and Jasper let out the breath he'd been holding. "But keep it here. Hide it away and don't bring it to your games. Don't tell anyone else about it."

Uncle Fredrick stood and Mullans's bed creaked.

"You should get down to breakfast. You don't want to be late for your lessons nor your practice."

Jasper nodded. He opened the wardrobe at the back of the room and shifted the piles of clutter. He slotted Eamonn's stick into the very back. No one would know it was there, unless they were looking for it.

Uncle Fredrick was about to leave.

"What happened to Eamonn Moran?"

Uncle Fredrick stopped and turned to face Jasper.

"That's not for you to go digging into. Eamonn Moran is gone for good and it'll only cause trouble to go meddling into the past. You don't want to be making the same enemies Moran did. Jasper, promise me you'll leave this be."

The serious look on Uncle Fredrick's face made him seem like an entirely different person.

"Okay," Jasper said, crossing his fingers behind his back.

Days turned into weeks and before Jasper knew it, he had been living at the Players Pavilion for a month. He had fallen into a comfortable routine, attending class and going to practice nearly everyday. Since their big win, the team had yet to play another game. As it turned out, the Eridares team only crossed the Breakwater Channel when Emperor Black was in the mood. In the meantime, the Magmelland team was expected to keep practicing. They needed to be ready should the Emperor send word he was brining his golems over for a game.

He had only played in one game, but Jasper was treated like a hero every time he went out into Tara. Complete strangers asked to shake his hand or offered up their babies for him to hold. They gave him baskets full of homemade cakes and bottles of brightly coloured drink. At first, Jasper accepted these gifts with a thank you and a smile. He had always been told this was the right and polite thing to do. However, when Mullans suffered a two-day bout of non-stop vomiting after eating a plate of what he thought were cookies, Jasper declined all future gifts with, "Thanks, but I'm not allowed".

With Uncle Fredrick's warning in mind, Jasper did his best to forget about Eamonn Moran. Uncle Fredrick was only trying to protect Jasper, and Jasper had promised to stay out of trouble, but even so, there was something about Eamonn Moran that Jasper just couldn't put aside. Every time he walked through the entrance hall, Jasper would detour to the Famous Five's alcove to look at Eamonn's portrait. Every night before bed, Jasper would pull Eamonn's stick from the back of the wardrobe and hold it for a while, running his finger over the initials carved into the stick end. Every goal he'd score in practice, Jasper would say to himself, "That was for Eamonn." The more he tried to put Eamonn Moran from his mind, the harder it became to stop thinking about him.

Uncle Fredrick came to visit as often as he could. Each time, Jasper would try new and different ways to ask about Eamonn, hoping his uncle might let something slip. The moment Jasper mentioned Eamonn however, Uncle Fredrick's hearing would fail him. Jasper soon gave up asking.

Following a particularly tiring practice, Jasper was sitting on his bedroom floor, staring up at the ceiling and thinking about Eamonn Moran. Mullans was nearby, on all fours and shifting through piles of clutter, searching for a particular pair of socks he claimed were his favourite.

Mullans suddenly became very still. He reached out a hand, signalling for Jasper to stop mindlessly flipping through the nearby rubbish. Across the room, there was a soft rustling. Near the base of a heaping pile of dirty towels, socks, shorts, and blankets, which Jasper had taken to calling Clothes Mountain, stood an imp. It was picking its way through the glittering beads and twisted bits of string strewn about the floor with quick, fluttering flicks of its spidery arms. The imp inspected each bit of rubbish for a moment before tossing it aside, looking for something better.

Mullans raised a finger to his lips. Jasper held his breath. The imp hadn't noticed them yet.

The imp's shimmering wings quivered and it flitted up to the shelves above one of the cluttered desks. Sifting through the junk there, it quickly tossed aside each piece, uninterested. Then, its mossy green hands closed on the puck that had been in the package with Eamonn's stick. Panic rose in Jasper's chest. He couldn't be sure, but Jasper guessed the puck had been a milestone goal for Eamonn. He knew it must be special, which was why Jasper had put it high on the shelf, safe from the tidal wave of clutter below. There was no way the imp was leaving with it.

The imp struggled to hoist the puck from the shelf, its bony legs trembling. Jasper made to lunge at the creature and grab the puck before the imp could fly away, but Mullans seized him by the shoulders, forcing him back to the floor.

"Stay," Mullans mouthed before slinking across the room in slow inches. Carefully, he unfurled into a standing position, blocking the nearest window.

Jasper stared as the imp lurched and fumbled with the puck. Just as it looked like the imp would lose its grip, the puck split in two, opening along the edge.

Jasper yelped.

The imp's head whirled around, noticing Jasper and Mullans for the first time. The puck dropped from its tiny hands and clattered to the desk. The imp's wings beat frantically, flying from the shelf and making for the window.

Mullans was ready. He reached out and caught the imp in a flash of his hand. The imp struggled and squirmed, beating its wings hysterically against Mullans's knuckles.

Jasper scrambled for the puck. A small brass hinge held the sides together and plush purple velvet lined the inside. It reminded Jasper of a jewellery box.

The imp's bulging eyes were trained on Jasper.

"You see!" came the imp's squeaky voice. "It's empty. Ol' Scuttlebutt didn't take nothing."

"But ol' Scuttlebutt was planning to," Mullans said, wagging a finger.

"I were only looking," Scuttlebutt said, crossing his tiny arms.

"You imps, you come in here all the time, treating our bedroom like the hobgoblin market," Mullans said.

Scuttlebutt looked offended.

"Says 'oo?"

"I saw another imp just two days ago. I bet you've got my favourite socks."

Scuttlebutt squealed a peal of squeaky laughter.

"That were me, and them socks is lovely."

Jasper grabbed the puck and shoved it right under Scuttlebutt's nose.

"What was in here?"

" 'ow should I know? Just 'cause I would've nicked it doesn't mean I know what it were." Scuttlebutt struggled against Mullans's hand once again, but Mullans's only laughed and said, "That tickles."

"Seeing as you've no reason to detain me, if it pleases you kind sirs, I'll just be on my way."

"No. We caught you, fair and square. You owe us a wish," Jasper said, looking again at the empty velvet lining of the puck.

"*Ooooh*, I was hoping you'd forget that bit." Scuttlebutt heaved the heaviest sigh his little body could manage. "Right. Go on then."

Jasper looked at Mullans, who nodded.

"I wish to know what was in this case," Jasper said.

A moment passed. Jasper stared at Scuttlebutt, and the imp stared back.

"Well?"

"Well, what?" Scuttlebutt asked. "I'm hardly all-knowing, am I? I've got to do some groundwork, some research. I'll grant your wish, but there's going to be some processing time, d'ya know what I mean?"

"So.....you'll get back to us?" Jasper asked.

"Exactly. Give me a few days and I'll have your answer. One of the other imps is bound to know. The whole lot of us, we can't stop nicking things. Sticky fingers, you see. I'll check with my girl, Rumour. That lady's got a mind like a steel trap, and a mouth like one as well. Now," Scuttlebutt kicked his tiny feet against Mullan's hand. "If you don't mind...."

Mullans looked at Jasper, and Jasper nodded. Mullans loosened his grip and quick as a flash, Scuttlebutt was out the window, his wings a blur. The imp shrank to a dot and then disappeared into the sky.

"Do you think we'll ever see him again?" Jasper asked.

"Alas, even the wisest cannot see all ends," Mullans said.

Chapter 16

Eamonn's Last Game

The thought of when Scuttlebutt would return, and what news he might bring, rarely left Jasper's mind over the course of the next few days. The possibilities were endless as to what might have been hidden inside Eamonn's puck, and Jasper found himself constantly gazing out windows or staring up into the sky, scanning for Scuttlebutt's veiny green wings. After he told her about the hidden compartment inside the puck, Erin said she would ask Judith if she knew anything about it, although it was doubtful she would. Three anxious days and nights passed with no sign of the imp, however, and Jasper began to doubt Scuttlebutt would ever reappear.

Jasper might have grown distraught over the vanished imp had he not had another hockey game to prepare for. For the second time since his arrival in Magmelland, Jasper would be suiting up to play against Eridares. The entire city of Tara approached the coming game with spectacular enthusiasm. Early morning before the match, Jasper awoke to cheers echoing throughout the city. By the afternoon, the cheers had grown to a roar and the streets were a sea of scarlet and silver flags.

"We've never gone into a game knowing we can win," Mullans said on their way to Trillium Gardens. "I've never seen this sort of hubbub. This is mad!"

Flower petals and bits of colourful paper and ribbon streamers rained down on the team from all sides as they made their way down a wide street. Mullans did a few twirls in the centre of the laneway before bowing and scooping some flowers into his arms, much to the delight of all the girls nearby.

Even Emperor Black marked the match as a special occasion. Before the game began, and in front of a full to the rafters, rambunctious Trillium Gardens crowd, the Emperor made his way to centre ice to drop the ceremonial first puck.

As team captain, it was Troy McGee's duty to take the face-off. He squared up with the golem across the circle. The crowd cheered and whistled as McGee took his place, but immediately fell quiet as Emperor Black stepped onto the ice. His overly long legs moved steadily and surely across the slick surface. His pale, angular face looked severe in the flickering light of the torches and the shine of his heavy crown was absurdly bright in the dusky evening air. The sapphire gem atop his sceptre glinted beautifully blue and the ebony staff clicked against the ice with each step.

Emperor Black clutched the puck in his white, boney hand and, reaching the face-off dot, raised it. There wasn't a sound as everyone held their breath and waited.

"It is so *nice* to be back," the Emperor said. A smattering of applause and the crowd fell silent again.

Troy McGee bent forward, preparing for the drop. The golem sluggishly copied him, drool dangling from its open mouth onto the ice.

Emperor Black released the puck. McGee didn't move. Jasper guessed that even though Eridares was the visiting team, it was traditional for them to win a ceremonial face-off. The golem jabbed at the puck with its stick, but missed entirely. Another jab and another miss. McGee shook his head and then reached across with his stick, neatly scooping the puck back.

The crowd gasped. McGee bent to grab the puck and then offered it to Emperor Black.

Emperor Black's eyes grew wide, yet he still smiled,

showcasing two rows of impossibly long, pointy teeth. He was smiling so painfully wide that his lips were pulled back nearly to his ears. He laughed but his face was still, and his smile seemed to grow wider still. McGee looked terrified.

Emperor Black's hand shot out, ignoring the puck and grasping instead at McGee's throat. The bones in the Emperor's hand worked under his ghostly skin as his grip tightened. McGee clutched at the Emperor's wrist and kicked his feet as he was lifted from the ice.

"You've grown brave, haven't you?" Emperor Black said, shaking McGee like a rag doll.

McGee coughed and struggled for breath, his face growing red. Jasper made to hop the boards, but Coach Sparkle Pants grabbed his shoulder and held him firmly in place.

Emperor Black laughed again before tossing McGee to the ice. The puck skittered away as McGee reached for his neck, gasping, and Emperor Black smoothly bent to pick it up.

"Thank you," he said, and smiled.

Emperor Black patted McGee on the shoulder and then turned and strode off the ice. McGee carefully got to his skates and glided over to the Magmelland bench, bent double. The colour was fading from his face, but he still could not speak.

Soon after, the game was underway. Emperor Black, Lord Tan, the Black Queen, and Ms. Fearce watched from the black box, cheering whenever there was a particularly brutal check.

Magmelland won easily, but it was not without cost. Now that Eridares knew they would lose, the golems treated the game as nothing more than a chance to beat the Magmelland team to a pulp. Emperor Black found this highly amusing.

The golems had given up on playing proper hockey completely and instead, took every opportunity to hook, hold, trip, crosscheck, slash, spear, elbow, board, charge, bite, and fight Jasper and his teammates. By the end of the first period, the entire Magmelland team was bruised and bloodied. Emperor Black was having a grand time and he laughed and cheered for each increasingly worse infraction. The referee didn't call a single penalty.

The only upside was that Jasper's team was able to play to the best of their abilities. They easily outskated, outplayed, and outscored the golems, doing their best to stay out of the corners, which is where most injuries tended to occur.

Ten minutes into the second period and Magmelland was up by twelve goals, four of which Jasper had scored. He was zooming into the Eridares zone, aiming for another, when a nearby golem slashed its stick and knocked Jasper's legs out from under him. He hit he ice hard, his head rattling inside his helmet. Jasper heard the crowd gasp and scream and then darkness fell before his eyes and he heard no more.

The room smelled of fresh linen and crisp winter sky. A cool breeze puffed against Jasper's face as he lay upon the starched bed sheets. The heavy curtains lining the window struggled to flutter in the light breeze. Everything was clean, and cool, and calm.

The tender left side of Jasper's face felt swollen and strange. His head ached and his right eye smarted in the glow cast from the hanging lanterns, while his left eye remained stubbornly closed.

"Shh, *shhhh,* careful now," came a soft, sweet voice. "You took quite a beating."

A slim man with pale skin and white-blond hair stood over Jasper's bed.

"Who are you?"

"I'm Hazel. I'm a nurse."

Pale Hazel moved delicately about the room, straightening, then re-straightening, Jasper's blankets and pillows. He soundlessly pulled the heavy curtains closed and the night sky disappeared. The smooth, dark stones of the room's walls swallowed any light that came near.

Jasper struggled to a sitting position. His head gave a swooping ache and his stomach lurched. He squeezed his eyes shut, waiting for the pain to pass.

"Is this a hospital?"

Nurse Hazel bobbed his head and smiled a delicate smile that did not crease the perfectly smooth skin of his face.

"We're the only one in Tara," Nurse Hazel said softly, and Jasper strained to hear him.

There was a creak and scuff at the door and a short, sturdy woman bustled in. She and Hazel wore matching reddish-brown tunics. She approached Jasper's bed, her hand outstretched.

"Jasper, I'm Doctor Stowe." Jasper's teeth rattled as Doctor Stowe shook his hand in her painfully tight grip. "How are you feeling?" Her voice was loud and easily filled the room. Jasper's ears rang.

"Okay, I guess. My head hurts a little."

"I bet it does. That golem certainly had it in for you. He gave you a few extra whacks after knocking you out and the ref took his time pulling him off," Doctor Stowe said, shaking her head.

She bent over Jasper, gently tilting his head back so she could get a better look at his bruised head and swollen eye.

Nurse Hazel clasped his hands in front of his mouth and gave a soft sigh.

"Poor little guy," he said, and then left the room. He had a way of walking that made no sound.

Jasper didn't much appreciate being called "little guy", but his head hurt too much to protest.

"You'll need to stay here with us for a few days. No hockey for a least a week."

"But, practice -" Jasper started.

"The answer is no," Doctor Stowe said. Her loud voice reminded Jasper of Mrs. Jarvis and he argued no further.

Jasper slumped back onto the bed, his head swimming and his cheek throbbing. A whole week without any hockey. It would be torture.

"You'll need plenty of bed rest and quiet. We'll have you righted in no time," Doctor Stowe said. She straightened and made to leave. Nurse Hazel's appeared at the door.

His high cheek-boned face broke into a wide smile.

"You have a visitor!" he said. "Doctor, is it all right?"

Doctor Stowe considered Jasper once more. Jasper gave a one-eyed, lopsided smile that he was sure must look even worse than it felt.

"I suppose, but only for a few minutes. This patient needs to rest."

Doctor Stowe tromped from the room. Nurse Hazel followed behind with a flounce of his feet and a flutter of his fingers. Jasper struggled again to a sitting position, ready for his teammates to burst through the door.

Instead, in walked Mr. Brock, his tall frame cramped by the hospital room's low ceiling.

"Surprised to see me?"

"I just thought, you know, the team...." Jasper trailed off.

"They will be by tomorrow, I'm sure. It's after curfew now. They had to return to the Players Pavilion."

"But, you're allowed to be out after curfew?"

"Being a teacher has its perks. I have special permission to come and see you."

Jasper's heart lifted for a moment, then sank.

"We wouldn't want you to fall behind," Mr. Brock said. "I've brought your homework."

Mr. Brock unsnapped the leather satchel he carried and produced a parcel of books and papers.

"Here's a list of readings and assignments. Do as much as you can."

Jasper took the books without a word and deposited them on his nightstand without a look. The package tumbled to the floor and Mr. Brock stifled a laugh.

"I'll get it later," Jasper said.

Mr. Brock eyed Jasper's swollen head.

"That's a beauty," he said. "You'll have to get healed up soon. Tara will miss you. They haven't adored a player this much since

Eamonn Moran was around."

Despite his aching head, dozens of questions jumped to Jasper's mind.

"Did you know him?" Jasper asked. "Eamonn Moran, I mean."

Mr. Brock nodded his head once and looked on the verge of smiling.

"Yes. He was my coach. I used to play, you know. After Moran retired from playing, he coached for Magmelland," Mr. Brock said, gazing at the wooden rafters of the ceiling, remembering. "He was a great coach."

"I didn't know you played," Jasper said. He thought of the hockey stick tucked away in his closet at the Players Pavilion and he wondered again who had sent it. If Eamonn Moran had been Mr. Brock's coach, maybe he would have an idea.

"I played centre, like you," Mr. Brock said. "Not as good as you, of course. I never was a great goal scorer. I blame my skates. Maybe my stick, too."

Mr. Brock laughed and Jasper jumped at his chance.

"What kind of stick did Eamonn use? I mean, if he was your

coach, he probably did some practice drills with you, right?"

The smile disappeared form Mr. Brock's face. He thought for a moment.

"It's funny you should ask," he said. "I've never met a player who was more particular about their stick than Moran was. He had the same stick his whole career. I don't know how he managed it. Most guys break a stick every few games, but Moran's never broke. He said it was a lucky stick. He took that thing with him everywhere, now that I think about it."

Jasper thought of the initials carved into the handle of the stick in his closet. His fingers had traced the E.R.M a hundred times by now. His skin broke out in gooscbumps.

"What happened to it? Is it in a museum or something?"

Mr. Brock's face darkened.

"No," he said. "Eamonn Moran's stick, and everything else he ever owned, disappeared when he did. In fact, we shouldn't even be talking about this. It's dangerous and we can't be sure who might be listening."

Mr. Brock's eyes flashed to the window. Jasper thought of

the night angels, and the eagles that had perched on their shoulders. Might there be one outside the window now? Mr. Brock turned and walked swiftly toward the door.

"Wait!" Jasper said, then swallowed hard. His blood pulsed in his neck. "What if someone had Eamonn's stick?" Jasper asked, leaning out of bed and lunging a foot to the floor.

Mr. Brock halted but did not turn around. When he spoke, his voice was low, but steady. Jasper heard every word.

"If someone were to have such an item, it would be very dangerous." Mr. Brock turned and met Jasper's eyes. "Any association with Eamonn Moran can lead to serious consequences. You've heard of people disappearing?"

Jasper was frozen, half out of bed.

"Yes."

"If that stick hasn't been destroyed and if someone were foolish enough to have such an item in their possession, it would be best if it were kept secret and hidden."

Mr. Brock was breathing heavily. Jasper held his breath. Their eyes locked for a moment. The colour had drained from Mr.

Brock's face.

"Please, sir," Jasper said, his voice sounding small and far off. "What happened to Eamonn?"

Fearing Mr. Brock would refuse to say more, Jasper stood and crossed the room.

"Please," Jasper said.

Mr. Brock blinked once, very slowly, shook his head, and then began to speak.

"I last saw Moran twelve years ago. It was our season opener. Emperor Black was set to drop the the first puck. He likes that sort of thing. Ceremony and tradition and all that. Just like everyone else, Emperor Black adored Moran. So, Eamonn was told to lace up his skates for the opening face-off. You should have heard the crowd cheer to see him on the ice again," Mr. Brock said, a smile playing at his lips.

Jasper smiled, too. That would have been something to see.

"Moran skated out, all smiles and waves, and Emperor Black stood there, tapping his sceptre on the ice. Just as Moran came into the circle, he lost his edge and slid right into Emperor Black. You could have heard a pin drop in the Gardens. Black and Moran fell and I remember Black's sceptre smacking against the ice. We were terrified. Moran was a great skater. I couldn't believe what I was seeing."

"Was Emperor Black angry?" Jasper asked. Emperor Black seemed like the last person to take such a blunder lightly.

"No," Mr. Brock said, shrugging. "Moran had that affect on people. He could do no wrong."

"Did Emperor Black's sceptre break?"

"No. It made an awful bang when it hit the ice, but it didn't break. Although, perhaps, now that you mention it....." Mr. Brock's voice trailed off.

"Yes?" Jasper said.

Mr. Brock shook his head, waving his hands.

"It's nothing. There's no way," he said, meeting Jasper's eyes. "Definitely not."

"Then what happened?"

"A few days later, Eamonn Moran disappeared. That was it. No one's seen him since."

Mr. Brock frowned and shrugged and then turned to leave.

"Make sure you do your homework," he said, and then disappeared through the door, his head bent in thought.

"I will," Jasper said.

Jasper's mind buzzed with a hundred new questions. If everyone, even Emperor Black, loved Moran so much, why had he disappeared? Why had someone sent Moran's stick to Jasper if it were so dangerous? Was someone trying to get him in trouble? What would happen if he was caught with it?

Jasper knew the answer that.

"I'll disappear," he said to the empty room.

The sky darkened and Jasper curled under his blankets, his head still throbbing and his mind still whirring.

Jasper thought he might never be able to sleep again with such a heavy load weighing on his mind, but as the first notes of Somnia's song drifted up from the lighthouse at the water's edge, Jasper's eyelids began to droop. Just as he was drifting into the realm of sleep, his last thought was of Eamonn Moran skating into Emperor Black, and the Emperor's sceptre crashing to the ice and shattering into a million pieces. The sound echoed through his

dreams.

Chapter 17

Scuttlebutt's Return

Jasper slept late. Without an early morning practice to attend, and no Mullans to shake him awake with urgent tales of wild dreams, Jasper slept most of the morning away.

His stomach grumbled and he cracked open bleary eyes, only to come face to face with Nurse Hazel.

"How are we today?"

"*AHHHH!*"

Jasper scrambled away, sitting upright in his bed, and pulling the sheets to his neck.

"Did we sleep well?" Nurse Hazel asked, his voice cheery and soft.

Jasper rubbed the sleep from his eyes. His head felt heavy and his mouth was dry.

"I bet we're hungry. Are we hungry?" Nurse Hazel held a tray piled high with buttered toast and pastries and large jugs of water and a pinkish-purple juice, each with droplets of condensation beading on the side.

Jasper's stomach grumbled again.

"Yes. Yes, we're hungry," he said.

Nurse Hazel gently set the tray down on the bedside table. He spent the next ten minutes fussing and flitting about the room, fluffing Jasper's pillows and fixing the curtains. Jasper chewed and drank and watched Nurse Hazel at his work, thinking that he was a very strange man indeed.

When Nurse Hazel was finally satisfied with the state of the room, he gathered up the remains of Jasper's breakfast and turned to leave.

"Ill be down the hall if you need anything and remember, you're to stay in bed. Doctor Stowe's orders."

Jasper frowned but thanked Nurse Hazel before he left the room.

The day did nothing but drag and within an hour, Jasper was so bored the homework Mr. Brock had left was starting to look like fun. He was just reaching for one of the heavy history texts when a ruckus erupted in the hallway.

"Is he in this one, do you think?"

"Try it."

A door opened with a creak and then a shriek of surprise.

"*Oops! Sorry!*"

"Nice undies."

"What's going on out here?" It was Nurse Hazel. His usually soft voice verged on angry.

"We're looking for Jasper Jarvis. We've come to visit him." There was no mistaking the plucky voice of Erin Wickenheiser.

"He's in the room at the end of the hall, on the right. You may only stay for a few minutes. Jasper needs his rest!"

"Yeah, yeah," Erin said, and Jasper knew she was rolling her eyes.

They bounded down the hallway with all the grace of a herd of elephants and burst into Jasper's room without knocking.

"*Surprise!*" Mullans said, leaping across the room.

Jasper grinned. He was glad to see his friends and happy he had a reason to avoid his homework.

Erin followed behind Mullans, and then came Judith, stepping lightly. Judith looked nervously around the room and blushed when Jasper said hello.

Erin flopped onto the end of Jasper's bed, while Mullans poked through the cupboards on the far wall. Judith sat in a chair across the room and stared out the window.

"We won," Erin said, her freckly face breaking into a smile.

Jasper raised his arms above his head and cheered.

"I could get used to this winning thing," Mullans said, wrapping his head with a roll of bandages he'd found in the cupboard. "You're really shaking things up here, Jasper. You're an absolute beauty."

"Glad I could help," Jasper said, grinning from ear to ear.

"That golem really had it in for you. It was a brutal slash," Erin said.

"Does it hurt?" Judith asked, turning her eyes away from the window.

In truth, Jasper's head was still throbbing and his eyes stung with every blink.

"Nah," Jasper said. "I'm fine, but they're making me stay here for a whole week. No hockey."

Judith gave a shy smile. "I'm glad you're okay," she said, before turning back to the window.

"No hockey for a week?" Erin said, jumping up on the bed. "Are they crazy? You'll miss practice. And what if we have another game?"

Jasper shrugged.

"Doctor says no."

"Maybe we can bust you out, like a prison escape," Mullans said. He was completely wrapped in bandages now and looked like a mummy.

Jasper laughed.

"We could make a rope ladder and I could climb out the window in the middle of the night."

"Or we could sneak you out in a bag of laundry."

The three of them joked and planned all the ways they might free Jasper from his hospital prison, until they were interrupted by Judith.

"*Imp!*" she yelled, jumping from her chair and pointing out the window.

Mullans and Erin rushed over, craning their necks. Jasper leapt out of bed, his head spinning with a sickening swoop, and joined them at the window sill.

The speck on the horizon grew to a spot, and the spot grew to a smudge, and the smudge soon became Scuttlebutt. The buzzing wings and shimmering green skin swam into focus as the imp neared.

"You came back!" Jasper said as Scuttlebutt lazily buzzed over their heads, coming to a slow stop atop Jasper's headboard.

"I said I would, didn't I? I'm an imp of his word, have no doubt," Scuttlebutt said, making himself comfortable on the bedpost.

"All right, I'm sorry."

"You haven't been easy to find, I'll have you know. Send ol' Scuttlebutt off to fulfill a wish and you haven't the decency to be at home when I come to call with your answer," Scuttlebutt said.

"What did you find out?" Erin said, crawling onto the bed and bringing her face very near to Scuttlebutt. She was getting impatient.

"Hold on, hold on, don't rush me now," Scuttlebutt said. From the pouch at his hip he removed a tiny wooden pipe. He jabbed it in his mouth and struck what must have been a match (for it was much too small for Jasper to see) against the smooth, grey stone of the hospital wall. A tiny flame sparked to life as Scuttlebutt puffed on his pipe, sending a string of smoke curling towards the low ceiling. The four of them watched in a amazement for a moment, and then they all spoke at once.

"Please, Mr. Scuttlebutt, we've been waiting so long-"

"I've been in here with a concussion and I haven't been at the Players Pavilion-"

"If you don't hurry up, I'm going to squish you and then-"

"That's the tiniest pipe I've ever seen!"

"All right, All right. Let's settle down." Scuttlebutt leaned back, crossed his legs and took another long drag on his pipe. "It was about this hockey puck of yours, yes?"

"Yes!" All four of them said together.

"Right, well, I've had it from me gal Rumour, who talked to her Uncle Ack Ack, who heard from his neighbour Gossip, who knows an imp who knows an imp who may or may not have originally nicked it," Scuttlebutt paused to take another drag on his pipe.

"Yes? *And*?" Jasper said.

Scuttlebutt puffed at his pipe and sent a tiny smoke ring spinning towards the ceiling.

"Your hockey puck held a gemstone on a silver chain."

No one spoke, but Jasper's mind raced. Why would Eamonn Moran hide a necklace? What could be so special about that? He said as much to Scuttlebutt, but the imp only shrugged his bony shoulders.

"Don't know, but apparently it was a real beauty. The deepest, truest blue sapphire you ever did see."

"Maybe it *was* just a piece of jewellery," Judith said. She had been so quiet, Jasper had forgotten she was there.

Scuttlebutt shook his head and puffed on his pipe again.

"Not likely. Whoever owned that necklace went through a lot of trouble to hide it in that puck. That case was specially made. Leprechaun make, you see. The leprechauns are real clever, they are. Always hiding their gold. They know how to make near anything into a chest for stashing treasure. Their work's good, and expensive, and they're none too keen on outsiders. Whoever ordered that case made must've been a real charmer to convince the leprechauns to make it, and real keen to keep that necklace hidden."

Scuttlebutt puffed his cheeks again and a small cloud of smoke wafted into Jasper's face. From what Jasper knew of Eamonn Moran, he had certainly been charming.

"Well, what's this necklace look like?" Erin asked. Jasper's mind had gone to the same place. If they were going to find it, they'd need to know what they were looking for.

Scuttlebutt jabbed his pipe into the corner of his mouth.

"Thought you might ask," he said as he reached into the tiny leather pouch at his hip and began rooting around. After what seemed an inordinately long time for such a small pouch, Scuttlebutt's scaly hand reemerged holding a tiny square of paper which he proceeded to carefully unfold.

"Here," Scuttlebutt said, giving the little square of paper a shake. "This is what you're after."

Jasper pinched the corner of the paper with his thumb and forefinger. It was no bigger than a postage stamp. Mullans, Erin, and

Judith crowded closer for a better look.

"How do you know that's what it looks like?" Jasper asked. On the paper was a tiny, neatly drawn picture showing a gemstone set in a metal backing, hanging from a heavy chain. Where the chain and backing met, a small crest was fashioned of silver.

"I told you, I had it from me gal Rumour, who asked her Uncle Ack Ack, who talked to his neighbour Gossip, who-"

"All right, we get it. So, Rumour drew this picture?" Erin said.

"She did, she did. A real talented artist, if you ask me. Look at those lines!"

The four children leaned closer for a better look. The picture was very carefully done, Jasper had to admit.

"But how sure are you that this is really what was inside? It sounds like a lot of hearsay," Jasper said.

"No, no, Hearsay wasn't involved. It was Gossip who knew the imp who knew the imp who may or may not have originally nicked it," Scuttlebutt said, hopping to his feet. "It's the best you're going to get. Even though we misplace, lose, or sell most of what we steal, an imp never forgets what he's taken."

Mullans leaned in closer to the drawing. His breath puffed against Jasper's hand as he studied the picture.

"Are those moose antlers? With three stars between them? In the crest. There," he said, pointing to where the chain and gemstone met.

"Aye," Scuttlebutt said. "A little strange if you ask me, but it's a family crest, most like. No idea whose, mind you, but if you knew that then you'd know who owned this fine piece of jewellery before its journey through the hands of imps."

Jasper and Erin shared a look. They had a good idea whose family crest it was.

"Where's the necklace now?" Jasper asked.

Scuttlebutt squeaked a nervous laugh.

"I was hoping you wouldn't ask," he said, eyes trained on his little feet in their pointed shoes.

"Hey, a wish is a wish and a deal's a deal. You've got to tell us," Mullans said.

Scuttlebutt scrunched his face in a most unflattering way.

"Right, well, as it turns out, it seems that this particular piece of jewellery was nicked, only to be sold away."

"Why take it if you're not going to keep it?" Erin said, kicking at the bed post.

Scuttlebutt tottered on his perch on the bedpost.

"It's all about the chase, m'dear. All about the chase. We imps steal a lot and often, but we lose interest quickly. You know how it is."

Indeed, it would seem neither Jasper, Erin, Mullans or Judith *knew how it was.* Instead, they glared at the imp, angry with the careless, thieving ways of his kind.

"Right, right. Don't get your feathers all ruffled," Scuttlebutt said, tapping out his pipe. "I can't say for certain, but I might have an idea of where this necklace of yours is."

Mullans clapped his hands and did a little dance, taking Erin by the elbow and coaxing her to join in. She did not.

"It would seem that the imp who nicked it may have sold it back to the leprechaun who made the case. Leprechauns will only make cases for treasures they think are worthy, so the the leprechaun who made this particular case must have liked what he saw."

"But how do you know which leprechaun made the case?" Judith asked.

"Every leprechaun has a maker's mark, and yours is on the bottom of the case. I saw it when I was having a look meself. Three hoops around a hammer, that's the mark of Fergal Foley, that is," Scuttlebutt said.

"Fergal Folely?"

"Aye."

"Where's he live?"

"Leprechaun Town, last I heard. He was an old, crusty grump the last time I saw him, and that was years ago. If he's still alive, he'll be an older, crustier grump yet."

The four of them fell silent. Jasper wondered again who had sent him Eamonn Moran's old things, and more importantly, why.

Scuttlebutt packed his pipe back into his leather pouch.

"Well, methinks my work here is done. Consider your wish," Scuttlebutt unfurled his wings and they began to beat in a frenzy, "Granted."

Scuttlebutt rose into the air, winked and nodded, then zoomed out the window. His shimmering wings shrank from view, then disappeared all together.

Jasper carefully refolded the drawing and stashed it under his pile of heavy textbooks for safe keeping.

"I've seen that crest before," Jasper said. "It's carved into the bench in the locker room, right in front of my stall."

"People say that's Eamonn Moran's old stall," Erin said.

"Why would anyone have moose antlers as their family crest?" Mullans asked, removing the bandages he had wrapped around himself earlier and clumsily stuffing them back into the cupboard.

"I don't know, but it sounds like it's the Moran family crest," Jasper said.

"If it is, and that necklace really did belong to Eamonn Moran, then he went through a lot of trouble to hide it," Judith said.

"But why would someone just give it to you? No one talks about Moran since he disappeared," Erin said.

"Uncle Frederick told me to keep the stick hidden. He said I would get into serious trouble and maybe even," Jasper paused, his head had begun to ache again. "And maybe even *disappear* if I was caught with it."

"Maybe whoever sent the package didn't even know what it was. Maybe that's why Moran used a puck in the first place. He really wanted to keep that necklace hidden. I mean, who turns a hockey puck into a treasure chest?" Judith said. She was holding her chin, her eyes cast to the floor, thinking hard.

"Yeah," Erin said, nodding. "Maybe he just told everyone it was a regular game puck. A souvenir, for scoring his 500th goal, or something like that."

Another moment of quiet passed, each of the four lost to their thoughts.

Finally, Jasper said, "We need to find it."

"Jasper's right," Erin said. "We have to find it. Eamonn would want us to."

"It could be anywhere by now. Sure, that imp might have sold it back to Fergal Foley, but what's to say Fergal will still have it?" Judith said.

"It doesn't matter," Jasper said. "Eamonn Moran wanted to keep that necklace hidden because it was important and now it's lost. We need to find it. I just know it. We have to."

The other three shared a look, before nodding and turning their eyes back to Jasper.

Erin flashed her lopsided smile, "You're right, and we're going to help you."

Chapter 18

Down to Leprechaun Town

Jasper's recovery from his concussion was slow and lonely. Most days, he only had Nurse Hazel for company. Dr. Stowe would stop by to check on him, but otherwise, he was left alone. Erin, Mullans, and Judith visited when they could, hoping each day would be the last day of Jasper's hospital stay. They all agreed to wait until Jasper was out to venture down to Leprechaun Town in search of Fergal Foley. Jasper wanted to be there when they found the necklace.

"We'll go tomorrow," Jasper said. The four of them sat on Jasper's bed. Erin and Mullans had stopped by after their morning skate and Judith's lessons were done for the day.

Mullans cheered at the news.

"You're getting out of here!"

"Yeah, finally. Dr. Stowe says I can start practicing tomorrow, but no contact for another week."

"Ha," Erin said. "Tell that to the golems."

"You'll get to enjoy some of the nice weather we've been having," Judith said. "It's getting warmer."

Jasper had been indoors for the past week, but he had noticed the change in the weather. When he had arrived in Magmelland, Tara had been under a heavy blanket of snow. Now, the icicles lining the trees dripped, and great chunks of snow slid from the slanted roofs to land in the muddy, grey streets below. Spring was on its way.

"I hate the spring," Erin said. "It means the hockey season will be over soon."

Jasper didn't want to think about the end of the season just yet. He was much too excited about getting out of the hospital, and going to Leprechaun Town in search of Eamonn Moran's necklace.

Jasper didn't sleep much his last night in the hospital. Thoughts of finally rejoining the team and strapping his skates back on kept him awake. The next morning, Nurse Hazel was sad to see him go. He gave Jasper a tight hug before patting him on the head and telling him to "be good." Dr. Stowe's advice was much more specific.

"Wear your helmet and keep your head up and absolutely no contact for a week," she said, baring Jasper's exit from the hospital with her bulky frame.

"Yes, ma'am!" Jasper said, ducking under her arm and hurrying off towards Trillium Gardens.

The morning practice flashed by. Jasper got friendly bops on his helmet from the gloved hands of his teammates and even a few light slaps to his shins with their sticks. He couldn't stop the smile spreading across his face. It was good to be back with the team.

"Welcome back," Coach Sparkle Pants said. "We've got a game coming up. Friday, next week. Think you'll be ready?"

"Definitely."

Soon after, Coach called an end to practice. While the rest of the team went back to the Players Pavilion for lunch, Erin, Mullans, and Jasper went into the city to meet Judith.

"Judith's waiting for us at the junction," Erin said, leading the way. "We'll get something to eat along the way."

Erin took them on a winding path through the cramped, colourful streets of Tara, turning here and there, over footbridges and under archways. After a quick stop at a wooden stall which seemed to exclusively sell food on sticks, Erin handed the boys meat wrapped in orangey puff pastry. Jasper, who was used to trying strange foods thanks to Mrs. Jarvis, did not hesitate and took a big bite. He was glad he did. It was delicious.

"Thanks," he said, his voice muffled through his full mouth.

"Welcome," Erin said, taking another bite.

Mullans's mouth was so full he couldn't make a sound, and so just gave Erin a thumbs-up.

The three continued on and soon arrived at a crowded intersection of five large laneways.

A crush of people moved this way and that, pushing carts, leading horses, and carrying armloads of parcels and dragging canvas bags full to bursting.

Judith was waiting for them under a tall signpost at the centre of the junction. Five splintering wooden signs sprouted from the top of the post, each a different colour and written in a different hand, and each pointed down one of the five laneways. "Gorgon Estates" lead down a well-kept and wide street, lined with dull grey buildings fronted by large windows. "Hag Hill" pointed to a murky and muddy street with lines of laundry criss-crossing high above the road. Everything from lampposts and benches to tree trunks and rocks had been covered in swathes of chunky crochet and knotted knitting. A herd of stray cats wandered at their leisure. Jasper squinted. One of the cats looked suspiciously like Hercules, his white coat looking a shade of yellow against the snow. Jasper gave the cat a wave, and the cat promptly returned the gesture with a flick of his chin. That was Hercules, all right. "Giantsdale", unsurprisingly, lead down a wide street lined with hugely tall and clumsily constructed buildings. The archway leading to "Elvinhood" was draped with shimmering hanging vines, hiding the street from view. Pearly cobblestones were just visible below the curtain of greenery, and the whole laneway glowed with soft, warm light.

"Were you waiting long?" Erin asked.

Judith shook her head. "How was practice?"

"Good," Jasper said. "We've got a game next week. Friday."

"Let's go find this leprechaun!" Mullans said, pointing down the laneway marked "Leprechaun Town".

While the rest of Tara was paved with flat cobblestones, the streets of Leprechaun Town were covered in spongey moss. Despite the snow, everything was extraordinarily green. The houses seemed to grow right out of the ground. The wooden walls were covered in bark and filled with knots and protruding branches. The roofs were lumpy and covered in earth and ivy. Smoke curled from the chimneys and chimes tinkled in the wind. Somewhere, a harp was gently strummed.

The leprechauns themselves were dressed in all shades of green, with a splash of yellow or black or red here and there. They were taller than Jasper had expected, reaching nearly to his shoulders. They walked about on the street, their brightly polished shoes padding on the soft earth, chatting amongst themselves. They paid very little mind to the new arrivals.

Jasper's hand slipped into the pocket of his trousers and felt for the slip of paper Scuttlebutt had given him. He had studied the drawing while in hospital and he now had it memorized. Still, he felt braver knowing it was there.

"Where do we go?" Jasper asked, looking up and down the lane.

"Scuttlebutt said the leprechaun's name was Fergal Foley," Judith said. "Someone here must know him."

Erin nodded and walked straight over to the nearest leprechaun, a woman with shockingly red hair and a face wrinkled like a raisin. Erin gripped the lady leprechaun's shoulder, stopping her in her tracks.

"I'm looking for Fergal Foley, the chest maker," Erin said.

"Are you, now?" the woman said, her eyebrows shooting up her forehead and her mouth drawing to a tight line. "It seems you've got the wrong leprechaun, dearie, so you have. I've no beard, so I can't possibly be Fergal Foley."

"Well, do you know where he is?" Erin said, sighing. She was getting annoyed.

"Perhaps I do, but I won't be telling a twit like you. Now," the leprechaun woman craned her face upwards, stamping on Erin's toes. "Take that hand of yours off my shoulder or you and it will soon be parting ways."

Erin snapped her hand back and the leprechaun walked off, shaking her head.

"What's her problem?"

"Maybe we should be a little more polite. Leprechauns are

known for distrusting outsiders," Judith said in a small voice.

"I was being polite."

Jasper and Judith exchanged a look.

"Maybe Judith should do the asking," Jasper said.

Erin rolled her eyes and crossed her arms over her chest, but she did not argue.

They continued down the laneway. The road was bumpy and filled with hidden holes and even the odd tree or bush poking up through the moss. The going was slow and there was much to be seen. Mullans admired the snow coated shamrocks covering every surface in sight, while Judith politely asked the friendlier looking leprechauns where they might find Fergal Foley.

Mostly, the leprechauns ignored Judith, though some growled or grumbled at the question. Taking no offense, Judith kept on in her gentle, meek way. At last, a young leprechaun, with a beard like spun gold and icy blue eyes, gave them directions.

"Aye, yer man Foley lives down there." The boyishly handsome leprechaun jerked his chin towards an alley branching from the main road. "He'll be in the last house on the left, if he's at home."

"Thanks!" Judith said. Smiling, she lead the way.

The noise and light of the main street faltered and died as the four of them turned down the alley. It was dark and quiet here. The doors were closed and the shutters drawn. Nothing moved and no one spoke. They walked slowly, their steps cutting a path through the unbroken snow.

Some houses had fallen into disrepair, with splintered roofs and broken windows. Others were decaying, their wooden walls rotting above tree roots long dead. Black and green spotted toadstools lined the narrow alley, and a moldy, putrid smell filled the air.

Judith slipped back from her place leading the group, and now walked slowly next to Erin, hiding behind her cousin's arm. The four of them tread lightly, with many backward glances.

They came to the last house on the left and stopped. This house looked just as dark and lonely and uninhabited as all the others.

"I guess we should knock?" Jasper said, stepping up to the crumbling wooden door. A crow shaped door knocker stared out at him.

"Go on," Mullans said, patting Jasper's shoulder. "I'm right behind you."

Before Jasper could bring his fist down to knock, the crow sprang to life, shaking its head and rapping its beak against the door. Bits of rotted wood showered the front step and Jasper lurched back, his heart in his throat.

"Visitors! *Caw! Caw!* We've visitors!" the crow said in a most unnatural voice.

From inside the hovel, a gravely voice boomed, "Who's there?"

A nervous glance was exchanged between the four on the front stoop. Judith sidled closer to Erin.

"We're looking for Fergal Foley," Jasper said, trying to stop his voice shaking.

"Ha?" the voice beyond the door barked.

"Fergal Foley," Mullans said, enunciating each syllable carefully. "Do you know him?"

There came a scratchy chuckling from behind the door. The

crow joined in, laughing as best a crow could.

"Know him?" said the voice.

The door swung back to reveal a gnarled leprechaun in a red waistcoat and battered black bowler hat. "I *am* him."

Fergal Foley limped his way forward, leaning heavily on the twisted tree branch he used for a cane. The silver buttons of his coat had gone to rust and his cravat was yellowed with age and sweat. A gust of stale, sour air poured out of the old house, making Jasper cough. A web of wrinkles etched themselves into Fergal's face and one eye was milky white with blindness.

"What do you want?" Fergal said, rapping Mullans smartly on the knee with his cane.

Mullans jumped back, clasping his knee. "You're a mean little man, aren't you?"

"None meaner," Fergal said, surveying the four of them with his good eye. His head lolled and bobbed with a queasy flexibility, as if his neck were about to snap.

Erin pushed at the small of Jasper's back, urging him forward. "Go on," she said in his ear.

Jasper reached a shaking hand into his pocket and pulled out Eamonn Moran's puck. It was warm and slick with sweat in his hand.

"We're looking for the leprechaun who made this," Jasper said, careful to hold it in front of Fergal's good eye.

Fergal Foley staggered closer, his knuckles whitening as his grasp tightened on the cane. He narrowed his seeing eye and stretched a trembling hand towards the puck. Then, his eyes grew wide and he snapped back his hand, clutching the knobbly knuckles to his chest.

"I've not seen that before in me life, so I haven't." Fergal's mismatched eyes darted from Jasper's face to the puck and back. "You be on your way. I'll have no trouble here."

The old leprechaun turned to hobble back inside his hovel. In three quick steps, Erin darted past him to block his way.

"I'll thank you to move out of my way," Fergal said.

"We don't want any trouble," Erin said. "We only want to ask you a few questions."

"Please," Jasper said, joining Erin on the lopsided stoop.

Mullans took Judith by the elbow, and stepping forward they

completed the small circle around the leprechaun.

Fergal Foley's eyes flicked up the alleyway. It was deserted and he would have no help. He was breathing hard, clearly not accustomed to these sorts of shenanigans.

"Five minutes of your time, that's all we want. Then we'll be on our way and it'll be like we were never here," Erin said. "But if you refuse, who knows? This puck just might make its way into the hands of the night angels, along with a little rumour or two about it belonging to Eamonn Moran."

Jasper was surprised, and impressed, by Erin's boldness.

Fergal swayed from his good leg to his bad leg, blinking his good eye then his bad eye, thinking. He exhaled a heavy breath, kissed his teeth, then spat on the ground.

"What do you want to know?"

Before the leprechaun could change his mind, Jasper flipped the puck over in his hand to show the hammer circled by three hoops carved there.

"This is your mark, isn't it?"

Fergal's good eye contracted once again, despite having

already recognized his handiwork.

"Could be," Fergal said, his mouth curling to a knot.

"You made this case for Eamonn Moran, didn't you?"

At the mention of Eamonn's name, Fergal Foley's head whipped around, but now, he was relieved the alley was deserted.

"I don't know who you're talking-"

"Stop. Just stop," Erin said.

"It won't do to be heard speaking of Moran, it just won't do!" Fergal said, colour rising in his cheeks.

"We'll be in just as much trouble as you," Erin said. "This can be our little secret."

"The sooner you tell us, the sooner we'll stop talking about him, and the sooner we can leave you alone," Mullans said, as if it were the most obvious thing in the world.

"All right, all right. Yes, I made it for -" Fergal's voice dropped. "Eamonn Moran, but that was years ago."

"Years ago, maybe, but I bet you still remember why he wanted it. You knew what he wanted to hide inside of it, didn't you?" Jasper said.

"What's it to you?" Fergal said, his crunchy disposition returning.

"Look, we know it was a necklace. We're just trying to find out what happened to it. An imp friend of ours -"

"I'd call him more of an acquaintance, really," Mullans said.

" - imp *acquaintance* told us you might have the necklace," Jasper said.

Fergal scratched at his patchy beard and fiddled with his rusted buttons. He sighed, then coughed, then spoke again.

"Fine. Yes, one of those imps recognized my mark on the puck. Once he grew tired of his new trinket, he thought he'd sell the necklace to me for some quick cash."

"And you bought it? Knowing it was stolen?" Erin towered over the now red-faced leprechaun.

"It was a lovely piece of jewellery. How could I say no? And at that price! A steal of a deal if I ever saw one."

Erin bent forward, coming freckled nose to crooked nose with Fergal Foley. "We'll be having it back, then. Thanks."

Fergal rapped his cane on the stoop with a jingling, nervous giggle.

"Will you now?"

"Yes. Please. Is it inside?" Judith asked.

The murky dim of Fergal Foley's humble abode yawned before them. Mullans craned his neck but could catch no sight of the necklace and he wrinkled his nose as he caught another whiff of the stale air.

"I've haven't got it," Fergal said between a nervous, sheepish grin.

"*Ohhhhh!*" Erin stamped her foot, then kicked a nearby rock. It pinged and clanged down the alley. "Where is it *now*?"

"Times are hard. The demand for leprechaun-made, custom treasure chests just isn't what it used to be," Fergal said. "So, not long ago, I sold it."

Jasper's heart sunk. They might never find it. This might be where the trail went cold. He suddenly felt very tired.

"To who?" Jasper asked.

"To whom," Mullans said.

"To whom?" Jasper asked.

"You've gone 'round the bend if you think I'll be telling you that. Proof I've had dealings in illegal activities? You're off your head."

"We'd get in just as much trouble looking for Eamonn Moran's necklace as you would for selling it." Jasper didn't know if this were true, but it sounded right. "We just need to know. We don't want any trouble for you."

"And the sooner you tell us, the sooner we'll leave you alone," Mullans said, smiling a smile that looked out of place in the dingy alley.

Fergal Foley looked through his doorway, no doubt longing to rest his wobbling knees.

"I sold it to the museum."

"The Historic National Institute of Culture? What would they want with something like that?" Judith said.

"Search me. Perhaps they can appreciate a good piece of jewellery," Fergal said. "Now, if you'll excuse me -"

Judith stuck out her pudgy arm to stop him.

"Wait. What about the crest? It's the Moran family crest. The museum wouldn't take something with that crest on it. Too many questions and likely trouble for them."

Fergal gave Judith a sidelong glance.

"Clever," he said. "I flattened the crest with me trusty hammer. I told them I found it whilst digging in my garden. Had them convinced it was a few hundred years old."

"You little liar!" Erin said.

"Clever," Judith said, lowering her arm.

"Now," Fergal Foley said, straightening to his full height, uneven shoulders as broad as they'd go. "If you you'll excuse me."

Erin and Jasper parted and Fergal passed between them. The old leprechaun slammed the door behind him without another word.

The alleyway was silent as the four children looked at one another. They hadn't found Eamonn Moran's necklace, but now they knew where to look.

"Looks like we're going to the museum," Mullans said.

Chapter 19

The Historic National Institute of Cultural

(or HNIC, for short)

The trip to the HNIC had to wait a few days. Try as they might to find a spare moment, Jasper, Erin, and Mullans were kept constantly busy with hockey practice and school lessons. Coach Sparkle Pants had decided on an intensified training schedule in anticipation of the upcoming game that Friday. The Sunday after their visit to Leprechaun Town was filled with long, rambling meetings dedicated to strategy. "We just need to drive hard and get pucks to the net" was repeated so often, the phrase had now lost all meaning. By the time they finished for the day, the sun was sinking in the sky and they scampered back to the Players Pavilion to avoid the night angels. Monday was dedicated to endless passing and forechecking drills.

The team's exhaustion did not go unnoticed and Coach Sparkle Pants took pity on them.

"All right, all right," Coach said and practice ground to a halt. "Good work everyone. We'll have an easy day tomorrow. A light morning skate, your lessons in the afternoon, then you'll be free to do as you like for the rest of the day."

Erin whipped her head around and gave Jasper a wink. They knew exactly what they'd be doing.

"I'll tell Judith to meet us at the museum tomorrow afternoon," Erin said as she skated by on her way to the girls locker room.

Jasper was sweaty and tired, but pleased. His legs burned and his ankles ached but he couldn't wait to start searching the HNIC for Eamonn's necklace.

After a quick change in the locker room, Jasper and Mullans met Erin at the main doors of Trillium Gardens. They walked slowly and carefully on tired and tender feet. The once snow-packed cobblestone streets of Tara were now filled with grey slush and puddles of ice melt.

Erin sighed.

"The ice won't last much longer."

"Almost time to say goodbye to another season," Mullans said, stifling a yawn.

"Is that how it works, then? Once it gets warm, the season's over?" Jasper asked.

Both Mullans and Erin stopped to stare at him.

"Yes," they said together.

"What? Have they got magic ice where you come from?" Erin asked, scoffing.

"I wish *we* had magic ice," Mullans said.

"Ice in warm weather isn't nearly as strange as using dragons for goal buzzers. No, we have..... ah, never mind." Jasper was far too tired to explain how the NHL playoffs ran into the warm months of May and June and that there were teams that played all their home games in Los Angeles, California or Tampa Bay, Florida.

At the Players Pavilion they found Ding and Bogg roasting a side of bacon over a small cooking fire just beyond the enchanted front doors.

" *Coo-roo-coo-coo-coo-coo-coo-coo!* Just a little late night snack, eh? Nothing better," Ding said, warming his hands while his brother tended to the bacon.

They said goodnight to Ding and Bogg and followed the

winding hallway up to their rooms. The hanging lanterns swayed on their chains in the evening breeze, casting dancing shadows onto the walls. It was quiet in the Pavilion and Jasper's eyes began to droop.

"We'll go to the HNIC tomorrow. Right after practice. Sleep well." Erin continued on, farther up the twisting hallway and out of sight, to her private room at the top of the Players Pavilion.

Jasper climbed into the top bunk, not even bothering to change into his night clothes. He was asleep before the first notes of Somnia's song reached his ears.

A light rain was falling. Jasper stretched his aching legs and opened his eyes. It was a dull, grey morning. Drops pattered on the window ledge and Ikarus shivered in his nest.

"I think the rain smells nice, like the world is taking a bath," Mullans said as he climbed carefully out of bed only to trip over a pile of clutter. He landed with a thud. He let out a long, heavy sigh. "I don't want to go to practice."

"Me neither, but," Jasper leapt down from his top bunk. "We have to."

After a sleepy-eyed, open-mouthed, groan-filled breakfast, the team made their way to Trillium Gardens for their morning skate.

Jasper's sweater was soaked through by the time they got there. The light rain had become a steady downpour.

True to his word, Coach made that morning's practice a light one. Indeed, lighter than he had intended. Coach was willing, but the Trillium Gardens ice wasn't able.

Instead of spraying Reid Roy, the team's starting goalie, with snow, today Mullans gave him a shower as he pulled off a spin-o-rama in the shootout.

"*Mullans!*" Roy yelled, shaking the water from his mask. "Knock it off or I'll shave that pretty hair of yours while you sleep."

"You do that and I'll put my stick in your locker before the next game."

Roy's eyes grew wide.

"You wouldn't dare."

Mullans only laughed and winked and skated off.

"He's very superstitious," Mullans said, gliding to a stop next to Jasper. "He doesn't like our sticks to touch his before a game. He thinks it's bad luck."

"Goalies are strange," Jasper said.

"Some of the strangest people you'll ever meet," Mullans said. Coming from him, this was a particularly potent statement.

Mullans and Jasper had both scored in the shootout and now they waited along the boards to see who would be last.

It came down to Yitzi Dionne and Luca Tremblay. Try as he might, Tremblay just couldn't get the puck past Roy and it was Dionne who was at last able to sneak one past the goalie's five-hole.

"Nice one, Yitzi!" Mullans said, rapping Dionne's shin with his stick.

"Luca," Coach said. "Ten laps around the rink. Everyone else, we'll call it day."

"Could be worse," Luca said, his broad, good-natured face breaking into a grin as he skated off down the rink and the rest of the team skated toward the locker rooms.

They met Erin in the front hall and left Trillium Gardens through the main entrance. They were finally on their way to the Historic National Institute of Culture.

"Ahh, the good ol' aitch-nick," Mullans said as they walked. The rain had stopped but the day remained cold and cloudy.

It was a long walk, with many ups and downs and throughs and arounds. Some streets were now ponds of water and others were crowded with people who had been forced to find alternate routes. It was a most indirect way to travel.

Judith was waiting for them when they arrived. She was squinting down at a creased map of the HNIC.

"This museum is huge," she said by way of a greeting.

As with most of Tara's buildings, the HNIC was a teetering, towering monstrosity that looked like it might topple over at any moment. Mostly it was made of granite bricks, but additions of wobbly wooden compartments and asymmetrical annexes in sheeted copper had been tacked on at random across the storeys.

"How many floors?" Jasper asked, craning his neck upwards. The whole building seemed to slant dangerously to the right.

"Nine...." Judith checked the map again. "And three-quarters. There's floors in-between floors and staircases that lead to nowhere."

Erin sighed.

"Let's get started," she said, making for the mishmash of

differently coloured, shaped, and sized bricks that made up the entrance stairs.

If the outside of the HNIC was disorienting and imposing, than the inside was an absolute chaotic whirlwind of disaster.

The poorly lit foyer smelled of dust and mould and neglect. The ceiling vaulted high but was lost to the gloom. Everywhere were stacked musty boxes and rotting books and crumbling artefacts. It was almost as bad as Jasper's bedroom back at the Players Pavilion.

"I like this place," Mullans said, looking around and giving an approving nod.

Across the cluttered floor, a hunched custodian was sweeping rubbish into a heap. With his dustpan piled high, he shuffled a few steps and then upended the load into a crammed corner in a cloud of filth. He then hacked a wet, wheezing cough and didn't bother to cover his mouth.

"Let's get this show on the road," Erin said. "Judith, where to?'

"Well, this place isn't very well organized."

"You don't say."

"There's no logical groupings of any of the artefacts. It's just nine floors of.....stuff."

"We've got that drawing, from Scuttlebutt. Couldn't we just show it to someone who works here and ask if they've seen that necklace?" Mullans said.

Jasper's hand slipped into his pocket and felt for the drawing. It was still there, safe and sound.

"The drawing has the Moran crest. Even if Fergal Folely really did hammer the crest flat on the necklace, we don't want anyone to recognize it from the drawing and connect it back to the necklace," Judith said.

"Judith, what would we do without you?" Erin smiled and Judith blushed at the praise.

"We'll have to look for the necklace ourselves. I say we start at the top floor and work our way down."

"Sounds good to me," Jasper said.

The four of them walked slowly up the spiralling main staircase, craning their necks to take in the peeks and flashes of the floors as they passed. The entire museum was packed to the brim.

The staircases on the upper floors were unsurprisingly placed at random. Some had wide, flat steps and others narrow, shallow risers that were easy to miss. They climbed from floor to floor, passing an endless stream of rooms jammed with display cases, cabinets, boxes, chests, and shelves. The echoes of their footsteps banged loudly off the walls. It would seem they were the only visitors to the museum that day.

At last, the staircases came to an end. Dusty beams of sunlight streamed through long rows of stained glass windows.

"I guess we should look for cases with jewellery in them, or ornaments," Judith said, her sweaty face glowing in the orangey light cast from the windows. "Anything that's shiny, really."

Jasper pulled Scuttlebutt's tiny drawing from his pocket.

"I agree," he said. "If you see this, or anything like it, yell out."

And so, the search began.

It was slow going. Each display case had too many items inside for anything to be seen properly or clearly. Everything from clay pots and metal coins to wooden toys, tattered shoes, and crumbling maps were stacked and shoved together behind thick panes of glass. Each display case was wrapped in a set of thick

golden chains knotted together by a heavy lock the size of Jasper's

head. Jasper's heart leapt at the sight of any necklace chain dangling

inside one of the cases, but each time, after a closer look, he was

left disappointed. As the minutes passed into an hour, and one hour

passed into two, Jasper felt hope slipping away. The Historic

National Institute of Culture all at once felt impossibly large.

When they made their way down to the fifth floor, Mullans

decided it was time for a break. The other three did not object.

"Just about halfway," Mullans said as he lay on a wooden

bench, stretching his long legs.

Judith took a few sweets from her pocket and passed them

around.

As they sat quietly, chewing on the candy that tasted of

strawberries and fizzed and crackled with each bite, Jasper once

again pulled the drawing from his pocket. His stomach churned and

he clenched his jaw. If they couldn't find the necklace here, he didn't

know where else they could look.

Jasper was just about to suggest to the others continuing

their search, when a lofty, cold voice broke the easy silence of the fifth floor.

"There. Over there. That case."

Jasper recognized the voice at once and sprang to his feet.

"What-" Erin began but Jasper clamped a hand over her mouth. He motioned for them to follow him.

Jasper walked on tip-toe, leading the way towards the sound of the voice, down a narrow corridor branching off the main hall. Up ahead, a dimly lit, low-ceilinged room waited.

Pressing himself flat against the wall, Jasper edged just far enough forward to peer around the corner.

Ms. Fearce stood across the room, looking especially pressed and prim against the confused disarray of her surroundings. Her black, cold eyes were fixed on a nearby display case. She wore an angry, annoyed, and meaner-than-usual-for-her expression. Next to her, cowering and shaking, stooped a young woman with curly red hair, bulky glasses, at least six scarves wrapped around her neck and a pair of fingerless gloves on her hands. Despite the large wooden horse on display in the centre of the room blocking his view, Jasper knew her at once as the woman he had collided with on his first day in Tara as Uncle Fredrick had walked him to the Players Pavilion.

"Over there, you silly girl. That necklace, with the blue stone. Show it to me."

Erin dug her fingernails into Jasper's shoulder. Their wide eyes met and shared a shocked look.

"I'm s-s-sorry, Ms. Fearce, but I can't," the woman said, her hair shockingly red next to her pale face. She blinked her watery green eyes and a tear trickled down her cheek.

"You are the curator of this poor excuse for a museum, are you not?"

The curator's mouth opened and closed, but no sound came out.

"Well?" Ms. Fearce said, banging the flagstone floor with her chrome cane.

"Yes!" the curator said, jumping in surprise.

"Then surely you have a key for this case. Open it."

The curator's hand dropped to her right hip. A keyring hung from her belt, packed with brass, gold, silver, and copper keys. She clutched the keyring in her small hand, her knuckles going white.

"I do," the curator said, pinching a tiny brass key between

her thumb and forefinger. "I've got the only keys."

"Well?" There were tiny patches of red high up on Ms. Fearce's high cheek bones.

"You haven't filled out the proper paper work. Anyone wishing to see an artefact must complete the requisite form and the request then has to be approved by our collection manager. The process can take," the curator drew a shaky breath. "Up to six months."

Ms. Fearce howled and swung her cane. The curator jumped out of the way and Judith let out a frightened squeak. Erin and Mullans both slammed a hand over Judith's mouth. Ms. Fearce paced and fumed and thankfully, seemed to have not heard.

"Do you know who I am?"

The curator's head bobbed up and down.

"And you know who I work for?"

One slow nod.

"Good, because I also know who you are. Valland, isn't it?"

"Yes, Ms. Fearce. Lily Valland."

Ms. Fearce smiled and her eyes grew colder.

"And your family, they live in the Muse District."

Lily Valland's face grew impossibly paler. She didn't say a word.

Ms. Fearce stepped nearer to Lily, stooping so their faces were mere inches apart.

"In the red brick house, covered in ivy. At the top of Thalia Lane. Isn't that right?"

Lily's lip trembled as another tear slipped down her cheek.

Ms. Fearce stepped back and drew herself up to her full height.

"Now, why don't you open that case?"

Lily took a slow step back.

"I'm very sorry, but it's against museum policy," she said, her voice just above a whisper, her shaking hand still clutching the keyring.

A wild look came into Ms. Fearce's black eyes and she lunged for the keys.

Lily sprinted to the other side of the room, putting the wooden horse between her and Ms. Fearce. They moved in circles.

Lily ran and Ms. Fearce chased, but the big wooden horse, its head bent low in want of a pat, kept Ms. Fearce at bay.

Letting out another howl, Ms. Fearce raised her cane and whacked it against the thick glass of the display case with a heavy *thunk*. The case wobbled, but the glass pane held.

"Please, don't," Lily Valland said, peeking her head above the wooden horse.

Just as Ms. Fearce was aiming her cane for a second blow, there came a lumbering shuffle and heavy breathing. Across the room, a giant was crouched on all fours in the hallway, poking his big, bumpy, bald head through one of the many archways opening into the room.

"Me hear bang," the giant said, blinking slowly and looking from Lily to Ms. Fearce.

Ms. Fearce lowered her cane and Lily let out a shuddering breath.

"Museum no bang," the giant said. He scratched his head with a huge hand and then wiggled his enormous shoulders into the small room. The walls shook with the strain. "Is Miss okay?"

Lily flicked her eyes to Ms. Fearce.

"Yes, Hugo. I'm fine. Thank you."

"Hugo keep museum safe."

"Yes. Thank you."

"I am good job."

"Yes." Lily let out another shaky breath.

Hugo kept his large, round eyes trained on Ms. Fearce. He was dimwitted, but not stupid, and knew a threat when he saw one. Ms. Fearce considered the giant for a moment, then turned away. She straightened her corset and top hat, brushed her pristinely clean clothes down with a few pats of her gloved hands, and made to leave the room.

Then, she stopped and turned on her absurdly high-heeled shoe.

"Keep that necklace safe, will you? I'll be back for it."

Lily looked over at Hugo, then squared her shoulders and brought herself up to her full height.

"Why do you want it so badly? The museum only recently acquired this artefact and it is of......questionable provenance." Lily bit her lip a moment, then pressed on. "Do you know who it belonged to? Or its significance? There was a crest, but it's been flattened."

Ms. Fearce smiled her cold smile once again, but this time, it did reach her eyes.

"That," she said. "Is the business of Emperor Black. In fact, I believe I shall bring him with me when I return."

Ms. Fearce snapped her neck around, her body following in a sickly twist, and walked briskly from the room.

Jasper's heart pounded in his ears and he clamped his hands over his mouth to stop himself screaming. Lily Valland waited until the sounds of Ms. Fearce's heels clicking against the flagstones faded, then she sank to the floor and wept.

Chapter 20

A Hole in the Plan

The journey back to the Players Pavilion was a dreary one. They had waited in the gloom of the fifth-floor corridor of the HNIC, sweating and shaking and barely breathing, for as long as they could stand. Long after the *clickclack* of Ms. Fearce's heels had disappeared and the sobs and sniffles of Lily Valland had faded, they quickly and quietly rushed from the museum, spilling into the late afternoon light of Tara and gasping at the fresh air.

"That woman scares me," Erin said, throwing a look over her shoulder. Ms. Fearce was nowhere to be seen.

Judith's wide eyes scanned the busy museum square.

"Perhaps we shouldn't talk here. We don't know who might be listening."

"Good idea," Jasper said.

The four of them walked along in silence, each lost to their thoughts.

The thrill Jasper had felt in finding Eamonn Moran's necklace had gone as soon as it came. Ms. Fearce wanted it, and so did

Emperor Black. Jasper just couldn't work out why. Maybe Emperor

Black wanted to erase every trace of Eamonn Moran from

Magmelland, but Jasper couldn't be sure the Emperor even knew it

belonged to Eamonn in the first place. What he could be sure of was

getting the necklace back just became much more difficult.

They walked on. The sky darkened. Jasper's stomach

growled. When they reached Hobgoblin Town, Judith turned to go

home.

"I'll come to the Players Pavilion tomorrow afternoon when

school's done for the day. We'll think of a plan. I don't know what yet,

but we have to do *something*."

Jasper nodded and Erin said goodnight to her cousin. The

three hockey players continued on their way towards the Players

Pavilion, with their minds on dinner and a quiet corner to discuss

what they were going to do next.

Dinner was no trouble, as Christof the cook had outdone

himself once again with an amazing spread of chicken and pasta and

bread and roasted vegetables, but a quiet corner to talk was another

matter.

The dining hall was buzzing by the time Jasper, Mullans, and Erin arrived. Asher Orr and Yitzi Dionne had a run-in with Ms. Fearce that afternoon.

"She was fuming mad about something," Orr said, doing his best impression of Ms. Fearce's scowl. "We were down in the Muse District, right by the docks."

"That's not too far from the HNIC," Erin said. She, Jasper, and Mullans sat around a small, uneven table. "Orr and Dionne must have seen her after she left."

Jasper tilted his head towards Orr and Dionne sitting across the room. The dining hall was filled with chatter and the clicking and clanking of cutlery.

"She was swinging her cane at everything that moved, growling like a dog," Dionne said, stroking his patchy moustache. Orr barked a few times and Dionne laughed. "So, of course, Orr asked her what was wrong."

The dining hall erupted into laughter.

"She chased after us, swinging her cane all around, but we were faster. She was so angry, but we just couldn't stop laughing," Orr said.

There were cheers and high-fives all around.

Suddenly, Jasper had a thought.

"You said you were down by the docks?"

"Yeah, right by Somnia's lighthouse," Orr said.

"Did you see where she went afterwards?"

"After she gave up trying to catch us, we watched her walk back down to the water. She got on one of the boats, headed for Eridares, I'd guess."

"Bit strange, that," Dionne said. "She doesn't usually leave Lord Tan in charge for long, if she can help it. He's completely useless. I guess she must have important business with the Imperial Majesty himself across the Breakwater Channel."

Orr and Dionne did matching floppy-handed salutes before someone blew a raspberry and the laughing started again.

Mullans groaned.

"Emperor Black knows," he said.

They quickly finished their dinner and then escaped to the quiet of the bedroom Mullans and Jasper shared.

"She's definitely gone across the Channel to tell Emperor Black about the necklace," Erin said before the bedroom door had even closed. "Whatever we do, we have to do it quickly."

"Agreed," Jasper said. "Our next game is this Friday. I bet Emperor Black will go to the museum then. We have to get the necklace before he does."

"But how?" Mullans said, flopping down on the lower bunk. The straw-filled mattress crunched and the ropes underneath sagged.

They all thought for a moment.

"What if we just went to the museum, broke the glass case, took the necklace and ran away?" Mullans said.

It was the simplest solution, and the least likely to work.

"That glass looked thick. Who knows if we could break it? Besides, the place is so quiet, the noise it'd make would bring the security giants running," Jasper said.

"Or waddling, anyway," Erin said. "And I don't fancy the idea of trying to outrun one of those beasts in that maze of a museum."

Erin looked from Mullans to Jasper.

"No, if we're going to take it-"

"Steal it," Jasper said. He wasn't entirely comfortable with the idea.

"Fine, *steal* it, then we're going to need the keys."

"The keys the curator had on her belt?" Mullans said, propping himself up on his elbow.

"Those ones, yes."

Jasper had a sick, queasy feeling in his stomach.

"I don't like this," he said. "Maybe there's another way?"

"Like what?" Erin said.

Jasper didn't have an answer.

"I know it's stealing and I know it's not the best plan, but if we don't do it, Ms. Fearce is going to bring Emperor Black to the HNIC and then he's going to take it."

"*Steal* it," Mullans said.

"Right, okay." Jasper let out a heavy sigh. The idea of Emperor Black stealing the necklace made him feel even sicker. "How do we get the keys?"

Erin bit her lip and then said, "Judith."

"What?" Jasper and Mullans said together.

"She's so quiet, and light on her feet. She sneaks up on people all the time and she doesn't even mean to. When we were younger I would always talk Judith into snatching keys and coins out of my mom's pockets when she wasn't looking."

"You turned your cousin into a pickpocket?" Mullans said, his mouth hanging open.

"We were young! I didn't know we shouldn't. I haven't gotten her to do it in years, but I bet she still could," Erin said, crossing her arms over her chest.

"Okay," Jasper said, thinking hard. "But if Judith can manage to take the keys, and we can manage to take the necklace without getting caught, won't they notice it's missing?"

"That's a lot of 'ifs' and 'buts'," Mullans said. "This isn't a very good plan."

"It's the only one we've got and we haven't got much time," Erin said. She tossed her tangled hair and began to pace up and down the cluttered room, stepping over mounds of junk as she went.

"We'll just have to do it quickly," Erin said.

"And quietly," Jasper said. "If we're very quiet, and we have a lookout, maybe we could pull it off. Judith can talk to the curator and keep her distracted while Mullans keeps an eye out for the security giants. Then, you and I can steal the necklace."

"What about the keys? How will we get them back to Valland?" Mullans said.

"The same way we got them in the first place," Erin said.

Mullans raised his eyebrows.

"Carefully."

The three of them looked at each other. The room had grown dark. On the horizon, the lamp of Somnia's lighthouse cast a beam along the coast, scanning smoothly down the edge of Tara. It was time for bed.

Satisfied they had concocted the best plan they were capable of putting together, Jasper said goodnight and climbed into his top bunk.

Erin paused on her way to the door and then turned and walked back to the bunk beds. Her eyes peeked above the top rail, reflecting the moonlight.

"I didn't like you when you first got here," she said. Jasper didn't know what to say. "But now, I'm glad you're here."

Jasper still didn't know what to say, which was just as well, as Erin left the room before he could say anything.

A moment of silence, then:

"*OHHHH*, Jasper's got a girl-"

Mullans very quickly had a face full of Jasper's pillow.

The next morning passed in a blur. The team had a morning skate, followed by lessons in the early afternoon, but Jasper could keep his mind on none of it. Every thought drifted toward the plan they had made the night before and whether or not it could work.

When lessons were done for the day, Judith arrived at the Players Pavilion. Her face, as usual, was nervous and pale, and it grew more nervous and pale as she was told of the plan to steal Eamonn Moran's necklace from the HNIC. When Erin finished explaining, Judith looked like she might be sick.

"I have to take the keys?" she said in a small, shaking voice.

Without a word, Mullans emptied a brimming garbage can onto the messy bedroom floor. He handed it to Judith.

"You look like you're going to puke."

"I know you can do it if you try," Erin said. "You're light on your feet and so quiet."

"And you've got soft mitts!" Mullans said, flexing his fingers and smiling.

"This isn't a very good plan," Judith said.

Mullans nodded but Erin was annoyed.

"Have you got a better idea?"

Judith shrank away from her cousin.

"Maybe if we just ask the curator nicely, tell her why-"

"I don't think that will work," Jasper said. "If we tell her why we want it, she's going to want to keep it for the museum."

Judith's lower lip trembled, but she nodded her head.

"Good. We're all agreed, then," Erin said.

Erin checked the pocket watch hanging from a silver chain around her neck.

"I think it's a good idea if we go back to the museum for a second look before we try anything. We need to find the fastest way out."

"Yeah! Let's case the joint!" Mullans said, jumping to his feet.

"If we go now, we can get to the museum with time to spare before it closes," Erin said.

The four of them made to leave and a sudden wave of hope washed over Jasper. They might just manage to pull this off.

They walked down the curving, sloping hallway with quick steps. The corridor was quiet and the entrance hall was empty.

"Where is everyone?" Mullans asked.

"Doesn't matter, we've got to hurry," Erin said, making for the open enchanted doors and the drawbridge beyond.

Bogg stepped out of the guard booth and blocked her way.

"Just where do you think you're going, eh?" Bogg said, his frayed toque slipping forward as he looked down at Erin.

"None of your business."

"Just stepping out for a stroll."

"Official team business."

"KEYS!"

The four of them spoke all at once, their words tripping over each other. Now, they didn't just look guilty, but sounded so as well.

Bogg scratched his head, chuckled, and then flashed a smile missing more than a few teeth.

"Three of you are going nowhere but Trillium Gardens. You've got a game to play."

Jasper felt panic rising. Had they gotten the days wrong? He was sure Coach had said the next game was on Friday and it was only Tuesday.

"What? Since when? Our next game is on Friday," Erin said, trying to edge her way around Bogg. Then, Ding appeared from the guard booth to block Erin's way. She tossed her frayed hair in annoyance, messy braids and frizzy dreadlocks flopping every which way.

"*Coo-roo-coo-coo-coo-coo-coo-coo!* Things have *ch-ch-ch-changed*," Ding sang. "Look out at the harbour, there. You can see Emperor Black's dragon boat. He only ever crosses the Breakwater

Channel when he wants to see a game. Must be he's decided he'd fancy a game earlier than Friday."

In the distance, the hulking ship with the dragon prow was just visible, already anchored in the harbour and its sails furled.

Jasper knew a hockey game wasn't the only thing Emperor Black had on his mind. The panic he felt could be seen on Mullans, Erin, and Judith's faces.

Before Jasper could even think how this changed everything, the rest of the Magmelland hockey team spilled out of the lounge in a tidal wave of chaos. There were shouts and yells, with players running and jumping here and there. They moved in a herd towards the enchanted doors, the din echoing off the high ceiling.

"There you are!" Asher Orr said.

"McGee's been looking for you. You three missed the team meeting," Felix Gallant said.

Team captain Troy McGee appeared and encircled Mullans, Jasper, and Erin in his bulky arms, giving them a shake and a squeeze.

"You three ready for the game?"

Jasper's one ray of hope was gone. He thought that maybe they could slip away without being noticed, but with Troy McGee personally escorting them to Trillium Gardens, there was no way.

They did their best to smile.

"Very excited," Erin said, her voice flat.

"Good!" McGee said, slapping her on the back. Erin tumbled to the floor, but quickly righted herself without anyone's help.

McGee clamped his big, burly arms around their shoulders and began marching the three of them out the enchanted doors. Judith hurried along beside, jogging to keep pace with Jasper. Her eyes were wide and a shaking hand covered her mouth.

Jasper's brain raced. He needed an idea and fast. He looked to Erin. Her brow was creased as she stared at the ground, McGee hauling them along, thinking hard.

Then, it came to him. A small square of light at the end of a long tunnel.

Jasper pulled Judith's head toward him, and spoke directly, and quietly, into her ear. Erin tilted her head closer and strained to listen.

"Go to the museum. Now. Find the curator and get those keys. Follow her to Trilium Gardens if you have to, but *get those keys*. You have until the start of the third period." Jasper wanted to give Judith as much time as possible. "Then, meet us outside the equipment room. It's in that narrow hallway near the locker rooms, take a right after the last lantern and it's the third door on the left." Jasper spoke quickly as tears formed in Judith's eyes.

"The equipment room? But why?"

"Let's move it!" McGee shouted. They had crossed the drawbridge and were heading into the crowded streets of Tara. "Jarvis, come on!"

"No time," Jasper said, just as McGee yanked him around the collar and began dragging him around a corner.

"Please," Jasper said to Judith. "Do it."

Looking more frightened than he had ever seen her look, Judith said, "I will."

Chapter 21

Fight Night

The walk to Trillium Gardens soon became a run. The streets buzzed with frantic energy as the people of Tara shoved and shouted and scrambled on their way to the arena. The team geared up in the locker room in such a rush that Jasper didn't have a spare moment to tell Mullans his plan. Erin was, of course, with the other girls in their locker room and so Jasper was left to go over the plan again and again in his head, searching for holes.

In a bulky, waddling single file line, the team walked down the tunnel leading to the ice. Jasper caught Mullans's eye. Mullans looked as worried as Jasper felt. Jasper tried a smile, but it felt stiff and strange on his face.

The team took to the ice and the crowd roared. The stands were packed full and scarlet and silver flags fluttered everywhere as the people screamed and cheered.

Jasper circled the Magmelland end of the ice. His legs felt clumsy and his feet felt heavy, and more than once, he nearly tripped over his own blades. Jasper watched as his teammates stretched and took shots on Reid Roy.

Jasper didn't know how long he had been standing and staring, going over the plan in his head, when he was hit with a heavy thump to the back.

Jasper jumped and spun around.

"You're a million miles away," Yitzi Dionne said, flipping a puck towards the goal.

"Just getting my head in the game, you know? Got to visualize the win," Jasper said, trying to keep his voice calm.

Dionne nodded, his curly brown hair bobbing against his forehead.

"I know that feeling."

Dionne tapped Jasper's shin with his stick before skating off.

Nearby, Mullans, who usually wore a far-off and dazed look, was looking especially distracted as Erin absentmindedly shot pucks into the corner. Just as Jasper was about to wave them both over, the trillium flowers sprouting around the arena barked to life. Ms. Fearce was in the black box and did not waste any time making her introductions.

The velvet curtains parted and Lord Tan, the Black Queen, and Emperor Black appeared to the lackluster cheers of a less than impressed crowd. Jasper's mouth went dry and his stomach churned. He hoped against hope that Emperor Black had come straight to Trillium Gardens when he arrived in Tara. The museum and the Gardens were on opposite sides of the city and with any luck, the Emperor had been in a lazy mood.

Lord Tan, the Black Queen, and Emperor Black took their seats and a quiet hum of excitement crept back into the crowd. Ms. Fearce disappeared behind the heavy curtains, only to reappear a moment later. Jasper's heart sank to his feet.

Cowering next to Ms. Fearce, her eyes wide and her frizzy red hair a mess, was Lily Valland. Ms. Fearce grabbed the curator roughly by the elbow and pulled her along, shoving her into a seat at the end of the row. Lily hunched low in her chair, shrinking away from Ms. Fearce and eyeing the curtains behind her.

Instantly, Mullans and Erin were at Jasper's side.

"The keys," Erin said, biting her lip and staring up at the black box. "Oh, Judith."

Jasper had hoped Judith would have the first two periods of

the game to sneak the keys away from the curator, but with Lily

Valland sat between Lord Tan and Ms. Fearce in the black box, the

situation was looking grim. Judith had no chance of getting anywhere

near the keys now, no matter how light she was on her feet.

"We'll just have to hope Judith got the keys before the start

of the game. Maybe she got to the museum before Ms. Fearce did,"

Jasper said.

Erin looked worried.

"She can't run all that fast."

Jasper thought of Judith, her cheeks flushed and her face

sweaty, running through the crowded streets of Tara, saying,

"Excuse me" politely to every person she had to pass.

"We stick to the plan. I told her to meet us at the equipment

room for the start of the third. That's what we're going to do."

"But how? We'll be playing in the game," Mullans said.

"What's the plan?" Erin asked.

The referee's whistle sounded shrilly, calling an end to the

warm-up.

The Magmelland players skated to their bench, scooping

Jasper, Erin, and Mullans up as they went. There was no more time for talk.

The match began and the crowd cheered and soon Magmelland was up by five goals, but Jasper couldn't concentrate on the game. More than once, Coach Sparkle Pants had to give him a shove in the back when it was time for a line change. Jasper's shifts passed by in a blur. He couldn't help but keep looking up at the black box. Emperor Black was enjoying himself, smiling his foul, evil smile, while Ms. Fearce looked annoyed and kept checking her pocket watch. Lily Valland had sunk so far into her seat that only the top of her frizzy red hair could be seen above the edge of the black box.

Before he knew it, they were nearing the end of the second period. Jasper was so distracted that he made a cross-ice pass straight onto the stick of a golem, who then sluggishly skated down the ice and suckered punched Reid Roy before slapping the puck into the net.

As the golems whacked each other in celebration, Jasper skated over to Roy.

"Are you okay? Sorry, that was my fault."

Roy gave his head a shake before flicking the puck out of the back of his net. He gave the crossbar a tap with his blocker.

"It's not your fault the golems are goons, but what's the matter with you? Two periods and only one goal and one assist? You're getting soft, Jarvis."

"Just not my night, I guess," Jasper said and patted Roy's helmet before skating back to the bench.

The last grains of sand slipped through the hourglass, the gong sounded and the second period came to an end.

Twenty minutes, Jasper thought, only half listening to Coach Sparkle Pants's intermission pep talk. *Twenty minutes until it's go time.*

Mullans, who normally liked to gear-down to just his skates between periods sat nervously on the bench in his full equipment, bouncing his leg and running his fingers through his sweaty hair. Erin, who was on Mullans's other side, was carefully re-taping her stick. Coach's speech came to an end and the team let out a small cheer.

"Let's go," Jasper said.

"Let's go," Erin said.

Mullans just nodded, his shiny hair flopping.

The team walked down the tunnel and Coach Sparkle Pants signalled for Jasper's line to take to the ice.

Jasper glided out on to the centre dot. His stick felt heavy in his hands and the arena air felt especially cold in his lungs.

"Follow my lead," Jasper said to Mullans and Erin before each of them took their place at the wings.

Jasper eyed the golem across from him at centre ice. It was time.

"Does your coach know you're out here?" Jasper asked, looking over to the Eridares bench where the gruff looking coach stood. Jasper did his best to look surprised and concerned.

The golem grunted and huffed.

"It's a good thing your team doesn't wear jerseys. They'd have to put "SCRUB" on all the backs and the ref would get confused," Jasper chirped.

The golem's mouth hung open, drool dripping from its chin. The golem swung its heavy head in a wide arc, looking to the winger. The wingman only shrugged, its mismatched eyes staring in different directions.

Jasper had never been one to chirp. He preferred to just play the game and let others do the trash talking. Now, he thought that was probably a good thing, as he was rather rubbish at it.

Undaunted, and with the plan in mind, Jasper reached across the face-off circle and gave the golem a shove.

"You're got a face only a mother could love," Jasper said.

Mullans, who had thankfully picked up on what Jasper was trying to do, joined in.

"Yeah, and I bet she's not even sure because she probably wears glasses. *Ohhhh,* gross, myopia. Or possibly hyperopia. Blech."

Mullans gave the golem next to him a shove, but drew his hand back quickly. He had pricked his palm against the golem's pointed armour.

The referee was skating over. They were running out of time. Jasper got right in the golem's face, slamming his heavy helmet against the golem's thick skull.

"Jasper,*what are you doing?*" Erin said.

"I saw that goal you got before. It was total garbage. Pigeon!"

Jasper gave the golem another shove, harder this time. The golem grunted again, louder this time.

"Yeah, you're all pigeons," Mullans said, and he cooed like a pigeon, just like Jasper had heard him do back and forth countless times with Ikarus before bed.

The golems looked at each other, their heavy brows furrowed in confusion. The referee came to a stop outside the face-off dot and pulled the puck from his pocket.

Erin, finally cottoning on to what Jasper was trying to do, spoke up.

"I've heard better chirps from dead birds," she said. "That's not how you start a fight. *This* is how you start a fight."

With that she dropped her stick and gloves and swung at the golem across from her, throwing all her weight behind the punch. Her fist landed square on the golem's jaw and there was a *pop!* as two of Erin's knuckles exploded.

Jasper and Mullans didn't waste any time. They dropped their sticks and gloves, and Mullans tossed his helmet aside. The golems weren't far behind and soon, it was all out chaos. Punches and jabs flew in a flurry, teeth chomped, and sticks slashed.

Jasper couldn't be sure if any of his punches landed, but he grabbed a hold of the golem's shoulder and just kept swinging. He lost an edge and tumbled to the ice, dragging the golem with him. They landed with a heavy crunch and all the air was knocked from Jasper's lungs.

A coppery, sour taste filled Jasper's mouth. The left side of his face felt swollen and tight. He pressed his forehead to the ice, gasping for air. He fought to stay calm. Every breath was shorter and harder to catch.

Jasper felt dizzy and the edges of his vision greyed. His eyes drooped and the noise of Trillium Gardens dimmed. Then, the golem's crushing weight was hauled away and the world shot back into focus. He gulped at the air and struggled back to his skates.

The referee was red in the face and furious. Mullans and Erin were already skating towards the tunnel. Relief flooded through Jasper. Erin was cradling her hand against her chest and Mullans was holding his head.

"You," the referee said, jabbing his finger at Jasper. Jasper turned to listen.

"That's two for instigating, five for fighting," Jasper held his breath, "And a game misconduct. You can't do that. You're out of here!"

Jasper raced to follow Erin and Mullans to the tunnel. The crowd groaned and booed.

As he skated past the Magmelland bench, Theo Howe gave Jasper a pat on the back.

"A goal, an assist, *and* a fight. Not bad, Jarvis, " Howe said.

Jasper tried to smile but his mouth was full of blood, so he nodded instead.

Down the tunnel and safely out of earshot, Jasper put the plan in motion.

"Change. Quick."

Erin dashed to the girls's locker room and Mullans and Jasper went to theirs.

In a flurry of equipment and clothes, they were all changed and dressed and back in the hallway in a minute flat.

"Let's go," Jasper said, and they took off running.

Mullans's face was swollen with bumps and bruises and Erin still cradled her hand against her chest as she ran.

"Sorry about that," Jasper said.

"Never mind. Just tell us what this plan is," Erin said.

They were flying down the corridor, their footsteps smacking and echoing off the walls.

"First, Judith will need to have gotten the keys."

"Even if she did get them, we can't leave. There're night angels posted all around the Gardens. No one can leave until the game is finished," Erin said.

"That's why we're going to the equipment room," Jasper said.

They rounded the last corner, breathing hard, and came to a stop outside the equipment room. Judith was nowhere to be seen.

Jasper, Erin, and Mullans looked up and down the wide corridor, Erin's messy tangle of hair swinging wildly. The corridor was deserted. Jasper tried to recall the frantic directions he had given Judith. Had he told her the wrong way? Was she lost, wandering around Trillium Gardens somewhere? Worse yet, had she simply lost her nerve?

"Judith," Erin said, her voice hissing down the corridor.

"Judith?" Mullans said, louder. "Oh, *please* be here."

A moment passed. Then, another. Jasper felt the precious seconds ticking by with every heart beat pounding in his ears.

The door of the equipment room creaked open. Judith's pale face peered out.

"I was afraid someone would see me if I waited out there," she said, her yellow curls falling in her eyes. "I have the keys."

Jasper's knees went weak with relief.

"When I saw Lily Valland up in the black box, I was worried," Jasper said.

Judith pushed the equipment room door open. Sour, sweaty air spilled out and they all coughed.

"It smells the way sweaty socks taste," Mullans said, wrinkling his nose.

Jasper didn't have time to ask.

"I got to the museum just in time, I think," Judith said, pulling the keys from her pocket and handing them to Jasper. "The security trolls were banging away at a rotten staircase and the curator was distracted. I snuck up behind her and took the keys right off her belt. She didn't even notice. As soon as I had them, I left as fast as I could. Ms. Fearce walked into the HNIC as I was running out."

"Lucky," Erin said. "Ms. Fearce must have been on her way to fetch the curator and drag her to Trillium Gardens."

"And I'm sure they'll be headed back to the HNIC as soon as the game is over. Come on, the third period is underway and we don't have much time," Jasper said.

He stuffed the keys into his pocket and pushed his way into the equipment room and the others followed. Judith closed the door behind her.

"We don't have much time, yes, so what are we doing in the equipment room?" Erin asked, tossing a battered pair of goalie pads out of her way.

"There's a trap door," Jasper said. "I found it on my first day here, when I was getting my gear."

"But what good is that?" Judith asked, struggling to push past a heap of heavy helmets.

Mullans held his breath while trying to shift as much equipment as possible, and so said nothing.

Jasper didn't answer. He was too focused on finding the trap door again. The room seemed to have doubled in size and disorder since the last time he was here. The darkness was complete. He hadn't brought a lantern this time. More than once Jasper thought he had found the round, metal ring on the floor, only to pull back and come away with a hockey stick or a dull skate blade in his hand.

Soon enough, there was success. His hand closed around the perfectly round brass ring. He remembered the feeling of it. The metal was cold and the ring almost too large for his grip. He heaved and the trap door creaked open in a tumble of dust and hockey equipment.

"This trap door leads to a tunnel that runs under Trillium Gardens and out into the city," Jasper said. He cleared his throat, thankful it was too dark in the equipment room for the others to see his face. "I think."

The silence said it all.

"You think?" Erin said, and Jasper knew she wanted to punch him in his face.

"This is almost as bad as our first plan," Mullans said.

"It's the best we've got," Jasper said, painfully aware of the time they had already wasted and were continuing to waste.

"Where does it lead?" Judith asked.

Jasper shifted his weight.

"I don't know."

"You didn't check?" Erin asked, her voice filled the cluttered room.

"I didn't need to know until now."

"But you know it leads out of Trillium Gardens."

"I said I *think* it leads out of Trillium Gardens."

More silence. Jasper sunk to his hands and knees and swung his head down into the tunnel. Up ahead, a dim square of light was just visible. Jasper hoped it was the night sky he was seeing.

"Well, needs must," Mullans said, joining Jasper on all-fours. "There's only one way to find out where this tunnel leads."

There was a scuffling and a drop and Mullans was gone, down into the tunnel below.

"It smells like feet down here," Mullans said, his voice drifting up from the trap door.

Jasper followed, then Erin, and finally Judith. In the darkness they had nothing to lead them but the dim square of light up ahead.

They ran for it.

Chapter 22

A Secret Tunnel and a Horse's Secret

It was dark. Nearly black. Jasper opened his eyes as wide as he could, but it made little difference. Erin, Mullans, and Judith were just murky shadows next to him. They ran on towards the square of light up ahead, their breath coming in gasps and huffs as their feet slapped along the sandstone tunnel.

It was smooth and dry down here. Nothing like the earthy tunnel Ms. Fearce had forced Jasper and Uncle Fredrick through on their journey to Magmelland. The pale sandstone walls rounded smoothly into the ceiling and the path under their feet followed a perfect line.

Jasper skimmed his fingers along the wall as he ran, using it as a guide. He hadn't expected there be other tunnels running off this one, so when the wall at his fingers suddenly disappeared, he tumbled sideways, his breath catching in his throat.

"Jasper!" Erin said, skidding to a halt. Pebbles skittered down the tunnel.

"I'm all right," Jasper said, pulling himself to his feet. "There's another tunnel leading off this one."

An arched doorway of darkness opened in front of them, visible only by the darker shadows filling the opening.

"I wonder where it goes," Judith said, taking a small step towards the archway.

"Who knows?" Erin said. "But we've got no light and no time. We stick to this path and keep moving toward the light, or else we're bound to lose our way."

No one argued and soon they were off running again, faster now they had had a break.

Jasper fingers still skimmed along the wall as he ran and each time the wall disappeared, he counted. One, two, three, four, five, and on, and on. If there were tunnels leading out of all those archways, there must be tunnels running under all of Tara.

Jasper only had a moment to wonder at who had made the tunnels, and why, when the four of them arrived at the square of light they had been chasing.

Mullans was doubled over, breathing hard. Judith had sunk to the floor, gasping for air. Erin's face was flushed and sweaty as she pulled Judith to her feet. Jasper wiped his brow on his sleeve and tried to slow his breathing.

It was a window. A simple, four pane glass window set deep into the sandstone wall. Jasper reached forward. The glass was cool against his clammy hand. He gave a gentle push and the window swung soundlessly open.

Cool night air gushed in and chilled the sweat on Jasper's face. Slowly, he poked his head out through the window. He squinted as his eyes adjusted to the light.

They had arrived at a deserted alleyway, between what looked like two rows of tall houses. It was about a four foot drop to the cobblestone road below. The other three pushed their faces through the window and had a look.

"Wow," Erin said. "We made it all the way down to the Muse District. This tunnel is huge."

Erin heaved herself onto the window ledge. Jasper tried to give her a boost, but she swatted his hand away. She landed with a soft *thump* on the cobblestones below.

"Help Judith. She's not tall enough," Erin said, her voice

echoing in the empty alleyway.

Mullans got down on all fours beneath the window and Jasper offered his arm. Blushing furiously, Judith took Jasper's hand and climbed clumsily onto to Mullans's back. After a bit of heaving, and a lot more blushing from Judith, she was up and over the ledge, landing in a heap below. Jasper and Mullans followed easily behind.

"Smell that salty air," Mullans said, taking a deep breath. "We're down by the docks."

"The Muse District isn't far from the HNIC. We're close. Let's keep going," Erin said, taking off down the alleyway. The others followed behind.

The streets of the Muse District were narrow, hemmed in by towering rows of colourful buildings lining every inch of the cobblestone roads. Neat rows upon neat rows of windows ran across the faces of the houses and every door was a shocking shade of red, purple, or blue. Graffiti covered nearly every surface. Artists lived here.

The four of them moved as fast as they dared, hugging the walls as they urged forward, stopping at each corner to check the coast was clear.

"I know everyone's at the game, but I thought we'd at least see a few night angels," Erin said as they paused in their pursuit to check around the next corner.

"I'm sure if we look hard enough, we'll find some," Judith said, looking nervous.

"Don't worry Judith, we're almost there," Erin signalled for the others to follow and they were on the move again.

Soon, the cramped, narrow alleys of the Muse District widened into well-kept roads. They were getting close. Up ahead, the teetering top floor of the HNIC was just visible above the dull grey buildings of the Gorgon Estates.

They kept moving, ever mindful of night angels possibly lurking around every corner. The eery quiet of Tara pressed in around them as the darkness gathered. Every breath, every step, every flutter of clothing rang in Jasper's ears. By the time they mounted the stairs of the HNIC and pushed through the heavy front doors, Jasper's clothes were soaked through with sweat.

On their first visit, the HNIC had been quiet, but now, it was like a tomb. Night air breezed through an open window set high into the wall, sending dust swirling through the air. The boxes and crates littering the floor fused together to form menacing, shifting shadows. As the twilight sank into gloom, they plunged forward.

"Judith," Jasper said, cringing as his voice bounced and echoed down the cluttered corridors. "Do you remember the way?"

"Yes. I brought the map from last time." Judith pulled a neatly folded square of paper from her pocket. Jasper only had a moment to admire Judith's thoughtfulness before they were on the move again, headed for the fifth floor.

The heels of their shoes clacked against the stone floor. Each of them walked in a hunched over, nervous shuffle, trying to take up as little room as possible. Jasper couldn't stop himself throwing nervous looks over his shoulder. Every dull twinkle and shadowy shape was a night angel, lying in wait.

They approached the room that held Eamonn Moran's necklace using the same corridor they had travelled down on their previous visit. Without the stand-off between Ms. Fearce and Lily Valland, and the hulking head of Hugo poking into the room, it seemed much larger, almost spacious.

A row of four small, square windows let the evening glow fall into the room. The case with Eamonn Moran's necklace stood in the beam of light. The rest of the room was bathed in darkness. Jasper took the keys from his pocket.

"It's the small brass one, remember? That's the one she was holding," Erin said.

Jasper deftly shuffled through the keys, willing them not to clink.

The little brass key looked dull, almost dirty, in the low light. Jasper pinched it between his fingers and stepped to the display.

The gold chains encircling the case were heavier then they looked and Jasper's wrist bent back as he lifted the lock. He pushed the key into the keyhole.

"Please work," Erin said, standing right at Jasper's shoulder.

The key clicked and turned smoothly and the lock popped open. All four of them let out a heavy breath. Jasper pulled the lock free. Mullans and Erin were there to ease the heavy chains to the floor. Jasper pulled open the glass pane door and Judith held it for him.

Jasper had studied the picture Scuttlebutt had given him for so long, there was no mistaking it. Eamonn Moran's necklace was within arm's reach. The silver of the chain was muted in the light but nothing could dampen the magnificent blue of the stone.

In one quick motion, Jasper snatched the necklace from its stand. It was smooth and cold and heavy in his hand. His heart beat in his ears as he put the necklace in his pocket and closed the glass case.

"We should put the chains back, and lock it," Judith said. "Maybe they won't notice it's gone, since the case is so crowded."

"Right," Jasper said and they set about lifting the heavy chains back into place.

The lock clicked closed with the same ease as when it opened. Jasper was just reaching for his pocket to take out the necklace again, when he heard it.

The hard clack of heel against stone. They were not alone.

"Oh no," Judith said, sounding on the verge of tears.

"Someone's coming!" Erin said, looking frantically around.

The echoes of the approaching footsteps bounced against the walls and around the room. There were several corridors leading out of the room, but it was impossible to tell from which direction the footsteps were approaching.

"We're trapped," Erin said, edging closer to the nearest corridor and daring to peek around the corner. "I don't know which way to go."

Judith let out a strangled sob, but quickly quieted herself.

The sweat on Jasper's brow turned to ice. His breath came in short gasps. The footsteps grew louder.

Jasper looked from one corridor to the next, straining to guess which might be empty. With every second, the banging echoes of the nearing footsteps grew louder. Jasper couldn't think straight.

Jasper thought he might as well just choose a corridor and hope for the best, when Mullans spoke.

"This horse's stomach has a door in it. Neat."

"Wait, what?" Jasper said, running over.

Mullans was lying on his back, under the huge wooden horse standing in the centre of the room. It did, indeed, have a small trapdoor opening out from its underbelly.

"He must be hungry because his stomach is empty," Mullans said.

"Mullans, you're a genius!" Erin said.

"Thank you."

"Judith, quick, inside!" Erin said, and Jasper felt relief wash over him. If they couldn't run, they could hide.

"It's big enough for all of us. We'll hide inside. Hurry," Jasper said, helping to give Judith a boost.

Erin went next, followed by Jasper, and Mullans, with his long arms and impressive upper body strength, came last. Erin pulled the trap door shut and clicked the inner latch in place. It was dark inside the wooden horse, and they were crammed against each other awkwardly. Elbows, knees, hands, and feet were mashed together in a tangle. Jasper was lying on a slant, positioned uncomfortably in the horse's neck. Judith's face was shoved into the crook of his elbow.

There they lay, breathing heavily and sweating, waiting, in the dark.

It would seem Mullans had discovered the horse's secret just in time, for as soon as they had gotten themselves hidden and settled, and their breathing was beginning to slow, the clacking of the heels grew painfully close.

Then, Ms. Fearce spoke. There was no mistaking her cold, lofty voice.

"This way, your Imperial Majesty," she said.

With his face mashed against the wooden planks of the horse's neck, Jasper had the slimmest of views through a crack. He squinted and the stiff frame of Ms. Fearce swam into focus.

Ms. Fearce walked with her head high, pointed chin leading the way. Her shoulders were thrown back, so far back as to be almost humanly impossible. Her preposterously high-heels clacked against the stone floor in a deafening rhythm.

Behind Ms. Fearce came Emperor Black himself. He didn't walk so much as glide, taking long, fluid steps, his cloak billowing out behind him. He carried his sceptre aloft, its sapphire glittering. Emperor Black was taller than the already tall Ms. Fearce. He cast a shadow over her as he came to a stop beside his henchwoman.

Last came Lily Valland, shaking with fear. With every small step the tower of scarves twined about her neck shook. She pulled her knitted shawl tighter about her. Lily's eyes were wide and shining as she looked about the room. There was no Hugo, nor anyone else, in sight. The game was still on and it seemed Lily

Valland was alone with Ms. Fearce and Emperor Black.

"Hurry along," Ms. Fearce said, her crisp voice breaking the nervous silence.

Lily scuttled forward, closing the remaining distance between herself and Ms. Fearce and the Emperor. Lily came to a stop near the neck of the wooden horse. Now, all Jasper could see was the dull grey of Lily's shawl. He shifted ever so slightly for a better view. He felt like he had been holding his breath forever and couldn't remember the last time he breathed.

Emperor Black's deep, rumbling voice sounded throughout the room.

"We've left the game early, Ms. Fearce. This had better be important."

At the sound of Emperor Black's voice, there was a quick intake of breath and Lily stepped back, pressing herself against the drooping head of the wooden horse.

"It is, your Imperial Majesty, I assure you. Now is the perfect time. The city is distracted and captive inside the Gardens. We shall not be disturbed."

Emperor Black and Ms. Fearce continued to speak in low voices.

Jasper had a moment to be glad they had thought to lock the case again, as he didn't want it to look like Lily Valland had anything to do with the necklace disappearing. Jasper hoped that the curator was creative, or at least a good actress, and that she might be able to convince them the necklace had never been there to begin with.

He clutched his hand tighter around the keyring for a moment, and then, his heart sank. The keys. He was still holding them. How would Lily open the case for them? These were the only keys and Lily Valland was about the look very guilty.

Carefully, Jasper extended his arm down the horse's neck, towards its open mouth. There was a sharp pinching on his calf. Erin saw what he was doing and was not impressed. Jasper ignored the pain and kept going.

Lily was pressed right back against the wooden horse, which made Jasper's job all the easier. Ever so carefully, as gently as he could, Jasper clipped the keyring back onto the curator's belt. The keys swung once, twice, and then they were still. Lily Valland noticed nothing.

"And where.....?" Emperor Black said.

"This case. Here," Ms. Fearce said, pointing with her cane. "The keys, you silly girl. The keys!"

For a moment, Jasper thought Lily would refuse once more to give the keys to Ms. Fearce, but in the presence of the Emperor, she meekly complied.

"Yes, Ms. Fearce. Here. I always keep them at my right--" Her hands went to her right hip, but her voice stopped short and Jasper realized his mistake. He had put the keys back on the wrong side of the curator's belt and she would know they'd been taken. "That's not right."

Lily's shoulders began to rise and fall in jerky spurts as her breathing quickened. Her shaking white hands patted all the way around her waist, searching for the keys and finally jolted to a stop when she found them.

"I must have misplaced--"

But Ms. Fearce didn't let her finish. She snatched the keys from Lily's belt, dragging the little curator forward and to the floor. Lily's hands slapped against the flagstones as Ms. Fearce turned on her heel, and stalked toward the display case.

Jasper strained his eyes as he peered through the crack in the horse's wooden shell. Lily slowly climbed back to her feet.

Ms. Fearce reached the case, stopped, and spun her head around while the rest of her body remained still. Her neck was sickly twisted in an alien way, but it did not seem to cause her any pain.

"Which key?" Ms Fearce said so loudly that Judith jerked back in surprise. Jasper clamped his arm around her, willing her to be still.

"The little *b-b-b-brass* one," Lily said.

Ms. Fearce twisted her head back around, deftly located the brass key, and opened the lock. She let the heavy gold chains fall to the floor with an ear shattering clank.

There was some rustling and banging as Ms. Fearce searched the cabinet. Her pointed shoulder blades slithered and worked under her sharp grey dress as she searched. Emperor Black let out a sigh.

"This is very trying, Ms. Fearce," the Emperor said.

Ms. Fearce ceased her searching and spun around to face them.

"The necklace is not here," she said. She was breathing heavily and her eyes were as wide as a cat's before a pounce.

"But, that's impossible," Lily said. "I have the only key."

Ms. Fearce flicked her wide, staring eyes to the curator.

"Do you, indeed? Perhaps you are to blame for the necklace disappearing!" Ms. Fearce said and she swung her cane out, pointing it directly at Lily's chest.

The little curator shrunk back.

"I would never! These artefacts are too precious. Please! I didn't," Lily said, sounding on the verge of tears. She paused for a moment, then continued. "Perhaps you....."

But her voice trailed off.

"Speak up," Ms. Fearce said, poking her cane roughly into Lily's chest and knocking her to the floor again.

Lily's voice trembled when she spoke.

"Perhaps you were mistaken. M-m-maybe it was a different necklace you saw. There's plenty in there."

Ms. Fearce's nostrils flared and she loomed over Lily where she sat on the floor.

"You DARE to question me? Foolish, insolent girl!" Ms. Fearce said. She swung at Lily with her cane. The curator ducked and Ms. Fearce went back over to the display case. She reached her spidery, long arms inside the case and grabbed an armload of artefacts, which she promptly flung across the room.

"I. Do not. Make. Mistakes," Ms. Fearce said, each word punctuated by an armload of artefacts flying across the room. Bracelets, coins, tiaras, and clay pots went flying, crashing and smashing all around.

"Please, don't," Lily said, ducking as Ms. Fearce hurtled an antique wooden jewellery box at her head. "Those still need to be accessioned."

"Enough," Emperor Black said, and Ms. Fearce ceased immediately.

Jasper strained to hear Emperor Black. He spoke in a low, purring rumble. Each of his words melted seamlessly into the next.

"Please, Ms. Fearce, tell me exactly what it is you saw in this case."

Ms. Fearce squared her shoulders and gave Lily Valland a cold stare before answering.

"It was a necklace, your Imperial Majesty. A silver chain hung with a jewel."

"Ah, then, perhaps our young curator is correct. Perhaps what you saw is one of these fine artefacts you have tossed to the floor."

Lily got to her knees and nodded her head vigorously. Jasper had to stop himself from nodding along with her.

"No," Ms. Fearce said, and Jasper clenched his jaw.

Please, no, he thought.

"It was not just any necklace, your Imperial Majesty, for from this particular necklace hung a jagged shard of blue stone. The deepest and truest of sapphires, the likes of which I have only known one to exist."

Emperor Black shut his eyes and swallowed slowly. He closed his long, bony fingers tightly around his sceptre.

"You're certain?"

"I do not make mistakes."

Emperor Black took a slow, steadying breath and then moved his deep, black eyes to where Lily crouched. She crumpled under his gaze.

"Tell me, did you see this jewel? This deepest of sapphires. Was this what hung from the necklace? Do not lie to me."

Jasper couldn't think, couldn't even breathe. He felt a hot splash of liquid on his arm. Silent tears wear rolling down Judith's face.

In a whisper, Lily said, "Yes. It's true. It was the bluest stone I've ever seen."

"And now the necklace and the stone are gone."

"Yes."

"And you have the only keys."

"Yes."

Emperor Black sighed again.

"I am very disappointed. Another promising lead, dashed," he said. The Emperor walked over to Lily, who made to scoot away, but Emperor Black offered her his hand instead.

Delicately, shaking, she took it and he gently pulled Lily to her feet.

"I'm so sorry to have troubled you," Emperor Black said. He flashed his cold, pointed-tooth smile, and his eyes twinkled.

"It's no trouble, your Imperial Majesty. Had I known it was so important, I would've tripled security," Lily said with a small smile. Some of the colour had crept back into her face.

"Alas," Emperor Black said, his eyes growing wide and the skin at their corners crinkling as his smile became unbearably broad. "Now you do know just how important it is."

Emperor Black raised Lily's hand to his mouth and placed a soft kiss there before releasing it. He walked toward the corridor to exit, but then, he stopped and turned.

"Good evening," he said to Lily and then nodded to Ms. Fearce.

Lily Valland made to reply but Ms. Fearce's cane was already pressed against her throat, choking her.

Lily Valland struggled and squirmed, kicked and clawed, and gasped for air, but soon, she was still. Ms. Fearce released her grip and the curator's body dropped to the floor in a heap. Ms. Fearce stepped neatly over it and then pulled a tiny notebook from her pocket. She made a single stroke with her pencil, closed the notebook, and returned it to the folds of her dress. Ms. Fearce and

Emperor Black exited the room.

    All was quiet.

Chapter 23

Season's End

No one moved. No one spoke. The seconds became minutes and time stretched on. Jasper didn't dare to breathe. The silence was deafening.

The pile of scarves and sweaters covering Lily Valland's body remained motionless. There was no rise and fall of breath and there wouldn't be. Jasper's eyes were opened painfully wide. Watching. Waiting.

With every second, Jasper's heart beat louder and faster, pounding in his ears until he felt he might scream.

"*Out,*" Jasper said. "Everyone out."

As fast as she dared, Erin undid the latch and jumped lightly from the horse. Hers were the only sounds. Emperor Black and Ms. Fearce had certainly gone.

The other three soon followed and Mullans closed the door in the wooden horse's stomach. On silent feet they gathered wordlessly around the curator's body, which was face-down on the floor, her hands stretched outward for help that would not come.

Then, they were running. Running away from the shock and the fear and the guilt. Their footsteps smacked and pounded against the stone floor in a noisy racket, a storm of echoes bouncing wildly. Hot tears streamed from Jasper's eyes, but he was running too fast. The tears slipped from his face and were lost behind him.

The creeping infiltration of the HNIC had given way to a panicked escape. Corridors and staircases flew past in a greyish-blue blur. Jasper couldn't even be sure they were going the right way. He had to keep running. That was all that mattered.

The heavy doors of the main entrance were light as feathers when Jasper reached them and pushed. The four children burst into the night air. Heavy rain poured from the sky in an endless stream. Soon, they were soaked through.

"The ice," Erin said with a dazed look. "The ice will melt. Trillium Gardens hasn't got a roof."

Judith cried her silent tears, unhidden by the rain.

And so the hockey season came to an end.

Jasper clutched Eamonn Moran's necklace tightly in his fist.

This necklace with the blue stone was worth killing for. Jasper felt sick and dared not look the others in the eye. Not yet, not now. He had to think.

In silence they ran toward Trillium Gardens. Jasper had the vague idea their absence would be noticed and that they should really do their best to be seen back at the Gardens.

"They'll wonder where we've gone," Mullans said, his voice flat. He picked up his pace and took Judith gently by the elbow, urging her onward. Judith let out a little sob but did not protest.

Panting and lungs near bursting, they came upon the crowd. Scarlet and silver scarves and flags fluttered and flew in a pulsing mass. There were screams of delight and cheers and smiles all around, and the sight of it all made Jasper's head swim. The home team had won.

Soon, Jasper, Erin, and Mullans were spotted by the crowd and they were swept up into the chaos.

"That was a nice fight," a man with knobbly grey skin and a long hooked nose said, thumping Jasper so hard on the back he nearly fell over. "Haven't seen a tilt like that in years!"

"Thanks," Jasper said, forcing a smile.

Up ahead, Troy McGee and Asher Orr were hoisted onto the shoulders of cheering fans. Gui Morenz was there too, crowd-surfing and high-fiving everyone in reach.

Before they could protest, which Erin most certainly would have done, the three of them were hefted up into the air and bounced along a stream of hands. Judith struggled to keep up below.

"There you are!" McGee said, reaching for Jasper's shoulder and giving it a squeeze. "I was wondering where you three went."

"Nowhere," Mullans said, a little too quickly.

"We watched from the stands," Jasper said.

"Good game," Erin said, giving Orr a hug. She looked dazed, but was trying to smile, all the same. Jasper followed her lead.

The crowd kept up their chanting and cheering on the slow procession to the Players Pavilion. Jasper did his best to smile along with the rest, but flashes of Lily Valland filled his mind. Her eyes springing open in shock as Ms. Fearce's cane pressed against her throat, gasping for air as she choked, the rasping and gurgling sound, her frantic hands, clawing at the cane before becoming still......

"Cheer up, would you?" Erin said out of the side of her mouth. "We just won our last game of the season. We're happy, remember?"

Erin plastered a huge grin to her face and let a loud cheer as she crowd surfed onwards. Mullans joined in, and soon, so did Jasper. There was nothing else for it.

By the time they reached the Players Pavilion, Jasper's hands were sore from countless high-fives and his cheeks ached from all the smiling. Thankfully, Ding and Bogg stood guard at the enchanted doors to stop the crowd of fans going any farther.

"Now, now," Ding said, bringing himself to his full height and straightening his ripped collar. "Residents only beyond this point. The rest of you best be getting home. Curfew is still in effect."

The crowd let out a stream of boos. Jasper was eased to the ground. He dashed inside, followed closely by Mullans, Erin, and Judith. Erin did her best to block Judith from view as they passed through the doors, but Ding and Bogg were so busy trying to hold the crowd back, they paid no mind to the non-resident.

The rest of the team made their way to the lounge to continue the celebrations, but the four thieves went straight up to the dorms.

When the bedroom door had closed, they stood in silence, staring at one another.

Ikarus poked his head from his nest and cooed a greeting. The warm glow of the bedroom's heating stove highlighted the swollen and bruised faces of Erin and Mullans, and Jasper reached up to check his own. It was hot and tender to the touch.

"We can't tell anyone," Erin said, breaking the silence. "I don't know why Emperor Black wants that stone or why it's so important, but he's willing to kill for it."

Jasper nodded.

"You're right. No one can know. What happened tonight stays a secret. Agreed?"

Jasper looked at them each in turn. Erin nodded, then Mullans.

"But, Lily Valland," Judith said, tears running down her cheeks again.

Jasper's stomach clenched and he felt queasy. His chest felt so heavy that every breath was a struggle.

"I know, but I don't think there's anything we can do, or anything we could've done."

"Emperor Black was going to do what he did, whether he got the necklace or not. You heard him. Lily knew how important it was to him, so she had to go," Erin said, and Jasper was impressed by her calm reasoning.

"But shouldn't we tell someone what happened?" Judith said, sniffling and wiping her runny nose on her sleeve.

"Like the night angels? Are they really going to haul Emperor Black off to prison?" Erin said. "No, he'll get away with this like he gets away with everything else. No one can stop him. Lily Valland and all memories of her will disappear."

"Just like Eamonn Moran," Mullans said.

"No," Jasper said, taking the necklace from his pocket. "Moran isn't gone. We have this. I don't know why, but this stone is important. Moran went through a lot of trouble to keep it hidden and we stopped Emperor Black from taking it tonight. We should be proud."

"You're right," Erin said. "And we are. Now we just have to figure out why it's so important."

"Well, we're on the right track," Mullans said, before gathering them all in for a group hug.

"Where will you keep it?" Erin asked, politely pulling away from Mullans as soon as she was able. She wasn't, and never would be, a big hugger.

Jasper opened his closet and reached far into the back. Next to Eamonn Moran's hockey stick, tucked neatly into the back corner, was the puck turned jewelry case that had started them on this hunt in the first place.

"It really is a pretty clever hiding spot," Jasper said, running his thumb along the edge and popping the puck open. The case wobbled in his hand and the velvet backing came loose. A piece of paper fluttered to the ground.

"A note!" Judith said, reaching for the paper. Without looking at it, she handed it to Jasper.

It said:

Eamonn,

*You were right. The stone is as you suspected, and the key to our success. Tell no one. **Keep it safe.*** *-R.D.*

Jasper read it aloud three times. With each read, the painful clench in his stomach eased slightly. Their heist had been a success and it was for the best. They were fighting the good fight.

"Who's R.D. ?" Mullans said.

"No idea," Jasper said. "But we'll have to find out."

"Yes," Erin said. "We will."

Erin had been right when she saw the rain. The ice in Trillium Gardens had melted, which meant the end of the season. Amongst a great many other changes in Tara and Magmelland, the end of the season also meant the emptying out of the Players Pavillion. Some of Jasper's teammates had families who lived in the countryside outside of Tara, like Mullans, and others had families to return to within the walls of the city, like Erin.

Mullans's version of packing consisted mostly of shifting piles of dirty clothes and old hockey equipment from one side of the room to the other, and he set about it with a gusto Jasper found tiring just to watch. Jasper packed his few belongings into a canvas sack Mullans had given him.

There was a knock at the door and Uncle Fredrick's face peered inside.

"Hello boys!" he said. "I meant to come by after the win last night, but Ding and Bogg wouldn't let me in. I saw your little friend though, Judith I think it is, walking home on her own. I made sure she got there safe and sound."

Uncle Fredrick took a seat on Mullans's cluttered bed. The bed frame groaned under his weight.

"Lads, great game. Never knew you were such a fighter Jasper."

"Me neither," Jasper said, reaching up to gently touch his swollen face.

"You're all packed, I see," Uncle Fredrick said, nodding to the canvas bag by Jasper's feet.

"I'm all ready to go," Jasper said, and frowned. He had been dreading this moment. Now that the season was over, he'd have to return home to Mr. and Mrs. Jarvis and his younger brother, Jake. He cringed at the thought. He loved it here in Magmelland and he would hate to go.

Uncle Fredrick laughed. "Why the long face?"

"I'm going home, aren't I? Back to Brantford?"

Uncle Fredrick laughed again.

"Goodness, no. This is your home now."

Jasper jumped onto Mullans's back and was promptly tackled to the floor.

"Really?" Jasper said, smiling as wide as he had ever done in his whole life.

"Of course. You'll stay with me in the off-season," Uncle Fredrick said.

Mullans made to give Jasper a high-five, but Jasper wasn't looking, so instead got a high-five to the face.

"And you'll have to come visit me in the counties," Mullans said, cramming some shoes into his already overflowing canvas bag.

Jasper couldn't believe it. No more Mrs. Jarvis nagging him, no more annoying Jake, a summer spent with Uncle Fredrick and a hockey season to look forward to. He couldn't believe his luck.

Jasper grinned.

"I can't wait," he said.

And that is how the hockey hero came home.

Made in the USA
Middletown, DE
27 November 2017